Berkley Prime Crime titles by Lila Dare

TRESSED TO KILL
POLISHED OFF

Polished Off

LILA DARE

BERKLEY PRIME CRIME, NEW YORK

THE BERKLEY PUBLISHING GROUP
Published by the Penguin Group
Penguin Group (USA) Inc.
375 Hudson Street, New York, New York 10014, USA

Penguin Group (Canada), 90 Eglinton Avenue East, Suite 700, Toronto, Ontario M4P 2Y3, Canada
(a division of Pearson Penguin Canada Inc.)
Penguin Books Ltd., 80 Strand, London WC2R 0RL, England
Penguin Group Ireland, 25 St. Stephen's Green, Dublin 2, Ireland (a division of Penguin Books Ltd.)
Penguin Group (Australia), 250 Camberwell Road, Camberwell, Victoria 3124, Australia
(a division of Pearson Australia Group Pty. Ltd.)
Penguin Books India Pvt. Ltd., 11 Community Centre, Panchsheel Park, New Delhi—110 017, India
Penguin Group (NZ), 67 Apollo Drive, Rosedale, North Shore 0632, New Zealand
(a division of Pearson New Zealand Ltd.)
Penguin Books (South Africa) (Pty.) Ltd., 24 Sturdee Avenue, Rosebank, Johannesburg 2196,
South Africa

Penguin Books Ltd., Registered Offices: 80 Strand, London WC2R 0RL, England

This is a work of fiction. Names, characters, places, and incidents either are the product of the author's
imagination or are used fictitiously, and any resemblance to actual persons, living or dead, business
establishments, events, or locales is entirely coincidental. The publisher does not have any control over
and does not assume any responsibility for author or third-party websites or their content.

PUBLISHER'S NOTE: The recipes contained in this book are to be followed exactly as written. The
publisher is not responsible for your specific health or allergy needs that may require medical supervision. The publisher is not responsible for any adverse reactions to the recipes contained in this book.

POLISHED OFF

A Berkley Prime Crime Book / published by arrangement with the author

PRINTING HISTORY
Berkley Prime Crime mass-market edition / February 2011

Copyright © 2011 by Penguin Group (USA) Inc.
Cover illustration by Brandon Dorman.
Cover design by Annette Fiore Defex.
Interior text design by Kristin del Rosario.

ISBN: 978-0-425-23986-5

BERKLEY® PRIME CRIME
Berkley Prime Crime Books are published by The Berkley Publishing Group,
a division of Penguin Group (USA) Inc.,
375 Hudson Street, New York, New York 10014.
BERKLEY® PRIME CRIME and the PRIME CRIME logo are trademarks of Penguin Group (USA) Inc.

PRINTED IN THE UNITED STATES OF AMERICA

10   9   8   7   6   5   4   3   2   1

For Don and Dolores, people of conviction. Rest in peace.

[ACKNOWLEDGMENTS]

If I said "it takes a village" to nurture a book from idea to manuscript to publication, my husband would gag, so I'll just say thank you to the many, many friends, colleagues, and publishing professionals who improved *Polished Off*, especially my critique group buddies—Amy, Lin, Marie; my agent, Paige Wheeler; my editor, Michelle Vega and all the wonderful people at Berkley Prime Crime; Greg Gillis and Ellory Gillis-McGinnis, amazing web designers of www.LilaDare.com; and Joan Hankins, my first reader and dearest friend. To my husband and daughters—thanks for the love and support and the grand adventure that is our family life together.

Chapter One

✂

THE DAY GOT OFF TO A ROCKY START WHEN A HYSTER-
ical bride-to-be pitched a hissy in the salon. We all have
bad hair days, but brides tend to look at lank locks, or humidity frizz, or a dye job that's more flaming idiot than
Flaming Auburn, as a catastrophe on par with a mud slide
burying their reception site. And this bride, twenty-year-
old Penny Williams, had a real problem: she'd tried to iron
her hair straight and toasted it.

"Look at it," she wailed from Mom's styling chair. She
was a tiny thing—barely topping five feet—with long hair
and brown cocker spaniel eyes, currently reddened by crying. She grabbed a hank of light brown hair and waved it. "I
can't get married now . . . I look hideous. Jarrett will want
his ring back." She waved her left hand, sparking a twinkle
off the diamond chip embedded in fourteen-carat gold.

"Jarrett loves you, Penny," Mom said soothingly, patting

the distraught girl's shoulder. The sun streaming through the wooden blinds made a halo of Mom's short, spiky salt-and-pepper hair and glinted off the lenses of her rimless glasses. Sixty years old, she still had smooth, relatively un-lined skin and deep periwinkle eyes. Her figure was com-fortably rounded and she favored practical clothes when working: washable cotton-knit or linen pants, sneakers, and blouses with pockets to hold clips and combs.

"But the wedding's Saturday!" Penny said despairingly. "It'll never grow out by then. I need to call my mom so she can cancel the flowers. And the photographer. And the—" She dug through her purse and came up with her cell phone.

Mom drew her fingers through Penny's hair. "Look, hon, it's just the ends that got a bit . . . crispy. I can trim those off in a jiff, do a bit of layering around your face, and you'll be a radiant bride."

"You think?" She hiccupped at her reflection in the mir-ror. A half-hopeful look flitted across her face.

"I know," Mom said firmly. "Let's get you shampooed."

While Mom led Penny to the shampoo sink that sits be-hind a half wall of glass bricks, I called Jarrett Noblitt, the groom-to-be. It struck me that a little reassurance from her beloved might help Penny put the hair fiasco in perspective.

"I'll be right over," he said. "Thanks, Grace."

I hung up smiling. Sometimes being part of a small deep-South community can be a blessing. Having lifelong friends and neighbors who care about you and know your business can be a huge help. Of course, having those same friends and neighbors meddle in your life can also prove frustrating and embarrassing. There's a thin line, I'd noted years ago, between caring and meddling. Like when your marriage ends up on the rocks and everyone has a theory about what went wrong. Or, worse, they want to fix you up with their friend/cousin/nephew/coworker who will be "just perfect for you." Since I'd returned to St. Elizabeth from Atlanta after my divorce, I'd fended off offers of blind dates from well-wishers ranging from clients to my landlady.

Heavy footsteps thudding up the stairs and across the veranda cut across my thoughts. Jarrett Noblitt burst through the door into the salon, which is the front half of my mom's Victorian home. Usually it seemed cozy, with a chintz love seat and chairs in the waiting area, two styling stations, and a shampoo sink separated by a half wall of glass bricks, wooden blinds canted to let the sun stream across heart-of-pine floorboards, and a profusion of violets and ferns. The womanly figurehead from the wreck of the *Santa Elisabeta*, a galleon that went down off our coast in the 1500s, provided benevolent supervision from a wall behind the counter. But Jarrett made the salon feel cramped. He was six and a half feet of former high school point guard turned welder.

Stella Michaelson, our manicurist, caught my eye and bit back a smile as she readied her polishes for the day. Her white Persian cat, Beauty, sat on a purple satin pillow beneath Stella's station in the Nail Nook, whisking her tail back and forth.

The groom rushed to Penny, who was now sitting in Mom's chair with her hair turbaned in a violet towel. He gave her a crushing hug that knocked the towel askew.

"Jarrett!" She got wide-eyed. "What are you doing here?"

"I just stopped by to tell you I love you in sickness and in health, with hair or without hair."

"That'll come in handy if I ever go completely bald," she said with a watery chuckle.

He frowned. "Why'd you go and try to iron out your curls, anyway? I like 'em. They're part of you."

"Oh, Jarrett."

They kissed.

"It's romantic, the way he came rushing over here." Stella had come up behind me and whispered in my ear.

I faced her, noting a wistful look in her eyes. Even at forty-one, her pale complexion usually had the sheen of a magnolia blossom, but today she looked pasty. She'd secured her auburn hair at the nape of her neck with two enameled chopsticks, but one lock escaped to straggle across her cheek. Strain was visible in the lines around her eyes.

"It's sweet. Young love." I fluttered my lashes in an exaggerated way. I remembered when Hank and I felt that way about each other. High school, maybe. I hoped I wasn't too old at thirty to fall in love like that again.

Stella's eyes brimmed with tears and she rushed toward the bathroom.

Before I could decide whether or not to follow her and ask what was wrong, the door opened to frame a woman on the threshold. She paused a moment, like the diva in an opera making sure the audience notices her entrance, before gliding into the salon. With russet hair and a sharp nose in a heart-shaped face, she reminded me of a fox. She was petite, maybe three inches shorter than my own five-six, but she wore heels and a tailored teal dress that made her seem taller. Her businesslike air suggested she wasn't one of the tourists that flocked to St. Elizabeth, Georgia, in the summer, enchanted with our Southern hospitality, white-sand beach, and antebellum mansions.

"Violetta Terhune?" Her drawl, honey dripping from each drawn-out word, told me she grew up around here.

She looked from me to Mom, waxed and plucked brows arched.

"That's me," Mom said, leaving her station and the still smooching couple to shake her hand. "How can I help you?"

"I'm Audrey Faye," the woman said. "My friend Simone DuBois recommended you."

Mom had been accused of murdering Simone's mother, Constance DuBois, at the start of the summer. We had found the real murderer and kept him from doing away with Simone in the bargain, so she felt she owed us.

"I can fit you in after I do Penny," Mom said. "Or Grace can take you now."

"Oh, I don't need a haircut," Audrey said, flicking the idea away with a wave of her hand. "I'm the coordinator of the Miss Magnolia Blossom pageant, which, as I'm sure you know, is being held right here in St. Elizabeth this week." She beamed. "Girls from across the region are competing for the chance to wear the crown and move up to the Miss Georgia Blossom contest next month. And then . . . Miss American Blossom."

She breathed it in the awestruck tones my Catholic roommate at UGA used when talking about meeting the Pope.

"I'm not sure—" Mom started, looking confused.

"I want to hire two of your staff to do the girls' hair and nails," Audrey Faye interrupted.

I got the feeling she interrupted a lot. She came across as one of those women who wanted to be the bride at every wedding and the corpse at every funeral, as my Granny Terhune used to say. She probably still said it, but she'd moved to Maryland with my Uncle Graham's family and I didn't see her often.

"This is my first year as pageant director and I can tell you I'm making some changes in the way we do things. Some long-overdue changes." She shot a sideways glance at her image in the mirror and brushed a speck of mascara off her cheek. "It helps to have a real beauty queen directing a pageant, don't you think?"

Mom nodded, although I was sure she'd never given it a thought.

"I was Miss American Blossom once, you know; it seems like yesterday." A reminiscent smile curved her full lips.

Since she was clearly in her mid-thirties, "yesterday" probably meant "fifteen years ago." Meow, I chastised myself, unsure why I felt so catty about the woman.

"It's like being queen for a whole year. I like to think I accomplished a lot during my reign."

I didn't think wearing a rhinestone crown and going to supermarket openings put her in the same league as Marie Curie or Eleanor Roosevelt on the accomplishments front. I put the brakes on my uncharitable thoughts; maybe she'd done good work with literacy or raising money for a disease. Just because she came across as a tad superficial didn't mean she was ungenerous.

Audrey Faye took a deep breath. "Anyway, some of the contestants are old pros at the pageant thing, but several are neophytes. I want to level the playing field"—she smoothed the air with beautifully manicured hands—"so we can send the best woman to Atlanta. Isn't that a brilliant idea? I'm determined that our Miss Magnolia Blossom will win the Miss Georgia Blossom crown this year." Her lips tightened. "That'll show them."

That would show who what? She'd lost me. "Show who?"

She looked at me, apparently surprised I'd spoken. "The state pageant directors who don't think we have a rigorous enough program here on the coast to compete successfully for Miss Georgia Blossom."

"Well . . . what did you have in mind?" Mom asked.

"Today's Tuesday. The finals are Saturday night. I need a stylist and a manicurist to do the contestants' hair and nails for their appearances and the competitions. Talent tonight, swimsuit tomorrow, local appearances on Thursday, semifinals Friday, and the crowning on Saturday." She ticked the events off on her fingers. "I'm running it just like one of the national pageants. Isn't that brilliant? I'm paying three hundred a day. Each."

Mom cast me a questioning look.

"I'm not too busy this week," I told her, turning the pages of the appointment book. August was our slowest month as many of our customers fled the sweltering heat of coastal Georgia for cooler holidays in the Carolina or Tennessee mountains. I turned to Mom. "You could take my clients, couldn't you?"

It sounded fun. I'd never been closer to a beauty pageant than a televised broadcast and I could use the extra money. I'd decided it was time to buy a house—I was thirty, after all—and was saving for a down payment. I was pretty sure Stella and Darryl could use the money, too. I looked around for Stella, but she was still in the bathroom.

Mom nodded. "If you want to, Grace. Althea can put in a few more hours."

Althea Jenkins, Mom's best friend, was our part-time aesthetician. She was a good stylist, too, but didn't much like cutting hair. Still, she could fill in.

"Super," Audrey said, taking Mom's comment as agreement. "We're at that old theater on Pecan Street. We're sharing it with a community theater group doing *Phantom*. The stage is perfect. I can just see our Miss Magnolia Blossom, wearing her new crown, crying, waving to the audience . . ." She gave a royal wave, hand cupped, and hummed a snatch of the familiar Miss American Blossom theme song.

I had a feeling she was seeing herself, not the soon-to-be-crowned winner.

"Anyway"—Audrey's tone snapped back to business-like and she looked at me—"plan to be there at noon. The girls will be rehearsing their talent numbers and you can meet them then."

"Sure," I said.

"Super." She turned on her designer heel and left just as Stella emerged from the bathroom.

"Who was that?" Stella asked, drying her hands on a paper towel.

"A woman who's hired us to do hair and nails for a beauty pageant," I said. "For three hundred a day."

I expected Stella's face to light up, but instead it twisted in consternation.

"You don't have to do it if you don't want to," Mom said, eyeing Stella with concern. "I thought you'd be interested."

"I am," Stella said with an effort. "We need the money." Looking wan, she settled into her chair and coaxed Beauty onto her lap. Stroking the cat, she stared at the door, a faraway look in her eyes.

Chapter Two

MOM FINALLY UNGLUED JARRETT FROM PENNY AND got on with cutting the bride's hair. Other customers trickled in and the three of us were busy for a couple of hours. Rachel Whitley, our shampoo girl, had asked for the week off and so we were doing our own shampoos, which put me a little behind. At eleven, I had a gap in my schedule and grabbed a diet root beer from the mini fridge. Taking an appreciative swallow of the foamy liquid, I slipped my sandals off and scrunched my toes—standing all day is murder on your feet. Stella had left for an early lunch, promising to meet me at the theater. My thoughts drifted to my last trip to Atlanta to see Marty, a man I'd been dating since we met in May. A political reporter for the *Atlanta Journal-Constitution*, he'd mentioned an upcoming interview with the *Washington Post*. We weren't serious or anything—he lived four hours away, for heaven's sake, and

I'd only known him three months—but I'd miss him if he moved north. The clatter of the wooden blinds against the door brought my head around. I stared for a moment at the tall, African American woman crossing the salon. I almost dropped my root beer. "Althea?"

Althea Jenkins, our aesthetician, was the same vintage as my mom, give or take a couple of years, and had been her best friend since before they both lost their husbands in the early eighties. Althea's husband was murdered, and my dad died of pancreatic cancer. They'd started the salon, Violetta's, together as a home business to make ends meet, doing hair and facials for friends in my mom's kitchen. Over the years, the business had expanded and taken over the front rooms—dining room, parlor, half bath—of the old Victorian my mom inherited. Althea was salt of the earth: a no-nonsense, Baptist-church-going, outspoken woman who had no tolerance for fools. I'd never seen her wear anything but polyester-blend pants and tops or loose cotton skirts and blouses from fashion emporiums like J.C. Penney and Sears. Today . . .

"Althea?" My mom's voice held the same disbelief swirling through my head. "What in the name of heaven are you wearing?"

A tall woman with a proud bearing, Althea always had a commanding presence. In the ankle-grazing—what was it? a caftan? a tunic?—red, green, and black patterned garment, she was impossible to miss. Her gray-flecked afro was shorter than when I'd last seen her, following the curve of her skull and throwing her prominent cheekbones and deep-set eyes into sharp relief. Large circular earrings—some kind of bone or a facsimile—dangled from her lobes. At my mom's question, Althea's chin, always tilted up a hair like she was ready to take whatever the world threw at her, jutted forward.

"Like it?" Her tone dared any of us not to. "It's a traditional African kente caftan." She spun slowly so the full sleeves, really just slits in the fabric, belled out.

"Is it machine washable?" Mom asked. She plugged in a curling iron to finish her client's hair. Close to eighty, Euphemia Toller had faded blue eyes that widened as she took in Althea's new attire.

"It's striking," I offered.

"Are you going to a costume party?" Euphemia finally asked, shifting on the booster Mom had to use to raise her high enough to cut her hair.

Althea glared at her. "I've decided it's time I explore my heritage," she said loftily, "and reclaim it for myself."

"Your hair? Did you lose it?" Euphemia asked, cupping a hand to her ear. She was deaf as a tree stump, except when it came to gossip; then, her hearing put a bat's to shame. "It does look shorter."

"Not hair. Her-i-tage," Althea said loudly. "My roots. My cultural history."

"What prompted this, Althea?" I asked. I crumpled the A&W can and tossed it in the recycle bin.

She looked down her nose at me, trying to decide if I was making fun of her. Apparently satisfied, she said, "Kwasi says it's important to know where you come from in order to figure out where you're going."

I didn't point out that she came from small-town Georgia, as did her parents and grandparents. She'd never been nearer the African savannah than watching *The Lion King* on DVD.

"Kwasi's the man you've been seeing? The teacher from the community college?" Mom asked, removing Euphemia's cape and escorting her to the counter. Euphemia counted out the correct change in crumpled dollar bills and quarters and left with a last disbelieving glance at Althea.

"He's a professor," Althea corrected her. "He's designed a cross-disciplinary major in Multicultural and Oppression Studies." Correctly interpreting our blank looks, she went on, "He enlightens students about the plight of oppressed peoples and cultures throughout history and shows the consequences of imperial and discriminatory mind-sets." She sounded like she was reading from a course catalog.

Mom and I exchanged a covert glance. "Sounds interesting," Mom said. "I hope we get to meet him soon."

One of Althea's neighbors had introduced her to Kwasi whoever six weeks ago and they'd been on several dates. She hadn't shared many of the details with us, but if appearances were anything to go by, she was more involved with him than I'd realized.

I could tell Mom felt the same when she said, "Why don't you and Kwasi come for dinner Friday? I'll make my fried chicken and a peach pie."

"Kwasi's a vegetarian," Althea said.

"I'm sure I can come up with something. Let's say six o'clock."

I knew that tone. It meant "be there or else." Alice Rose and I heard it frequently in connection with curfews, family dinners, and Sunday school when we were growing up. It even worked on Althea.

"I'll invite Walter," Mom added.

Walter Highsmith, rabid Civil War reenactor and owner of Confederate Artefacts a couple of storefronts down from Violetta's, was my mom's most frequent escort. I shied away from the word "boyfriend."

"Thank you, Vi. I'll check with Kwasi."

"You, too, Grace."

"If I can get away from the pageant," I promised. Speaking of which, I looked at my watch and realized I needed to get going. I kissed Mom's cheek and gave Althea a hug. "Later."

"What pageant? What's that girl going on about?" Althea asked as I grabbed the tote with my supplies and headed for the door. "Nobody tells me anything around here," she complained.

Chapter Three

✂

TEN MINUTES LATER I STOOD ACROSS THE STREET from the Oglethorpe Theater, having parked under a graceful magnolia tree. The theater was only a fifteen-minute walk from Violetta's, but strolling a block was enough to bring on heatstroke in the dog days of August, so I'd driven my old Ford Fiesta. I'd considered dashing to my apartment to change, thinking I should look more pulled together to hang out with pageant contestants, but I'd run out of time. My above-the-knee denim skirt and melon-colored blouse would have to do.

Crossing the street, I admired the lines of the building, with its peaked roofline in the Greek revival style and a series of white arches topped by a brick exterior. Rumor had it that both Robert E. Lee and Jefferson Davis and their wives had seen plays put on at the Oglethorpe. Since its heyday, it had hosted high school plays, been a movie theater for a short period, and played home to a variety of defunct community theater groups performing everything from Shakespeare to experimental stuff the local reviewer called "obscene." I'd seen a production of *Waiting for Godot* there as a teenager and had never been so bored.

I shook off the memory and noticed a small group of people waiting on the sidewalk and sitting in folding chairs outside the theater. What the heck were they doing? Two minutes in the August heat and humidity was all I could stand. Almost as wet as if I'd plunged into a pool, but not nearly so refreshed, I crossed the street.

As I drew abreast of the group—maybe twelve people, most of them women—they lifted posters and looked more alert. One young woman blocked my way and thrust her placard toward my face. It read: "The Objectification of Women Leads to Violence Against Women." The last two words were hard to read, scrunched to fit on the poster board.

"Are you in the pageant?" the young woman asked. With sandy hair pulled into a low ponytail, a halter top, and jean shorts, she looked about twenty. Sunburn pinked her bare shoulders.

"She's too old, Daphne," an earnest young man with a scraggly goatee called from the relative comfort of the shade cast by a pecan tree.

Too old? Ouch. Before I could reply, Daphne suggested, "Maybe she's a judge."

They regarded me for fifteen seconds before the young man said, "Nah, she's not famous."

"You can't really call the channel nine weatherman famous," Daphne objected. "It's not like he's Ashton Kutcher."

The man shrugged and pulled a Coke from the cooler at

his side, rolling it over his forehead. A sign saying "Pageants Kill!!!" was propped against his aluminum chair.

"Kill?" I asked skeptically. "That seems a bit over the top."

"A girl died competing in this pageant four years ago," Daphne said, her expression somber.

"She had a heart attack," the young man said. "Huge bummer. She was only twenty."

Daphne whirled to face him, her placard coming dangerously close to my face. "Seth, you know that's—"

"What did I tell you about blocking access to the building?" The new voice came from a man getting out of a Prius at the curb. He was African American, short, and fiftyish, with light brown skin stamped with cinnamon-colored freckles over his nose, cheeks, and pate. Short, tightly curled hair circled his bald spot. Narrow, rectangular framed glasses rested atop his plump cheeks. A loose shirt with white-on-white embroidery at the collarless neckline skimmed a small pot belly. An air of self-conscious intellectualism hung about him like a musky cologne. "We can demonstrate, but we have to allow free access to the public right-of-way."

"I'm not blocking the sidewalk, Dr. Yarrow," the girl blocking the sidewalk said. "I'm having a conversation with this woman"—she looked at me enquiringly and I supplied my name—"with Grace about the evils of beauty pageants."

Evils? That sounded harsh. Were beauty pageants the height of cultural achievement? Probably not. But did they portend the end of civilization? I didn't think so. I was tempted to ask what the evils were, but I sensed that listening to the answer would make me late.

"I'm going to be late," I said, edging around Daphne. "But I'd like to hear more another time."

"We are always happy to engage in dialog with the uninformed," the newcomer said. He extended a hand with thin, spatulate fingers. "I'm Dr. Yarrow. I'm a professor at Georgia Coastal College." He gestured at the other demonstrators. "This is a field exercise for the students—exposing them to the kind of activism and vigilance that make a difference in the way our society views oppressed peoples: Native Americans, African Americans, women, gays."

I shook his hand. His palm was damp. "Great," I said, not knowing what else to say. Did students get an A for having the best poster? Did they get extra credit for sunstroke in the name of the cause? I pushed a lock of sweaty hair off my forehead. "I've got to go. I'm sure I'll see you around."

"You can count on it," Dr. Yarrow said as I hurried up the walk, eager to reach the air-conditioned comfort of the theater. It shamed me a bit to realize I couldn't think of a cause I felt strongly enough about to spend the day demonstrating for in the nearly one-hundred-degree heat.

All thoughts of the demonstrators left me when I stepped into the narrow foyer. I shivered deliciously as the chilly air draped over me. Standing still for a moment, arms held away from my sides, I hoped some of the sweat would evaporate. Cool marble tiles in a black-and-white pattern extended about ten feet to two sets of double doors. A glass-encased ticket window anchored the lobby's left end. I wanted the old lobby to smell of greasepaint and glamour, but instead the scents of pine cleaner and a hint of mildew made me sneeze. Hearing faint voices, I crossed the lobby to the doors and pulled one open.

An auditorium large enough to seat maybe a thousand people sloped before me, with its rows of chairs covered in faded mustard velvet. Two carpeted aisles split the seating area into thirds. I stood at the top of the left aisle. A gaggle of people milled around on the stage and a piercing voice said, "I can't be expected to do my interpretive dance after Hayley's flaming-baton routine with the sparklers. There's little charred bits on the stage. They'll ruin my costume."

"There's not enough of it to matter," another girl said sweetly. "The audience would need a magnifying glass to see your costume, never mind any stains."

"Tabitha, Brooke! Miss Magnolia Blossoms never complain or treat each other unkindly." Audrey Faye stepped from stage right, a clipboard in one hand. "Tabitha, you didn't want to go after Morgan either because you said there was gun oil on the stage after she fieldstripped her M16. When—"

I lost the rest of what Audrey was saying in my puzzlement over the M16 comment. Last time I'd watched Miss American Blossom on TV, the talent had run more toward third-rate Celine Dion imitations and tap numbers than assault rifles. This might be even more entertaining than I had imagined. I made my way down the aisle as the argument concluded with Tabitha, a svelte blonde, scheduled to go last, right after a yodeler. Viewing Tabitha's satisfied smirk, I figured she'd been lobbying to be the final performer all along.

Audrey clapped her hands. "Right. Let's get back to it. Elise, you're up."

I caught Audrey's attention with a wave of my hand. She stared down at me blankly for a moment, then recognition dawned. "Right. You're the stylist. Sit there until we get done with this rehearsal, and someone'll show you around."

I obediently settled into a chair at the end of the front row, only a couple feet from the stage. The seat squeaked when I pushed it down and the velvet was worn smooth by thousands of rear ends over the years. I looked around but didn't see Stella. A disembodied voice from backstage announced, "Elise Metzger, a sophomore at the University of Georgia Tifton, will perform a flute solo."

A movement from the left caught my eye and I saw a man with a sophisticated-looking camera training it on the stage. A proud papa? He looked a bit young for the role, maybe in his late thirties, with a closely trimmed beard and crisp brown hair curling to collar length. Midway through the flute piece, he lowered his camera and slipped through a door I figured must lead to backstage.

Several other acts followed the flautist, including the previously mentioned Morgan, introduced as a member of the United States Army Reserve, who dismantled and reassembled her M16 in sync with the final movement to Tchaikovsky's "1812 Overture." Her camouflage-patterned hot pants and halter top added a sparkly note with their bugle bead fringe. When the cannons boomed at the end, she hoisted the rifle to her shoulder and mimed firing it before saluting and running off the stage.

Stella settled into the seat beside me as the crew spread mats on the stage for a tumbler. "Sorry I'm late," she whispered. "I went home for lunch and lost track of time." She sounded weary and looked wearier, slumped low in the seat, her hair matted with perspiration. "Did I miss anything?"

"No," was all I had time to mutter before the next performer bounded onto the stage, executing three back handsprings in a line from the far side of the stage to our end. She was a tiny thing, all green leotard and black hair whipping around in a ponytail. She flung her body into the air in a somersault and landed on the last mat, which separated from the others and slid toward the edge of the stage. The girl windmilled her arms but couldn't stop. Her mouth opened and her eyes widened as her momentum carried her sideways. She teetered on the edge before the mat slid off the stage, taking her with it. *Oof.* She slammed into my lap, one arm striking my nose and forehead, her feet thumping Stella's shoulder. She might only weigh ninety-five pounds, but it felt like two hundred dropping on me from stage height.

We sat there entangled for a few seconds. Shock, rather than injury, held me still. It had happened so fast. I took a deep breath as the girl shuddered and burst into tears.

"Are you okay?" I asked. I decided I wasn't seriously hurt, although my nose smarted.

"Kiley!" A voice called from the stage. "Are you all right?" Several faces looked down at us.

"Here, honey, don't cry," Stella said, helping Kiley swing her legs around and put her bare feet on the floor. "Can you stand?"

The girl sniffed and nodded. "I think so."

I helped by steadying her as she shifted her weight from my lap and stood. "My ankle!" she cried, collapsing to the floor.

Stella sank to her haunches and examined the girl's ankle. "It's swollen," she said.

The photographer was back, camera fixed on us. The man shifted to his right, trying to get a better angle. Before I could ask him what he thought he was doing, Audrey Faye arrived, clipboard in hand, and announced, "This is going to put us behind schedule." She ran a hand through her russet hair. "God! If it's not one thing it's another," she muttered.

Stella glared up at her, looking quite fierce. A sheepish look crossed Audrey's face; maybe she'd heard how uncaring she sounded. "We should call someone," she said, looking around. "Jodi!"

Trotting footsteps told me the unseen Jodi was responding. I called 911 since it didn't seem to occur to Audrey to do it herself.

Catching sight of the photographer, Audrey snapped, "Not now, Sam. For God's sake."

"You said I could have complete access," the man said, his flat Midwestern vowels in striking contrast to Audrey's drawl. He shifted slightly to get a better angle of Kiley and Stella on the floor. Audrey's frown didn't seem to intimidate him one whit.

"I won't be able to compete, will I?" Kiley said, tears trickling down her cheeks. She had a delicate, small-bosomed body and didn't look much older than Stella's twelve-year-old, although I knew she had to be at least sixteen to be in the pageant. In the green leotard, with her tear-streaked face, she looked like a sad pixie.

"Don't worry about that now," Audrey said. "We can talk—Oh, great, ice."

A lanky woman with brown hair and full lips extended a plastic grocery bag full of ice toward Audrey. The former beauty queen shrank from the dripping bag and Jodi handed it to Stella.

"Sorry about the drips," Jodi said. "The bag's all there was backstage." She made a shield of her clipboard, clasping it to her chest.

"Good thinking," Stella said. She placed the bag carefully on Kiley's ankle and the girl winced. "We really should prop your foot up."

I put down my bag of styling tools and helped Stella lift the girl's foot into place.

"Thank you," Kiley said in a small voice. "I want my mom."

"Of course you do," Stella said, looking from Audrey to Jodi. The latter said, "I called her already; she's on her way."

Audrey, becoming aware of the ring of girls peering over the stage, shooed them away. "That's it for today's rehearsal, ladies," she said. "Get changed and meet me out here in thirty minutes for notes."

"But I didn't get a chance to run through my number, and tonight's the talent competition."

Even before I looked up I knew the voice belonged to the dissatisfied Tabitha. She stood with one hand on her hip, staring down at us from the lip of the stage. She was undeniably beautiful, with cascades of blond hair, light green eyes, and a curvaceous figure tapering to long legs. Her beauty had a packaged air to it, though, like the Madame Alexander dolls I collected when I was little, with their pristine clothes and hair and perfect painted features. So perfect I didn't ever play with them; they weren't snuggly and fun.

"Like it matters, Tabby. You've been doing that routine for years—ever since you entered the Miss Vanilla Swirl contest." This came from the elegant African American girl Audrey had called Brooke.

"Well, it won me that title, didn't it?" Tabitha said in a self-satisfied voice, apparently impervious to the snideness of the comment. "And Miss Camden County and Miss Coastal Bathing Beauty and Georgia's Lovely Lady and—"

Tabitha seemed set to enumerate titles for hours, ticking them off on her fingers, but someone interrupted with, "But it didn't work for Miss Magnolia Blossom last year, did it? You came in—what?—third runner-up? Maybe you'd *better* practice—if you don't win Saturday, you don't get another chance, do you? This is your last year of eligibility. Next year you'll be too *old*."

A smothered giggle greeted this comment and Tabitha swung on her heel and stalked off stage.

Audrey heaved a sigh and seemed about to say something, but the EMTs and Kiley's mother arrived simultaneously and chaos ruled for a few minutes before they bore her off, Sam the camera guy trailing them to the lobby.

"Scratch her from the program," Audrey told Jodi as soon as Kiley was out of earshot.

Jodi hesitated, then obediently made a note on her clipboard.

"Where should I set up the manicure stuff?" Stella asked, indicating her kit.

Audrey made a "don't bother me" gesture.

"I'll show you," Jodi offered and the two women headed to the right.

I retrieved my tote and was about to follow them when a bald man, both thick arms covered from wrist to bicep with colorful tattoos, signaled Audrey from the stage. "Ma'am," he said, "you need to look at this." He held up a section of the mat.

"What now, Marv?" Audrey asked. Stairs at either end of the stage led down to audience level, and Audrey climbed the steps on our left. I trailed after her out of sheer curiosity.

"Look at this," the man said when we stood beside him. He bent to flip over a mat section, causing the waistband of his jeans to dip alarmingly. "You can see the Velcro strip's been cut off."

"What?" Anger and alarm rang in Audrey's voice.

I leaned over and fingered the mat. The textured plastic over a squishy core of some kind was supposed to have an inch-wide strip of Velcro on its end, I could tell by looking at the intact mats, designed to mate with a similar strip on another section and secure them together. But the damaged mat had nothing but a few snippets of thread where someone had cut away the Velcro. "Someone wanted the mat to slip," I said.

"Impossible!" Audrey said. She squatted to inspect the damage and ran a finger along the mat's underside. "Who would do this?" she asked in a less certain voice.

The man held up his hands defensively. "I don't know, ma'am, but it wasn't any of my crew. The boys brought the mats out and shoved 'em together. They didn't notice anything wrong, but they didn't have a reason to look. It's not their fault."

"Maybe they were defective when Kiley supplied them," Audrey said hopefully. Her eyes held a calculating gleam. "No one can prove they weren't, so no one can blame the pageant. The accident wasn't our fault. Just like the other incidents weren't anyone's fault." She looked from Marv to me, as if daring us to contradict her.

Marv's lips thinned at Audrey's words, but he didn't say anything.

"What other incidents?" I asked as Marv stacked the mats and shoved them toward the wings.

Audrey flipped a hand, as if to brush away a gnat. "Oh, nothing important. Just irritations. Somehow the sprinkler system in the dressing room went off and several of the girls' evening gowns were ruined. And when the programs came back from the printer, they had a typo that changed 'public' into 'pubic,' as in 'Huge Pubic Sale—Discounts Galore.' That furniture store withdrew as one of our sponsors. Stuff like that."

As she spoke, she crossed the stage to the wings and I followed. Scenery depicting white-topped mountains loomed to my right and a prop table sat immediately behind the heavy red curtains. Thick ropes and pulleys dangled like jungle vines, and I ducked around one. A gilt-framed mirror leaned against a wall and Audrey glanced at her reflection, rearranging a strand of her foxy hair. Above, catwalks and metal scaffolding for lights and other technical equipment crisscrossed below the roof. It smelled like sawdust.

"Do you think it's deliberate?" I asked.

Audrey shot me a look over her shoulder, as if surprised by the question. "Maybe. No. I don't know. I've certainly been involved with pageants where one or another of the contestants did . . . stuff to trip up a rival. Stains or tears on gowns, disappearing instruments or props, laxatives slipped into food—"

"Good heavens!"

Audrey gave me a condescending smile that said she found my surprise incredibly naïve. "Believe me, there's very little some girls wouldn't do to win a pageant, especially a big one with large scholarships and a prestigious appearance schedule at stake, like Miss American Blossom."

"I had no idea." I thought about it for a moment. "Were all the incidents aimed at Kiley?"

Audrey stopped and pinned me with a sharp look. "The incidents were not *aimed* at anyone. We've had a couple minor accidents, nothing more. Irritations. Certainly nothing the pageant could be liable for."

Audrey seemed a heck of a lot more concerned with how the pageant came off than what happened to the girls. I couldn't resist pushing her a little. "Kiley's accident was more than irritating," I pointed out. We were in a wide hall now, with doors opening to our left. "She could have been seriously injured."

"But she wasn't," Audrey said in a discussion-ending tone. She pushed open the door to a cramped room with a light-ringed mirror set above a narrow counter. A hanging rack on wheels held what looked like old costumes: a moth-eaten tuxedo with a toga draped over it, a cancan girl's petticoats, soldiers' uniforms from a variety of wars, six cheerleader skirts and vests, and a gray rabbit suit with pink-lined ears and big feet. Grotty carpeting that might have been laid down in Sarah Bernhardt's prime covered the floor, and the scents of acetone and, strangely, barbecue sauce lingered in the room.

"Here we are." Audrey hovered at the door, obviously eager to get on to more important things.

I eyed the straight-backed chair in front of the vanity. "Any chance we could round up an adjustable-height chair?"

"Ask Jodi," Audrey said. "She's my assistant. I've got to run and give notes to the girls. And, on top of everything, I've got to tell—Never mind. After that, they'll start getting ready for the talent competition which starts at six—we have to be done by seven thirty so the theater group can rehearse—so you'll be busy."

I nodded, wondering who she had to tell what. "Where's Stella?"

"Stella?"

"Stella Michaelson, the manicurist from Violetta's."

Audrey's mouth opened and she took a sharp breath. She

recovered before I could puzzle over her reaction, saying, "I didn't know that was her name. She's next door." Her head nodded to the right. "Now, if you'll excuse me . . ." She was out the door before I could think of anything else to ask her.

I rolled the costume rack into the corner and unpacked my kit, putting brushes, combs, curling iron, clips, gels, sprays, and my other equipment on the counter. It'd be cramped but workable. When I had everything set up, I wandered next door to find Stella. Her room was identical to mine, although period costumes, including a cape that looked like something *The Phantom of the Opera* or *Dracula* would wear, rather than cheerleaders and rabbits, hung on an extension rod that stretched the length of the room. The carpeting even had similar mysterious stains. Her polish bottles marched across the vanity in a neat line and a clutter of Q-tips and cotton balls obscured the countertop. Stella sat with her chin in her hands, gazing morosely at her reflection.

She jumped when I entered and pasted on a smile. "Hi, Grace. Isn't this pageant something else? I asked Jodi— she's really nice—how many girls we'll be working with and she says there are sixteen for tonight and the swimsuit competition tomorrow and then it'll only be eight after they announce the semifinalists. And they won't all want our help, Jodi said, but I still think we'll be busy."

"Sounds like it," I agreed. "Stella—"

She cut me off before I could ask what was bothering her. "I entered a beauty pageant once, you know," she said. "When I was a junior. I was pretty enough when I was younger—"

"You're gorgeous now," I said. She was: her auburn hair set off her creamy complexion and green eyes that tilted up a bit at the corners, and she had a slim figure that many a twenty-year-old would envy. Although laughter and smiles had left their stamp on her face, the faint lines actually made her more attractive, I thought, giving her a character and personality that silicone-breasted, Botoxed, plasti-girls didn't have. I could tell she didn't believe me, though, from the wry quirk of her lips.

"—but I felt so uncomfortable up on the stage. I withdrew before the swimsuit competition. That was the end of my pageant career!" She laughed but glanced at her reflection out of the corner of her eyes, like she was looking for the embarrassed teenager she'd been. "I still have the dress I wore for the evening gown competition. I thought maybe Jessie might wear it to prom one day, although if she keeps growing, it'll be too short. That girl has been shooting up like a kudzu vine. Darryl says—" She cut herself off and bit her lower lip.

"Let's see what the layout's like around here," I said. I wanted to ask her what was wrong, but the "No Trespassing" signs of expression and body language were too forceful to ignore. Stella followed me as I turned left in the hall.

We poked our noses into the rooms we passed and found another small dressing room and a cluttered office I figured belonged to Marv. A bigger dressing room at the end of the hall was clearly where the contestants gathered, with tatty sofas and occasional tables stacked with magazines and several clothes racks holding plastic-swathed costumes and dresses. We found our way out of the dressing room area to the auditorium, where Audrey Faye stood on the stage, reading notes from her clipboard to the upturned faces of the girls seated below her.

". . . and remember the new lineup for the closing number." She paused and knitted her brows. "There's just one other thing. Something has been brought to my attention that may affect a contestant's eligibility to compete in my pageant."

Her pageant? I turned a laugh into a cough.

Audrey lifted a hand to stave off questions from the wide-eyed young women in the audience. "I won't act without verification, so you will all perform as scheduled tonight. However, if the information proves correct, I will have to take action." She made eye contact with each of the contestants. "Any girl who suspects that poor choices in her past—that she 'forgot' to mention on the disclosure form—could tarnish the image of the Miss American Blossom pageant can talk to me after the show tonight. I'd certainly rather see a contestant resign of her own accord, with her privacy intact, than have to make a public display of . . . indiscretions."

Stella and I had paused halfway up the aisle to listen and I noticed the man with the camera directly across from us on the other side of the auditorium panning the girls' faces to get their reactions. They ranged from curious to nervous.

"What do you suppose it is?" Stella whispered, poking me in the back so I started moving again.

"Lingerie photos or something, probably," I said. "Who is that guy with the camera?" I asked, watching him follow the girls as they filed out of the auditorium.

"Sam Barnes. Jodi Keen said something about him filming a documentary on beauty pageants," Stella said. "He and Audrey Faye were at college together, Jodi said, so when he got the idea for the documentary, he naturally came to her. He interviewed Jodi on camera and she's hoping the exposure will help her land a position as a national pageant coordinator."

"Huh." I thought having the camera around was a little creepy, making the pageant feel like one of those "reality" TV shows where everyone's reactions are over the top because they know the camera's watching. And I suspected emotions around here were already running high enough.

Chapter Four

✄

THE NEXT COUPLE OF HOURS PASSED IN A BLUR OF curling, combing, teasing, and fluffing. A fog of hairspray hung permanently in the little room and I made a mental note to ask Jodi for a fan. She'd come through with the chair, and the contestants sat in a swivel office chair that could be raised and lowered about a foot. Not perfect, but better than nothing. Some of the girls sat tense and mute in the chair while others chatted away like little magpies, telling me all about their childhoods, dreams and ambitions, BFFs, and how or why they'd gotten into the pageant. Nerves, I guessed.

Threading a red ribbon that matched the lederhosen buttons through the yodeler's blond braids, I pronounced her done. "How many more girls are waiting?" I asked.

She peeked out. "Just two."

"Please ask the next girl to come in."

The elegant young black woman who'd been sparring with Tabitha glided through the door. She was average height but strongly built, with muscular arms and legs displayed by a sleeveless ivory vest over slim slacks. "Hi, I'm Brooke Baker," she said, marching forward with her hand out.

"Nice to meet you," I said, shaking her hand and introducing myself. Of all the girls I'd seen this evening, she was the most self-possessed by far. "What did you have in mind?" I studied her hair, running my fingers through the thick mass, which had obviously been relaxed and straightened so it hung to her shoulders with a slight flip at the end.

"It's a mess, I know," she said, as I worked my fingers through the dry strands. "But I have to straighten it. It doesn't pay to be *too* black in the Miss American Blossom competition." She said it matter-of-factly, not bitterly, with a smile that said she and I both knew how stupid that was, but what could you do? "And this bit flops in my face when I drum." She tugged at a hank of hair.

"You're a drummer?"

She nodded. "That's my talent. I've played since I was five. I did marching band all through high school and I play with an all-girl band called The Fabulosas. I wish they could be on stage with me tonight, but they'll be in the audience." She beat the air with imaginary drumsticks.

"Have you ever considered bangs?" I asked, appraising her oval face with its high cheekbones, strong chin, and beautiful brown eyes. "I think bangs would really make your eyes pop and emphasize your facial structure." I held up her hair to demonstrate. "And then your hair wouldn't get in your way when you perform."

She studied her reflection for a moment, then said, "Let's do it."

She held still as I cut, her eyes never wavering from the mirror. I could feel her assessing every snip, every bit of hair that fluttered to the floor. When I finished with her bangs, leaving them spiky and flirtatious so they just grazed her brows, I rolled and pinned the rest of her hair so it gently framed her face and hid the damaged ends.

"My eyes look so big," she exclaimed when I finished. "You are totally talented!"

"Thanks." I laughed, whisking hair snippets off her shoulders with a towel. "Good luck tonight."

Her face sobered. "Yeah, thanks. I really need to win. The Miss American Blossom scholarship money is my only hope for vet school after I finish my undergrad degree next May. I've got it all figured out. With what I make waiting tables and the money from the band's gigs, I still need to win Miss Georgia Blossom and be at least third runner-up at the national pageant. Thanks for the cut." She strode out, leaving the door open.

With a focus like that, I had no doubt she'd end up as a vet, or whatever she wanted to be. I thought of my own lack of focus at her age, the two years at the University of Georgia drifting from art classes to business classes, the decision to attend beauty school, hanging on to the relationship with Hank long after it was clear we had different priorities and values, my return to St. Elizabeth after the divorce. Maybe I needed to be more Brooke Baker–ish in my approach to life, I decided, slipping combs into the container of germicide. I needed goals. Not vet school or fame as a rocker chick, but something beyond "work at Mom's salon, live in an apartment, and see what turns up." I was saving for a house, but not in a really determined way. Maybe I should go around with a Realtor and look at what was on the market. Maybe that would inspire me to get more serious about my saving. Maybe I'd even get a part-time job to make it happen quicker.

I had resolved to ask my best friend, Vonda Jamison, if she could recommend a Realtor, when the door edged open and a soft voice said, "I think I'm last."

I turned, astonished, to see Rachel Whitley, the salon's shampoo girl, hovering on the threshold, her expression a blend of amusement and embarrassment. "Rachel! What in the world are you doing here?"

"I'm, like, a contestant," she said, plopping into the chair and spinning it around. The navy blue robe she wore over her costume belled out at her ankles.

"Really?" Seventeen-year-old Rachel, who would be a senior when school started up, had never struck me as the pageant type. With her style choices ranging from Goth to grunge and her makeup leaning toward kohl-rimmed eyes that made her look like a raccoon and matching black nails, Rachel struck me more as the anti-pageant poster child than a beauty queen wannabe. "Is this a joke?" I asked suspiciously, tempted to check the hall to see if Mom or Althea lurked out there, ready to burst out laughing.

"No," she said with an impish grin. "It's a dare."

"A dare?"

"Yeah. Like, some of my friends bet I wouldn't have the nerve to do this. If I make it to the finals, I get to drive Shannon's new Mustang for a week. If I win, I get it for a whole semester." She grinned at me and I noticed the Goth makeup was gone, leaving her great skin and Nile green eyes unadorned.

"What happens if you lose?"

She shrugged. "I have to wash it every week for the whole school year. And, like, wax it."

I cocked an eyebrow at her.

"It seemed like a good idea at the time," she said with a half shrug. "And it's a slick ride."

I surveyed her shoulder-length black hair with its multiple layers. She'd been known to hack at it with nail scissors and, for all I knew, hedge clippers . . . and it looked like it. At least it was free of the electric blue stripes she'd sported a couple weeks back. I didn't think there'd ever been a beauty queen with hair quite like this.

Correctly interpreting my silence, she said, "I need you to make my hair look more . . . more mainstream."

"How much time do I have?"

"I have to be on stage in forty minutes." She looked at me hopefully.

"Okay. The best we can do for tonight is make a few surface changes. Let me get Stella." I whisked out of the room to Stella's lair next door. She was just finishing up M16 Morgan's nails when I burst in. I explained the situation as concisely as possible and she rummaged in her purse for a makeup bag as she accepted Morgan's thanks.

"Oh, Rachel, this will be such fun," Stella greeted the girl with the first genuine enthusiasm I'd seen from her all day. "We don't have much time, so let's get to it. First things first: what's your talent?"

"I whistle," Rachel said, trilling a bar from "Whistle While You Work."

I'd always found whistling shrill and annoying, but Rachel's was surprisingly musical. "Isn't that from *Snow White*?"

She nodded. "I do, like, a Disney medley with part of a song from *Mary Poppins* and one from *Cinderella*."

"Let's see your costume," I said as an idea bloomed.

She rose and untied the robe, displaying a Cinderella-ish blue dress with white apron tied at the back, emphasiz-

ing her small waist. Lace-up black granny boots completed
the look. "My mom loaned them to me," she said, kicking
out one foot.

"Kerchief," I said, as Stella blurted, "Scarf." We exchanged a triumphant look.

"Your hair," I explained to the bewildered Rachel. "We
don't really have time to fix it, so we'll cover it with a kerchief for tonight, like the one Cinderella wears when she's
scrubbing the floor. I'll go find one. Stella, you get going
on the makeup."

"These brows—" Stella was saying as I hurried out the
door and down the hall.

I paused before the first door I came to past Stella's,
ready to knock, when an angry voice from inside said, "You
can't do this! I have rights. Elise is my daughter and—"

"Oh, please, Mama," a young girl's voice said. "I don't
even want—"

"I will ban you from the pageant if you don't return to
your seat in the auditorium, Mrs. Metzger." Audrey's tone
would freeze motor oil. "No one except staff and contestants are allowed backstage. I told you that yesterday."

"That's ridiculous. You can't exclude *mothers*." She tittered, but fury thrummed in her voice.

I backed away from the door, not wanting to interrupt
the argument to ask for a scarf. Turning, I bumped into
Marv, the bald man who found the mat sabotage. I didn't
know if he was the stage manager, the security man, or a
combination of the two. I asked him.

"I own this place," he said, apparently not offended by
my assumptions. "For my sins."

I was going to follow up on that, but the argument in the
room behind us got louder and we both looked at the door.

"Here we go again," he said lugubriously. "Just yesterday I had to show Miz Metzger out, but she's not the sort of woman who *stays* shown out, if you know what I mean. Miz Faye called me a coupla minutes ago, said she was creating trouble again. I don't know why I didn't just sell this place when Aunt Nan left it to me. Probably because no one would buy it," he answered his own question.

The door slammed open so hard it ricocheted against the wall. I jumped. A woman in her late forties stalked out— followed by Audrey and the young flautist—rage vibrating in every line of her massive figure. She probably topped out at close to six feet and two hundred pounds. Dyed blond hair showed darker at the roots. Her face with its slightly pug nose might have been attractive in an aging Doris Day-ish sort of way, if it weren't knotted into a scowl that would put a gargoyle to shame. At the sight of Marv, she stopped. "If you so much as lay a hand on me, I'll file assault charges," she said. She crossed her arms over an ample bosom.

"This way, Miz Metzger," Marv said, gesturing with one arm.

She wheeled to face Audrey. "Don't think I don't know exactly why you want to keep me out of here," she said meaningfully. "I know what goes on."

"I don't have a clue what you're talking about," Audrey said through clenched teeth. She held her clipboard like she wanted to bat the woman with it. "Nothing 'goes on,' Mrs. Metzger, except normal pageant activities." Before the other woman could respond, Audrey said, "I've got a dozen things to do before the show kicks off in half an hour. Thank you, Marv, for taking care of Mrs. Metzger."

"I don't need taking care of!" the older woman shouted after Audrey, standing on tiptoe to see around Marv. "My baby Elise needs taking care of." She clung to Elise's arm. "If she weren't so set on competing—"

"But, Mama, I don't want—"

Mrs. Metzger cut her off. "I heard what happened today with that poor girl falling off the stage. This place is a death trap. If my Elise so much as scrapes an elbow, we'll sue. I have a lawyer friend—"

"Okay, that's it," Marv said, his voice a good deal sterner. "Out. O-U-T." His bulk blocked the hallway and he stepped toward Mrs. Metzger, herding her toward the lobby. No small business owner wants a litigious troublemaker on the premises. Not waiting to see who triumphed—my money was on Marv—I hurried after Audrey, catching up with her before she entered the Green Room. A hum of conversation leaked out, punctuated by vocal warm-up exercises and what sounded like a dozen cats yowling. Bagpipes. Good heavens. I wondered briefly how anyone learned to play the bagpipes in this area. I didn't think you'd find much under "Bagpipe Lessons" in the Camden County yellow pages.

"Any chance you know where I can find a scarf or large handkerchief?" I asked Audrey.

She stared at me, distracted, and ran a hand through her hair. "I can't be bothered with that. Ask the girls."

I RETURNED TO RACHEL AND STELLA, TRIUMPHANTLY waving the blue and white kerchief a girl named Hayley had produced. Halting on the threshold, I gazed in wonder at the transformation Stella had worked on Rachel. She'd tweezed the thick brows into a clean arch and used liquid liner and earth-toned shadows to emphasize Rachel's beautiful Nile green eyes. Sheer foundation and a peachy blush finished the look. Rachel's squarish chin and strong jawline always looked a bit androgynous under the flat black-and-white Goth makeup she usually wore; now, she was striking.

"You look fabulous, Rachel," I said. "Your friend better plan on walking to school next month."

She beamed at me and could barely hold still long enough for me to secure the scarf around her head so just a few strands peeked out. "There. That'll do for tonight. I have a plan for tomorrow, so show up at Violetta's early."

"Will do," she promised. "Thanks."

Stella hugged her and said, "Break a leg," before Rachel danced out the door.

Chapter Five

THE TALENT SHOW BEGAN WITH A FEW REMARKS from Audrey and the introduction of the judges. The two men and a woman had seats at a narrow table shoehorned in front of the stage. Each stood and waved to the audience as he or she was introduced. The channel nine weatherman from Jacksonville, Ted Gaines, had heavy blond hair flopping onto his forehead and big white teeth that probably financed his dentist's last vacation. Audrey introduced the second judge as Renata Schott, a former Miss South Carolina Blossom and runner-up to Miss American Blossom 1990, who was now a motivational speaker and actress. Almost six feet tall, with a pronounced widow's peak, black hair, and lovely olive skin, she smiled a hello to the crowd. The third judge was a "prominent St. Elizabeth's businessman and major sponsor of the pageant." His attempt at a royal wave looked more like a drowning man signaling for help.

The evening got off to a rousing start with a fifth grader from St. Elizabeth Elementary School belting out the National Anthem. Seated beside Stella and Althea with my mom on the aisle (I had called them when I found out Rachel was competing), I gave Audrey props for knowing how to get the audience involved. Unfortunately, the first contestant was a singer who had considerably less talent than the ten-year-old and suffered by comparison. The audience, composed mostly of parents, friends, and supporters of the contestants, applauded politely. The baton twirler performed next, followed by Morgan with her M16. When the last booms of the "1812 Overture" faded, Althea whispered, "Well, at least knowing how to fieldstrip an M16 is a useful skill, unlike twirling. What does knowing how to toss a baton in the air get you?"

Still wearing the red, green, and black caftan, she might look like she'd wandered in from the Serengeti, but she had the old Althea's caustic sense of humor.

"Sssh," Mom cautioned us as the emcee introduced Rachel.

We fell silent, captivated by the sheer sense of joie de vivre Rachel exuded, as much as by the musicality of her whistling. Enthusiastic applause sounded when she finished and Mom beamed like Rachel was her daughter instead of her employee.

"Stella, however did you persuade Rachel to give up that black eyeliner and nail polish?" Mom asked. "She looks just darling with the new makeup."

Stella looked pleased with the praise. "She really wants to win, I think, and she's smart enough to realize that looking like Elvira isn't going to get her the crown. She—" Stella broke off, staring across the half-full auditorium. "What is Darryl doing here? I can't believe—" She jumped out of her seat and took off down the aisle.

Since the emcee announced a fifteen-minute intermission just then, she didn't disrupt the show. I watched as she came up to her husband, a wiry man with dark red hair, standing along the left-hand wall, halfway to the stage. Stella put her hand on his arm and he jumped. The crowd, milling in search of restrooms or chatting with friends, blocked them from view.

"What in tarnation is that about?" Althea asked. She, too, had watched Stella's rendezvous with her husband.

"I don't know," I said slowly, "but Stella's been weepy all day. I'm afraid she and Darryl are having problems."

"Every married couple does," Mom said calmly. "They'll work through it. It won't help them if their friends and acquaintances are gossiping about them."

"Mom!" I stared at her, surprised and hurt. "I'm not gossiping. Expressing concern is not the same as gossiping."

"You're right," she said, patting my arm. "I just know sometimes people need privacy to work things through." Her blue eyes behind the lenses of her rimless glasses looked serious. I wondered if Stella had confided in her. "Do you suppose it would be rude to leave now? I really came just to see Rachel. I'm dead on my feet. You'd've thought we were giving away free money, as many people as came to the salon this afternoon."

"I'm sorry," I said. "I should've been there."

"What, you think you're indispensable?" Althea asked. She stood and stretched, wooden bangles on her arms clicking together. She looked rather regal in the African garment. "I helped out and we did just fine. And, no, we can't leave yet, Vi," she said to Mom. "We've got to scope out the competition so we can strategize with Rachel in the morning."

My mom made a sound that was half sigh, half laugh

and said, "Well, in that case I'd better visit the little girls' room before they start up again."

"I'll go with you," Althea said.

"And I'm going backstage to collect my stuff so I can bug out of here as soon as the last contestant struts her stuff."

As Mom and Althea headed up the aisle to the restrooms, I threaded my way toward the stage and the steps leading backstage. It was quieter backstage, but not much. The contestants who had already performed laughed and chatted in small groups while the girls who had yet to display their talents warmed up or stood tensely, psyching themselves up like athletes preparing to storm the field during a championship game. Several parental-looking people, mostly moms but one or two dads, encouraged their daughters with cheery smiles and pep talks. So much for the prohibition against parents. Mrs. Metzger was huddled with Elise in a fold of the curtain just offstage. Her wagging finger and Elise's slumped shoulders clearly indicated she was haranguing her daughter about something. I didn't see Audrey or Jodi, but I spotted Marv on the far side of the stage, talking to a stagehand.

As I neared my little room, I noticed the door to Stella's room was closed. I raised my hand to knock but heard voices. Maybe she and Darryl were talking. I let my hand fall to my side and slipped into my room, quickly organizing my styling paraphernalia and tucking it into my kit. Stella's door remained closed when I came out, so I hurried through the narrow halls and returned to my seat just as the emcee announced Elise Metzger and her flute.

By the time the flautist finished, Stella still hadn't returned. Mom, Althea, and I exchanged a look. "Maybe she and Darryl went somewhere to have a conversation," Mom suggested.

"Maybe," I acknowledged, craning my neck to peer down the aisles. No sign of Stella.

Brooke Baker took the stage then, launching into a vigorous drum solo that brought the house down. She twirled her drumsticks when she finished and flung them into the audience, setting off a scramble as people lunged to get them. Brooke laughed and ran offstage, waving to the audience.

"That girl's something else," Althea said, shaking her head admiringly.

The talent competition finished up with Tabitha shaking her booty in a tiny costume that showed off her splendid figure. In fact, her abdominal muscles were so clearly defined I wondered if she used body makeup to enhance them. I was probably just jealous, I admitted to myself, surreptitiously patting my stomach. No six-pack there. Never very regular about exercise, I'd slacked off even more than usual in the summer's brutal heat, driving my car places I would normally have walked. I would do a few sets of crunches and squats when I got home, I promised myself.

As the contestants filed back on stage for their closing number, an interruption occurred. "Stop the exploitation of women," someone called from the back of the auditorium.

Virtually everyone in the audience turned his or her head. The protestors from outside marched single file down both aisles, headed for the stage. They carried their posters high, swiveling them from side to side so people could read their slogans: "Women are people, not objects"; "Beauty is only skin deep"; "Earn a degree, not a crown"; "Pageants promote violence against women"; and my personal favorite, "Get out of your bikini and into a classroom." I was pretty sure they didn't mean to encourage nudism in the classroom. Althea stiffened beside me.

The contestants looked stunned, the audience broke into nervous laughter punctuated with angry murmurs, and the emcee looked from right to left, hoping someone in the wings would defuse the situation. No one appeared—where was Audrey?—and Dr. Yarrow led his band onto the stage and calmly plucked the microphone from the emcee's fingers.

"You can't—" the emcee gobbled, but Dr. Yarrow overrode him with a calm, "Good evening," into the microphone. The contestants shuffled their feet uneasily behind him and Morgan sidled off the stage. I hoped she wasn't going for her M16.

"We're here tonight to educate you on the evils—yes, evils—associated with beauty pageants." His mellifluous voice rolled into the auditorium. "They range from fostering poor self-esteem to encouraging eating disorders to increasing violence against women. We—"

"Get off the stage, you freakin' feminazis!" A man's voice roared from the audience.

Dr. Yarrow ignored him. I supposed you got pretty good at ignoring hecklers if you taught college.

"Oppression of minorities starts by objectifying them. If a woman is no more than a collection of physical assets—hair, skin, reproductive organs—then she becomes something to possess, not an equal. Beauty pageants—"

Sam Barnes, the photographer, had been unobtrusive during the talent show. Now, however, he moved up the side aisle, camera trained on Dr. Yarrow and his band. He hugged the wall, advancing almost stealthily, a hunter creeping up on a pride of lions that might run if they spotted him. Or rip him to shreds.

"—undermine a woman's true self and take away her power." He held the microphone so close to his lips it made popping noises when he spoke.

"Amen!" a new voice declared from the back of the auditorium.

Before Dr. Yarrow could continue, Jodi Keen, looking as uncomfortable as a mouse facing a python, stepped onto the stage, followed by Marv. They advanced toward Dr. Yarrow, only to find their way blocked by the other protestors.

"We've called the police," Jodi called in a voice made thin by nerves. "They'll be here any minute."

"Good," yelled the protestor who told me I was too old to be a contestant. "We're not afraid of the po-po." She shook her poster fiercely.

Maybe I was wrong about their grades. Maybe getting arrested in the name of the cause got you an A+.

Marv trotted offstage, eluding Jodi's hand as she clutched at his arm like a drowning person grabbing at a rope. She stood there looking miserable, clearly undecided about what to do. I didn't envy her choices. She could rally the contestants to push through the line of protestors, possibly precipitating the kind of brawl that ended with combatants in the hospital or jail and earned unflattering headlines, or she could stand there and listen to Dr. Yarrow and his students diss her work and her contest. I wondered again where Audrey was. Maybe she was conferring with the police. A few people began to make their way to the exits. Others chanted, "Fight, fight!"

Dr. Yarrow fixed the audience with a stern look. "And those of you who come to gawk perpetuate—" His mic went dead. He tapped on it. Nothing happened.

Marv emerged from the wings, looking triumphant. He'd cut the power to the mic. I grinned. He handed Jodi another microphone. "This concludes the talent portion of the Miss Magnolia Blossom competition," Jodi blurted. "Thank you all for coming."

The protestors looked at their leader, who shrugged his shoulders fatalistically. He said something to his followers and they nodded. The protestors and the contestants gaggled together on the stage, gradually dispersing.

Althea stood, her head swiveling as she tracked the departure of the protestors. "I've got to get home," she said tersely. "See you in the morning, Vi." She sidled past us to the aisle and strode toward the doors.

Mom and I looked at each other, bemused. "What's up with her?" I asked.

"You don't suppose—" Mom said.

"No way," I said quickly. "Althea wouldn't date someone that . . . that militant."

"You're right," Mom said. "She's pretty much a live and let live kind of person. Sometimes she just gets a bee in her bonnet." She nodded toward Sam Barnes, who stood center stage, panning the departing audience, while Marv and his crew tidied the stage. "Is this really one of those reality shows?"

I explained about the documentary. "I'll bet he wishes someone had thrown a punch," I added. "Good TV."

"What a thought," Mom said. "I'm glad everyone had the sense to behave themselves. It's bad enough that the program got interrupted. Those poor girls work so hard on their routines." She tucked her purse under her arm. "Ready, Grace?"

"You go ahead," I said. "I just want to check backstage one more time for Stella."

"Okay, honey." Mom reached up to kiss my cheek. "See you in the morning."

*   *   *

THE BACKSTAGE AREA HAD EMPTIED OUT. NONE of the contestants lingered to hash over her performance or prep for the swimsuit contest the next day. A figure in a cape and hat—probably someone early for the *Phantom* rehearsal—disappeared around the corner at the far end of the hall. I could hear voices coming from the stage—Marv and his crew—but no chatter emanated from the Green Room or smaller dressing rooms. Stella's door remained closed but no light seeped from under it. I knocked. Nothing.

"Stella?" I called. Still nothing. I tried the knob. Locked. I felt chilled all of a sudden. Why would Stella lock the door? Assuming it was one of those locks where you push in the button to engage the lock, I ducked into my room next door and pulled a wire hanger from the rack.

Not stopping to analyze the sense of urgency that was driving me, I untwisted the hanger and returned to Stella's door. I poked one end of the stiff wire into the lock and maneuvered it, remembering the time Mom and I had used this trick to open the bathroom door when five-year-old Alice Rose locked herself in and refused to come out. The hanger jammed against part of the mechanism, then slipped. Darn. I wiggled it again, finally feeling it wedge in such a way I could twist it and pop the lock. Success! I turned the knob and the door swung open onto darkness.

The room smelled worse than it had, the musty scent overlaid with an odor that made me think there was a sewer backup. I wrinkled my nose, gagging. Light from the hall crept only halfway into the room, leaving the vanity and chair in near darkness. As my eyes adjusted to the dimness, I thought I could make out someone sitting in the chair. "Stella?" I whispered. No answer.

My fingers tingled like the blood had been cut off. I slid them up the wall beside me, seeking the light switch. Part of me knew what I would see when I flicked the light on, and I wasn't ready to face it. My fingers hesitated on the switch plate.

"What are you doing?" said a gruff voice directly behind me.

I stifled a shriek and jumped. The overhead light flared on, illuminating the woman's body in the chair, the reddish hair draping over the back, and the darker blood pooled on the floor and spattered across the wall and mirror.

Chapter Six

FOR ONE SHATTERING MOMENT WHEN I GLIMPSED the red hair, I thought it was Stella. But a second glance told me it was Audrey Faye with a knifelike implement plunged into her neck.

"Oh my God," Marv said behind me. "Aunt Nan told me about dry rot and warned me about mice in the dressing rooms, but she never mentioned anything like this." He bolted from the room and I could hear him being sick in the hall.

I didn't approach the body. There was nothing I could do for her and I knew the police would be pissed off if I intruded on the crime scene any more than I already had. I backed out of the room, careful not to touch anything, and found Marv leaning against the wall. He dabbed at his mouth with the hem of his tee shirt.

"Audrey Faye is dead," I told him. I pulled out my cell phone. "We need to call the police."

He nodded. "I'll get a bucket and mop."

Two patrol officers arrived just as Marv finished cleaning up. One of them, a woman about my age, with olive skin and dark hair, went into the room where Audrey's body slumped on the chair. The other, as luck would have it, was my ex-husband, Hank Parker. With thirty officers on the St. Elizabeth Police Department you'd think the odds would favor me occasionally and a stranger would show up when I dialed 911. But no. He didn't spot me immediately because I shifted half a step so Marv's bulk hid me. Hank's partner emerged after twenty seconds, conferred with Hank, and summoned help via her radio. Hank pulled out his notebook and lumbered toward us.

Two or three inches over six feet tall, Hank had the husky build of an offensive lineman, which is what he was in high school. In the twelve years since graduation, a small pot belly had added to his bulk, straining the buttons of his blue uniform shirt, and his brown hair had receded a bit from his forehead. He lived for the day he could shoot someone in the line of duty. So far, the best he'd managed was tasering a few gangbangers and assorted others when we lived in Atlanta.

I sneezed, drawing Hank's attention.

"Grace! What are you doing here?" He elbowed Marv out of the way and gripped my upper arm, leaning forward to kiss my cheek.

I ducked the kiss and shook myself free.

"Now, Grace, don't be like that. Can't a man even kiss his wife?"

Marv looked at us curiously. Hank's partner glared.

I kept a hold on my temper with difficulty. "I am not your wife. We are divorced. No relation legally or biologically. Get a girlfriend. Heaven knows, you had enough of them when we were married." Grrr. Hank's proprietary attitude was driving me crazy. I'd left Atlanta in part to get away from him, but he'd moved back to St. Elizabeth shortly after I did, ostensibly to care for his ailing mother who didn't look too sick when we saw her on the tennis courts or chugging mai tais at The Roving Pirate.

The female officer—her name tag read A. Qualls—threw me a suspicious look tinged with jealousy. Little did she know she had nothing to worry about; if she wanted Hank, she was welcome to him. More than welcome.

"I'm working for the beauty pageant," I said. "I found the body." I wrapped my arms around myself to stop the shivers that came on suddenly.

"Not another one!" Hank exclaimed.

"It's not like I go looking for them," I defended myself.

"Another one?" Officer Qualls stepped closer to me, her hand resting near the handcuffs clipped to her utility belt.

More footsteps sounded on the stairs and the door pushed open to admit a man about six feet tall, with close-cropped hair going gray at the temples. His flagpole-straight posture and air of command said "soldier" or "cop," even though he wore civilian clothes, a navy blazer, and an off-white shirt that set off his tanned skin. He had a square jaw and a longish nose that had clearly been broken at least once. His steely eyes swept the small crowd clogging the hallway, lingering for a moment on me. His brows rose a fraction. My heartbeat sped up at the sight of him. Special Agent in Charge John Dillon of the Georgia Bureau of Investigation. We'd met in May, when he investigated Constance DuBois's death, and there'd been a few sparks once he decided neither Mom nor I had stabbed Constance. But he'd been gone most of the summer, assigned to some special investigation on the other side of the state, and I hadn't seen him in two and a half months. How long had he been back? Maybe he'd returned weeks ago but hadn't been interested enough to call me. I suppressed a tiny ping of disappointment.

After a moment, his gaze moved past me and he said, "Who was first on the scene?" It took him less than a minute to take a report from Hank and Officer Qualls, prod them to put up crime scene tape, and assign Hank to keeping looky-loos from intruding. He disappeared into the room with Audrey's body. The coroner, arriving a few minutes later, joined him. More police officers showed up and separated Marv and me by putting me in the dressing room I'd used earlier. A sixteen-year-old copy of *People* I found in the vanity drawer kept my mind off what the coroner and crime scene types must be doing next door.

Finally, after what seemed like hours but was only twenty-five minutes by my watch, Special Agent Dillon stepped into the room. He paused on the threshold and gazed at me where I sat at the vanity. His eyes lingered a moment on the length of leg bared by my denim skirt. His mouth was set in a firm line, but a hint of humor lit his navy eyes. "Miss Terhune. I suppose I should've expected to see you here."

"I don't know why you say that, Marsh." I flipped a page of the magazine as if fascinated by the article about Pamela Anderson marrying Tommy Lee.

He sighed. I'd taken to calling him Marsh—short for Marshal Dillon—when we met during his investigation of Constance DuBois's death. His name was John, but it seemed like a liberty to use his first name. I wasn't sure why . . . I called everyone else I knew under fifty by their first names. And he couldn't have been more than forty or forty-one.

"Maybe because you're involved in every murder I've ever investigated in St. Elizabeth?"

I tossed aside the magazine and stood to shake the hand he held out. It was hard and callused and I remembered he had a horse and that he'd invited me to see it. An invitation he'd never followed up on. Not that I minded. Much.

"One," I said defensively. "This makes two. And I'm not 'involved.' I just happened to find the body. Well, after I picked the lock with a hanger." I resumed my seat.

"Exactly." He didn't quite smile, but a crease—not really a dimple—appeared in his cheek.

Damn. The almost-dimple made my pulse race in a way that was unnerving.

"I hope you're not going to tell me that the victim got a bad perm or a fright-night dye job at your salon this time."

I glared at him. He was referring to Constance DuBois, who was murdered only hours after threatening to close down Violetta's because her highlights turned orange. Through no fault of my mom's, I might add.

"Audrey wasn't a client," I said. I explained about Audrey hiring me and Stella.

He took out a notebook and a "let's get down to business" look appeared on his face. "Tell me about finding Ms. Faye."

I told him about coming back to look for Stella, about finding the door locked and using the hanger to open it.

"Who is Stella?" he asked. "And why were you concerned to the point where you picked the lock?" He flipped a page of his notebook.

I reminded him he'd met Stella at Mom's salon. The why I was worried part was harder. "I don't know," I said. "She'd been acting depressed and she seemed upset to see her husband here. When she didn't come back after intermission, well, we—Mom and Althea and I—were worried about her. I'd heard her and Darryl in there"—I nodded my head at the wall separating our rooms—"during the break and I thought she might be upset."

He shot me a sharp look. "You're sure you heard her and her husband?"

"Yes, I—" I stopped to think. I hadn't really been able to distinguish words or voices. I'd just assumed it was Stella. I told Agent Dillon as much.

"So it could have been Ms. Faye in there with . . . who? A man? A woman?"

"I don't know."

"What about when you came back here after the show? Did you see anyone?"

I closed my eyes, mentally retracing my steps. "Marv and a couple of his workers were on the stage—I heard them. There was no one—wait!" My eyes flew open. "Someone was at the other end of the hall when I came up the steps. He—or she—turned the corner just as I got to the hall."

"Description?"

"All I saw was a cape and a hat," I admitted. "I thought it was an actor here for the *Phantom* rehearsal."

"Midget sized? Shaquille O'Neal sized? Did he move like an octogenarian, an athlete, a kid? C'mon, Grace. You're a natural observer. Give me more."

His brusque tone undermined the compliment. I closed my eyes to visualize the figure at the end of the hall. "He was taller than me by at least a couple inches and moved like a young person, that is, he seemed vigorous." Opening my eyes, I screwed up my face in apology. "That's the best I can do."

"Man, woman? Black, white?"

I shook my head.

"When did you last see Audrey Faye alive?"

"Just a few minutes before the talent show started. I asked her to help me find a scarf."

"Did she have any enemies?"

I shrugged. "I didn't know her well at all. I never met her before she showed up at Violetta's today." I told him about Simone DuBois recommending us and he made a note. "She argued with one of the contestants' mothers today, though, and I suppose the protestors didn't like her." At his questioning look I filled him in on the spat with Mrs. Metzger and the existence of the anti-pageant protestors. "Oh, and she mentioned there'd been some mishaps, like the girl falling off the stage this afternoon."

He flipped his notebook closed when I finished. "About Stella," he said. "Does she have any history with Ms. Faye?"

His studied casualness put me on full alert. I sat up straighter. "Not that I know of," I said. "I don't think they'd ever met. Why?"

He paused as if debating whether or not to tell me. When he spoke, his voice was low and serious and his eyes watched for my reaction. "The murder weapon was a nail file."

Chapter Seven

"YOU CAN'T HONESTLY TELL ME THE POLICE SUSPECT Stella Michaelson of murder!" Mom said early the next morning as we readied the salon for opening. She looked refreshed by a night's sleep, wearing orchid seersucker slacks that complemented the grays, silvers, and white in her short hair. A matching tee shirt stretched across her plump bosom and over her stomach, hiding the drawstring waist. I didn't look so perky. It had been almost midnight by the time I got back to my apartment and I hadn't slept well with visions of Audrey's lifeless body sprawling in my dreams. Only caffeine—a cup of tea and a can of root beer so far—kept my eyes open. The only thing keeping me upright was the broom I was using to sweep around the styling stations.

"The police in this town don't see beyond the end of their noses, Vi," Althea put in. She stood by the coffeemaker, as if by looming over it she could intimidate it into faster production. The aromatic liquid slowed to a drip-drip and she pulled a mug from the cupboard. "Why, they suspected you of doing away with Connie DuBois." She snorted. Today's caftan was sand colored and fringed with knotted strings at the hem. I had to admit it looked good on her, setting off her dark skin and making her tall figure look graceful. An ankle bracelet of bells tinkled when she crossed the room to hand my mom her mug.

"Thanks," Mom said. "But *Stella*. No one could suspect Stella of violence."

"No one who knows her," I agreed. "I told Agent Dillon the idea was ridiculous."

"So he's back, is he?" Althea said with a knowing look at me. "Hmmm."

To my annoyance, I felt myself blushing. "There's nothing to 'hmmm' about," I said. "He was interviewing me about a murder, not asking me for a date." I plied the broom more vigorously than I intended, floofing the hair and dust I'd collected so it dispersed again. "Shoot." I swept more carefully and bent to scoop the pile into a dustpan.

"But he will," Althea said confidently.

"I'm worried about Stella," I said, dragging the conversation away from my social prospects. "Agent Dillon asked me for her phone number, but no one answered when he called. And then they sent an officer over to the house, but no one was home."

"He told you that?" Mom asked, her brows knitting.

"No. I heard his end of a phone conversation." He'd made me hang around until he finished interviewing Marv . . . I couldn't help overhearing the crime scene techs' conversations, the bantering of the other officers, and Dillon's phone calls. In addition to the tidbit about Stella and Darryl not being home, I'd learned that the coroner suspected Audrey had died within the last two hours (duh), and that whoever killed her would have been splattered with enough blood to impersonate an extra in a *Friday the 13th* movie. Dillon speculated that the murderer stole a costume from the rack to cover his or her bloodied clothes. It took me about two seconds to realize the caped figure I'd seen had probably murdered Audrey. It still gave me the shivers when I thought about it. I didn't mention it to Mom and Althea, not wanting to worry them.

"Good morning, all."

Stella's voice startled us. The three of us looked toward the door like our heads were on wires. Dressed in jeans and a pale pink polo shirt, Stella looked more tired than I felt. She held Beauty in her arms, but the cat jumped down and established herself on the wide windowsill where she could glare at the squirrels chasing each other around the old magnolia tree in the front. One of them scampered down the hammock's line and Beauty growled.

"Stella, honey, are you okay?" Mom asked, bustling forward to hug the surprised manicurist.

"A little tired, Vi, but nothing serious." Stella pulled away from Mom and looked at the three of us. "What's up? You all look so . . . so worried." A hint of unease crossed her face. "Did something happen?"

"It's just that when the police said you weren't home last night—" Mom started.

"The police?" Alarm rang in Stella's voice. "The police were here?"

"Not here," I said hastily. "At the Oglethorpe." When she just stared at me, wide-eyed, I said, "Audrey Faye was murdered some time during the program. I found her."

Stella's hand went to her mouth, covering it. She said

nothing. As we watched, she swayed and the color leached out of her skin. I'd heard of people turning white, but I'd never seen it happen. No spot of color remained in her cheeks. Her green eyes stood out like pools in the pallor of her face.

"She's going to faint," Althea said, springing forward. Ruthlessly, she pressed Stella's head down between her knees. "Deep breaths," Althea counseled. "In . . . out."

After a moment, Stella struggled against Althea's hand on her head. "I'm okay," she said. "I just need to sit down." With Althea's hand at her elbow, she tottered to the love seat and sank onto it. "What happened?" she asked.

"Someone stabbed Audrey," I said. I debated whether or not to tell her about the murder weapon but realized she'd find out sooner or later anyway. "With a nail file."

"Oh my God." Tears sprang to her eyes.

I was surprised. Sure, Audrey's death was a shock, but it wasn't a personal tragedy for Stella who hadn't even known the woman.

"Here." Mom thrust a mug of steaming chamomile tea at Stella, who took it automatically. "It's always a shock when you hear someone you know has died unexpectedly."

"When you said the police were looking for me, it's because they think I did it, isn't it?" Stella said, her gaze swiveling from Mom's face to mine. "Isn't it?"

"Of course they don't," I said. "But they need to question a lot of people. I'm sure they're talking to all the contestants and the crew and anyone who might've been backstage last night. You're just one on a long list."

"What'll happen to Jess if I'm arrested?" Stella asked, as if she hadn't heard a word I'd said. Her hands trembled so hard that tea slopped over the rim of the mug and splotched her slacks. "Ow." She set the cup on the end table.

Mom sat beside her and took her hand. "Stella, no one will think you had anything to do with Audrey's death. The police want to talk to you, but they're not going to arrest you. Your nail file was right there where anyone could pick it up, right?"

Stella nodded numbly.

"Agent Dillon will figure that out. It's not like you had a reason to kill Audrey Faye. Why, you didn't even know the woman."

"The police might be slower than three-legged tortoises," Althea put in, "but even they aren't going to figure you for a random killer, running around murdering people you don't even know."

Stella cried harder. She said something, but I couldn't understand her through the sobs.

I looked at Mom and Althea but they shrugged. "What?" I asked.

Stella raised her head. Tears ran down her face. Mascara streaked her cheeks and the tip of her nose glowed red. "They're going to arrest me," she said fatalistically. "Darryl and her . . . Audrey and Darryl . . . They were having an affair."

WE GOT SO QUIET YOU COULD HAVE HEARD A FEATHER land on a down comforter. Then, the three of us tried to talk at once.

"Stella, honey, I'm so sorry," Mom said.

"That bastard," Althea said, pounding her fist against her thigh.

"How do you know?" I asked. Maybe she'd misinterpreted something, jumped to the wrong conclusion. I didn't know Darryl all that well, but he'd always struck me as a solid guy. And he seemed to love Stella. They'd celebrated their nineteenth wedding anniversary in April and had spent a romantic weekend on Jekyll Island, leaving Jess with Stella's mother. Stella glowed for the whole next week.

Stella gave Mom a wan smile and looked at me. "He told me."

Oh. Not much chance she was mistaken then. "What did he say?"

Mom gave me her "mind your own business" glare. I pretended not to see it.

"They grew up on the same block over in Kingsland, so he's known her forever. He said they ran into each other about three months back and, well . . . you know. One thing led to another. They've been seeing each other a couple of times a week. Darryl's had a lot of time on his hands since they laid him off at the auto dealership up in Brunswick. He's been really frustrated that he can't find anything better than part-time work. You'd think with the economy being like it is, that people would need good mechanics to keep their old cars on the road so they don't have to buy new ones. That's what Darryl says. But it hasn't worked out that way."

"So what you're trying to say is he had an affair because he's feeling sorry for himself?" Althea asked bluntly. "Because he needs to get his mojo back? Don't tell me you're buying that hog swill."

Stella teared up again and Mom patted her hand.

"Why was he at the pageant last night?" I asked.

"He wanted to break it off," she said. She groped for the tissue box on the end table and blew her nose. "That's what he said. But when he got there, he realized it was bad timing, with all the people around and her so busy and me being there. He didn't know I would be there. We haven't talked much the last couple of weeks." She sniffed.

"Was she married?" Althea asked.

Stella nodded. "Her husband's name is Kevin. Darryl told me."

Wow. For some reason, I hadn't thought of Audrey as having a husband. "Does—did—she have children?"

Stella shook her head. "I don't think so. I didn't know them, you know. But Darryl told me her name, so when I found out that it was her that hired us for the pageant, I was torn. Part of me wanted to have it out with her, to ask her how she could do this to my family." Stella's voice rose and she clenched and unclenched her hands in her lap. "But the other part . . . Well, I just wanted to crawl in a hole and die when I met her and saw how young and pretty she is. Was."

"You're welcome to stay here for a couple of days, if you need to get away, get some perspective," Mom offered when Stella fell silent.

"That's kind of you, Violetta," Stella said, "but Jess and I have been at my mom's."

That explained why the police hadn't found her at home. It didn't explain Darryl's absence, though. "What about Darryl?" I asked.

She gave me a puzzled look.

"Is he still at your house?"

"As far as I know," she said. "Why?"

"The police may want to know where he was at going on eleven last night."

After a hesitation so brief I wondered if I'd imagined it, she said, "He was with me." Reaching for the mug, she took a sip of tea and kept her gaze on the liquid. "We were talking. You saw him at the pageant, right? Well, we drove around and talked."

"For four hours?" I wrinkled my brow.

"We had a lot to talk about." Her gaze fixed on Beauty, who was stalking the shadow of a leaf skipping across the wood floor as the breeze swayed the tree limbs outside the salon.

I didn't doubt that, but I did doubt her story. I didn't want to—I'd known Stella for almost fifteen years, ever since she came to work for my mom—but something about her airy tone and the way she wasn't meeting our eyes made me wonder if she was telling the whole truth. I let it go, but part of me couldn't help wondering who she was protecting—herself or Darryl?

Chapter Eight

✂

MOM TOOK STELLA INTO THE KITCHEN AT THE BACK of the house for another cup of tea and a tête à tête, as my favorite author, Georgette Heyer, would have said. As best as I could gather, that meant a quiet one-on-one conversation. Left alone with Althea, I finished sweeping and got to work dusting the wooden blinds. Althea rearranged the display of skin-care products, Althea's Organic Skin Solutions, moisturizers, masks, and cleansers from her family's recipes that she'd used for years as an aesthetician but had only gotten around to packaging and marketing last month. Setting the last violet-capped bottle in place, she turned to me with her hands on her hips.

"I assume you're going to nose around, find out who really killed this Faye woman?"

"It's a police—"

"Fah. Don't try to pull the wool over my eyes, baby-girl.

You know and I know that you could no more leave Stella swinging in the wind than you could design a rocket ship. What are we going to do first?"

"We?"

She looked down her nose at me and I caved. She was right: I *had* been thinking about doing a bit of investigating, not so much because I didn't trust the GBI to find the killer but because of the rumors that would spread while they plodded through their procedures. If word got around that Stella was a murder suspect, people would remember that a long time past when the real killer was convicted and stowed in a jail cell.

"All right, all right. Since I'm working at the beauty pageant anyway, I thought I'd talk to some of the girls, find out if they saw anything. And I also want to follow up on some of the incidents Audrey talked about. Maybe her assistant, Jodi, knows more about that. If you get a chance, maybe after work, you could hook up with the protestors and find out what they're all about."

Althea didn't respond and I turned to look at her. She looked uncharacteristically unsure of herself, pulling at a fraying thread on her cuff. "I don't know if I can do that," she said finally.

"Well, okay," I said, puzzled. "Maybe you could talk—"

"It's because of Kwasi."

"Your boyfriend? You don't think he'd like you hanging out with the protestors? They don't seem violent or anything."

"Of course he's not violent," she snapped.

"*He's* not—" I stopped. Dr. Yarrow was Kwasi. Her boyfriend was the protestors' ringleader. No wonder she'd gotten all stiff and huffy and run off immediately after the protestors invaded the pageant. I wondered if she'd known he'd be there. It didn't seem like it. I couldn't think what to say so I blurted the first thing that came to mind. Always a mistake. "I didn't think he'd be so young."

Her brown eyes darkened as she glared at me. "I'm too old for him, is that what you're saying?"

"No," I said. "I just didn't know—" I stopped before I could say something else stupid. The age difference had startled me, although he was probably only six or eight years younger than Althea. A moment's reflection told me my reaction was hypocritical; if he were older than Althea I wouldn't have blinked an eye. "He seems very . . . committed to his cause," I offered.

Althea's glare faded. "He's a passionate man," she agreed. A slight smile played around her lips and I got the feeling she was referring to more than his political opinions. I knew perfectly well that being sixtyish and unmarried did not mean a woman was celibate in this day and age, but in all the years I'd known Althea, I'd never gotten the feeling she was looking for more than casual friendship from the men she occasionally went out with. Maybe there was more to Dr. Kwasi Yarrow than met the eye.

"It's helpful that you know him," I said. "You can just ask him if he or any of his students saw something suspicious."

Althea twisted her mouth to the side. "I could do that, I suppose. Maybe I could even join them for a few hours. I've never had much use for beauty pageants. I could make a poster. How about 'Beauty is only skin deep, but ugly is ugly to the bone'?"

"Sounds good," I said, relieved that she didn't seem so touchy now.

Althea gathered up her purse, intent on buying some poster board and markers before the salon's first customer

was due. On her way out, she bumped into Rachel coming
through the door, munching on an apple. Althea congratulated the girl on her performance and bustled down the
stairs to her aged Ford LTD, anklet tinkling.

"I'm here for my makeover," Rachel said, spreading her
arms like an actress embracing her public. She spoiled the
effect by giggling. She sat at my station, pushing off with
her foot to spin the chair a lot faster than the manufacturer
ever intended.

"Just let me get Mom and Stella," I said.

She nodded, arcing the apple core toward the trash can
twelve feet away. When I returned with Stella and Mom,
Rachel was sitting in the chair, smock around her neck.

"It's weird to be a client," she said as I shampooed her
hair quickly and squeezed the water out with a towel.

"Okay, no looking until I'm done," I said when she was
back in my chair. I swiveled it so she faced away from the
mirror.

"Just like on *What Not to Wear*," she said. "You're not
going to make me look *too* mainstream, are you? I mean,
like, I don't want to be boring."

"You could never be boring," Mom reassured her.

I set to work, enduring a lot of "backseat styling" from
Mom and Stella. I had thought about this style a lot last
night and I cut quickly, leaving the hair longer at the front so
the ends softened her lantern jaw and keeping it short in the
back to display her swanlike neck. I gave her asymmetric
bangs she could either brush across her forehead or gel for a
spikier effect. I finished by working a wax through her hair
that gave volume to the newly evened-off layers that framed
her face, emphasizing her cheekbones and large eyes.

"Voilá," I said, spinning the chair so she could view
herself.

Mom and Stella applauded as Rachel turned her head from right to left to examine the cut. "It's, like, really cool," she said. "Not stodgy and dull."

I kept my mouth shut, but I wondered if her amazement meant she thought most of the cuts I did were boring. I tried to give customers what they wanted and sometimes that meant conservative or even out of date. I had to admit that my St. Elizabeth's customers were not, overall, as daring as my Atlanta customers had been. At Vidal Sassoon, I'd counted models and young junior league types intent on one-upping each other among my clients and they'd kept me on my styling toes.

"It suits you," Mom said. "Good work, Grace."

"Now, let me at her," Stella said, bumping me aside with her hip. "We've got to do something about those nails."

Rachel held out her hands, wiggling fingers with short nails still showing traces of black polish. "I guess black is out?" she said.

"Definitely," said Stella, taking one of the girl's hands. "I'm thinking coral with your skin tone."

The phone rang as Stella was finishing up the second coat of polish. Mom answered it. "It's for you, Stella. The police." She held the phone out.

Stella took it as gingerly as if it were a scorpion. Her end of the conversation was monosyllabic, and when she hung up, deep grooves bracketed her mouth. "They want to talk to me. Now."

"I'll drive you," I offered with a glance at my watch. We were due at the theater by ten to prep the contestants for the swimsuit competition. It was only eight now. If Agent Dillon kept it reasonably brief, we could be back from Kingsland in time to beautify the girls.

"Is this about Miss Faye's murder?" Rachel asked, still admiring her new 'do out of the corners of her eyes.

"How did you know about that, Rachel?" Mom asked.

The *St. Elizabeth Gazette* only came out once a week—on Thursdays—so news of the death hadn't been publicized in the newspaper.

Rachel gave her the kind of "how can you be so out of it?" look that only a teenager could perfect. "A tweet from my friend Shannon whose mom works in a funeral home. And Tabitha's blog. And an e-mail from Miss Keen this morning, saying the pageant would continue as scheduled. But we can't use the theater today. Everything's down at the yacht club."

I hadn't even stopped to think that the pageant might get cancelled.

"Goodness," Mom said faintly. "What's a tweet? I thought it was part of a stereo."

Stella and I left Rachel explaining the intricacies of twenty-first-century communications to Mom.

My cell phone rang before I got off Mom's veranda.

"How come I have to hear about you finding dead bodies secondhand?" Marty greeted me.

Martin Shears, political reporter for the *Atlanta Journal-Constitution*, was plugged into so many news sources, including the GBI and coroners' offices around the state, that I didn't even bother asking how he'd heard.

"It's good to hear from you," I said. Something in my voice made Stella smile and she continued to the car to give me some privacy. "I was going to call you later today. It's been hectic."

"Are you all right? Do you need me to come down there?"

His concern warmed me and I smiled into the phone. "I'm okay. It was gruesome, but I didn't know the victim very well. I *want* you to come down, if that counts."

He chuckled. "Maybe this weekend. I've got a new lead on the Lansky story—a developer who says he'll talk on the record about kickbacks—and I've got to chase that down."

Marty had a real bee in his bonnet about our governor, Beau Lansky, who had originally come from St. Elizabeth. We were convinced he was involved in the disappearance and murder of Althea's husband William twenty-some-odd years ago—whose body had only been found this last spring—but he was slippery and we hadn't been able to prove it.

"You can come down and cover the 'Beauty Pageant Murder,'" I said, investing the words with headline caps.

"Was Lansky sleeping with one of the contestants?"

"Not as far as I know." I laughed.

"Then I probably can't justify the trip. That would make a great angle, though," he said.

I heard clicking in the background and knew he was typing on his keyboard. "Look, you're probably on deadline so I'll let you go. If you come down this weekend, I'll get you a ticket to the pageant final."

"And if you think of a way to give the story a political spin, let me know. I'll drive right on down."

"Deal," I said.

Chapter Nine

STELLA SAT SILENTLY IN THE PASSENGER SEAT OF my Ford Fiesta as I headed out of St. Elizabeth on SR 42 toward Kingsland, a small town about twenty miles southwest. St. Elizabeth inhabits a point on Georgia's southeast coast bounded by the Satilla River to the north and the Atlantic Ocean to the east, so you pretty much have to go west to get anywhere unless you go by boat. A couple miles out of town, I-95 connects us to Jacksonville, Florida, forty-five minutes south, and Savannah to the north. When I lived in Atlanta, I was only four hours from home, but it felt like another universe.

Stella still hadn't said a word by the time I parked in the lot fronting the Georgia Bureau of Investigation Region Fourteen headquarters. Someone with a penchant for precision had clipped the hedges fronting the building into rigid rectangles. Narrow windows reminiscent of arrow slits scored the tan brick of the building. By the look Stella cast at the plain façade, you'd've thought she was entering the Bastille for an appointment with a guillotine. I gave her shoulders a squeeze. "It'll be okay," I told her. "Just a few questions and then we're off to work our magic on the contestants. What kind of swimsuit do you think Rachel will have?"

"Black," we said together. Stella gave a weak laugh and pushed open the door.

Special Agent Dillon didn't keep us waiting. We hadn't even sat down in one of the molded plastic chairs before the inner door opened and he motioned to Stella. "Thank you for coming in, Mrs. Michaelson," he said. He looked approachable in an open-necked shirt and navy slacks. I wondered if his lack of jacket and tie was a conscious attempt to set Stella at ease.

"I'll get a cup of coffee at the Perk-Up and meet you back here in half an hour," I said, emphasizing the time so Agent Dillon would know we were on a schedule.

Stella grabbed my arm, her ring snagging on the loose knit of my moss-colored cotton sweater. "No! I want you with me."

"I'd prefer to chat with you one-on-one," Agent Dillon told her with a smile, giving me a "get lost" look.

"No." Stella set her mouth in a mulish line. "This is hard for me. If Grace can't sit in then I want a lawyer."

"There's no need to get a lawyer involved," Agent Dillon said, his eyes narrowing.

From the look he gave me, I knew he thought I'd put Stella up to this. "I'll stay if you want me to, Stella."

Sighing, Agent Dillon held the door wider and escorted us both to his office. I'd been there once before, in May, when he first questioned me about Constance DuBois's death. It looked the same, with the large window admitting lots of light and a trio of photos on one wall showing Dillon's horse going over a series of jumps. Agent Dillon crossed to his desk and gestured at the two blue-padded chairs in front of it.

"I don't want to hear a peep out of you," he warned me as we sat. I settled into my chair, but Stella perched on the edge of hers like a finch ready to fly off at the first hint of danger. She clutched her purse on her lap, opening and closing the clasp. *Snick-snick.*

Dillon pulled a Baggie from his desk drawer and slid it across the polished surface. "Do you recognize this?" he asked, watching Stella's face.

Inside the bag was a nail file, six inches of rigid metal coming to a wicked point. Coated with diamond dust, it had a wooden handle stamped with the initials "SM." Darryl had given it to Stella when she graduated from cosmetology school. He'd had it specially made, she said, still impressed with his thoughtfulness years later. I couldn't count the number of times I'd heard her tell customers about the file as she used it to shape their nails. Even though she used a powered file for most of her nail work, she still finished customers' nails with her special file.

"It's my nail file," she said. She reached for the Baggie but Dillon pulled it out of reach.

"We have to hang on to this, I'm afraid," he said. "Can you tell me about your relationship with Audrey Faye?"

"I didn't know her," Stella said. "She hired Grace and me to do hair and nails for the girls in the pageant. I'd never met her before we arrived at the theater."

I waited for her to mention Darryl's relationship with Audrey, but she didn't. I tensed, thinking she'd be better off coming clean. Dillon had a way of ferreting things out.

"When did you last see her alive?"

Stella thought for a moment. "About half an hour before the talent show started, maybe? She walked past my room with one of the girls and her mother. They seemed to be arguing."

"Mrs. Metzger, I'll bet," I said.

The look Dillon gave me said he didn't want my input. "Any idea how your nail file ended up in Ms. Faye's neck?" he asked.

Stella gasped and a hand went to her own neck. "No! I mean, I left all my stuff in the room before I went out to watch the show. I didn't lock the door or anything—it's not like we had keys—so anyone could have . . ."

"Any idea who did?"

"No!" Stella seemed appalled at the thought.

"You went out to watch the talent show . . . then what?"

The *snick-snick* of the purse clasp opening and closing came faster. "My husband . . . I met up with my husband, Darryl, and we went for a drive. Just around, you know, talking."

Dillon nodded. "And later? Where were you when my officers came to your house about ten thirty?"

"At my mom's," Stella whispered.

"You spent the night there?" Dillon kept his voice neutral.

"Yes. Jessica—my daughter—and I have been staying there for a couple of weeks."

"And your husband?"

"He was at the house."

Dillon shook his head. "No one's been at the house."

"Then where's Darryl?" Stella asked, leaning forward. Her purse tumbled off her lap, spilling its contents. "Oh, no!" She bent and began trying to shovel wallet, lipsticks, coins, and other purse detritus into the bag.

"Let me," I said, gently nudging Stella upright. I dropped to my knees and patted the carpet in search of stray coins.

"You haven't been in touch with your husband?" Dillon asked. I couldn't see his face, but I heard the skepticism in his voice.

"I tried to call his cell," Stella said, "but he hasn't answered. Where could he be?"

She looked at me as I straightened, her face tight with worry. I put the purse back in her lap and squeezed her hand before reseating myself.

"That would be the sixty-four-thousand-dollar question, wouldn't it?" Dillon said. "Especially since I understand he had a relationship with Ms. Faye. A sexual relationship."

Stella jumped two inches, dumping the purse off her lap again. She started to cry and I glared at Dillon. He didn't have to hit Stella with it out of the blue like that. I stood to put my arms around Stella, hugging her and the chair awkwardly. Something from the purse made a crunching sound under my foot and I saw I'd pulverized a plastic container of breath mints. Drat.

"You don't have to answer any more questions," I told Stella. I'd learned a thing or two about legal procedure while married to Hank. "C'mon. Let's go."

Stella lifted her tear-blotched face to look at Dillon, who sat calmly behind his desk. I wondered how many years it took to become insulated to the violent human emotions—fear, anger, grief—that cops encounter almost daily. And what cost did that deliberate damping of sensitivity carry? A crow flew past the window, casting a shadow that obscured Dillon's eyes for a moment.

"H-how did you know?" Stella asked.

She sniffed and I hunted on the floor for the packet of

tissues that had spilled from the purse. She took it and blew her nose on a tissue, her gaze never leaving Dillon's face.

"A witness mentioned it," Dillon said. "When and how did you find out about the affair?"

I gave him credit for effective interviewing technique; startled by the way he divulged his knowledge of the affair, Stella had lost her opportunity to play dumb and say, "What affair?"

Stella squared her shoulders and took a deep breath. "Ten days ago." She told him about Darryl's confession and said he'd been planning to break up with Audrey. I didn't detect even a hint of doubt in her voice.

"But he didn't?" Dillon pushed.

"No. It was too chaotic last night. He was going to tell her today. Then, well, we were going to talk again." Stella's lips tightened and I could see the hurt in her eyes, but she had control of herself again. "I don't know where we stand right now." Her pain and confusion were almost palpable.

I thought I caught a hint of sympathy in Dillon's eyes before he jotted some notes. A lawn mower coughed to a start outside the window and I watched as a shirtless man began pushing it across the square of lawn behind the GBI building. I cleared my throat and looked ostentatiously at my watch.

Dillon arched one brow but didn't look up from his notes for a full thirty seconds. When he did, he addressed Stella. "We might have more questions later, Mrs. Michaelson, but I think we can wrap it up for the morning. If you hear from your husband, tell him to contact us immediately. It's important that we talk to him."

"Okay," Stella said, standing. "Oh, my stuff." A lipstick rolled across the floor.

"I'll get it," I said, nudging her toward the door. "You might want to splash some water on your face."

"Thanks, Grace."

As soon as Stella was out the door, I turned back to Dillon, who had moved around to the front of his desk and was leaning back against it, arms folded over his chest. "She didn't do it, you know."

Dillon picked up Stella's purse and held it open as I retrieved items and plopped them in. "It's early days yet," he said.

"I hope you know we'll be talking to people," I said, stuffing a hairbrush into the purse with unnecessary force.

"We?"

"Mom, Althea, and I."

"Great. Violetta's Vigilantes on the prowl again. Just what I need."

I stopped in mid-bend, a Kathleen Woodiwiss paperback in my hand. "What did you call us? Violetta's Vigilantes? It has a nice ring. But we're not vigilantes . . . We just ask a few questions, keep our ears open."

"Yeah. And it almost got all three of you killed just a couple months ago. Stay out of it, Grace."

I waved away his grim tone with a flick of my hand, picking up a metal container of paprika. Why in the world did Stella carry paprika in her purse? "All I'm saying is don't waste time and effort investigating Stella. She didn't do it."

"The affair gives her a strong motive," he pointed out.

"It gives Audrey's husband a motive, too," I said. "Have you talked to him?"

"He's the one who told us about the affair," Dillon said. He plucked the paprika from my hand and stowed it in the purse. "I really do know how to do my job, you know."

He looked at me from under his brows, his usually navy-colored eyes a tantalizing marine blue. His fingers grazed mine as he handed over the restocked purse and I felt a tingle all the way to my shoulder. From the sudden rigidity of his expression, I thought he felt it, too.

"I don't doubt that," I said a little breathlessly, "but your job is catching the killer and ours is taking care of Stella. So, you do your thing and we'll do ours."

"Just make sure your 'thing' doesn't interfere with my investigation," Dillon said. His manner wasn't threatening, but I sensed the steel beneath the words. "And make sure Mrs. Michaelson knows that lying to protect her husband would be a very bad idea."

Stella appeared in the doorway before I could answer. "Ready?" she asked.

I tore my gaze away from Dillon's and handed Stella her purse. "Yeah. Let's go."

Chapter Ten

I HAD TO BREAK A FEW SPEED LIMITS TO GET BACK to St. Elizabeth in time. Stella said little during the ride, but she seemed more composed, less tense, than on the way to Kingsland. We stopped by her house to pick up replacement manicure supplies since the gear she had at the Oglethorpe was trapped behind crime scene tape or stuck in a police evidence locker. She sat up straighter, peering through the windshield as we approached the small brick house, but her shoulders slumped by the time she returned to the car, manicure kit in hand.

"He's not there," she said. "I'm worried about him."

I wanted to ask if she thought Darryl could know something about Audrey's death but decided Stella would take such a question as a vote of no confidence.

The St. Elizabeth Marina sits just inside the Satilla River before it empties into the St. Andrew Sound. A variety of boats—from deep-sea vessels and ferries decked out with numerous radars and antennas to smaller pleasure and fishing craft that traveled up the river to sleek sailboats—rocked gently against the tire bumpers padding each slot at the dock. A park with greenery, fountains, and a gazebo popular for weddings stretches in front of the marina and runs for a couple of blocks on either side of it. In the summer, food vendors park their vans along the sidewalk so tourists can enjoy a hot dog or ice cream as they stroll along the water. The scents of briny water and baking mud told me it was low tide.

I found a place to park at the back of a dirt lot across the street from the marina. We arrived at the waterfront to find unusual crowds and an air of anticipation. Throngs of people—tourists with sunburned shoulders and cameras looped around their necks, and locals with folding chairs and dogs on leashes—jammed the street, sidewalk, and decks of restaurants overlooking the water. Clearly, the swimsuit contest was more popular with the general public than the talent contest. Either that, or word had gotten around about the protestors' invasion and Audrey's death and the crowds had turned out hoping for another disaster.

As if my thoughts had conjured them up, I saw the protestors setting up their chairs, coolers, and signs within easy viewing distance of the gazebo where the swimsuit contest judging would take place. Althea was helping Dr. Yarrow unload placards from a tan van. I waved but she didn't see me. The sunburned girl who had accosted me yesterday—Daphne—and her gangly, goateed cohort Seth were tag-teaming Tabitha when Stella and I walked by.

"Don't you see what you're doing to yourself?" Seth asked earnestly. His goatee waggled as he talked. "You're sacrificing your self-esteem to conform to an arbitrary standard of beauty that is meaningless."

Tabitha raised a supercilious eyebrow. "Meaningless? When I win the Miss American Blossom contest, I'll be making six figures in appearance money. That might not mean much to you, but it does to me. And my self-esteem is just fine, thank you." Wearing tight white jeans and a nautically themed tee shirt, she had a pair of tortoiseshell sunglasses pushed back on her head. Her green eyes glittered angrily as she tried to pass the twosome.

Daphne blocked the path with her body. "But you're too thin," Daphne said. "You probably have an eating disorder. This isn't worth it!"

"Too thin?" Tabitha said incredulously. Clearly, the concept was foreign to her. "Look, Pudgy, I don't want to be rude, but the only people who are against beauty pageants are the ones who are too . . . ordinary to be successful in them. So take your jealousy and your stupid slogans and get the hell out of my way." She shouldered past the stunned college students and stalked toward the St. Elizabeth Yacht Club.

Stella and I watched as Seth put his arm around Daphne's shoulders and gave her a squeeze. ". . . bitch . . . unenlightened . . ." drifted over to us.

Stella pursed her lips. "That was totally unnecessary," she said. "That girl didn't have to be so rude."

I didn't say anything. Tabitha had been brutal, but I could see where being told the choices you made were foolish could be wounding, too. And, I supposed, being attacked as "too thin" might rankle just as much as being called "too fat" to someone who was sensitive about it. Not that I thought "sensitive" described Tabitha.

Stella and I made our way to the St. Elizabeth Yacht Club entrance, where a big banner announced their support of the Miss Magnolia Blossom pageant. The SEYC had turned over its premises to the pageant for the swimsuit competition. "Yacht club" makes the facility sound grander than it is. A one-story wood building of weathered gray with a cupola at top, it has a bar and dining room with an expansive deck on the left end of the building, changing facilities, a game room, and the private docking area at the right end, with gas pumps and a small convenience store. A seventy-ish man in a red SEYC golf shirt directed us to the ladies lounge where the contestants were preparing. A somewhat upscale locker room, the lounge had wooden lockers in rows, shower stalls, toilets, and bulletin boards announcing regattas and sailing classes. Chaos reigned as the girls jostled for mirror space, brushed mascara onto their lashes and bronzer across their cleavage, and applied double-sided tape inside their bathing suits to keep them from riding up. At least, that was the only reason I could think of for Tabitha to stick tape inside her white bikini bottom.

As Stella and I entered the room, the girls swarmed us with requests for hair help—"make it look windswept and natural, like I've spent the day at the beach, but also like I could be headed to a hip club"—and pedicures since strappy sandals were the shoe of the day. We worked non-stop in the crowded quarters—I was tucked into a corner between banks of lockers—for two hours. The girls were more reticent than yesterday, subdued by the news of Audrey's death. No one eyed Stella with suspicion, so I assumed they didn't know about the nail file being the murder weapon. Word would get out. Interestingly enough, their suspicions seemed to center on each other. From just the other side of the lockers next to my "station"—out of sight but well within earshot—they speculated about who Audrey "had the dirt on" and was going to eject from the pageant. I was curling Elise Metzger's hair and she sat silent in my chair, both of us listening.

"Of course it's photos," one of the girls said in a world-weary voice. "Isn't it always in pageants? I mean, look what happened to that Miss California a couple years back. A few lingerie photos turn up—not even racy ones—and, poof! She's out on her ass."

"You're fired!" Brooke did a credible imitation of Donald Trump.

A couple girls giggled, then stopped abruptly as if afraid laughter was inappropriate this soon after a death.

"Or it could be drugs," another girl offered. "My roommate from the Miss Teen Angel USA pageant totally got kicked out for popping some E before the dress rehearsal. She was a real candy raver."

I couldn't remember the speaker's name, but she'd done a dramatic reading of Poe's "Lenore" as her talent. Her casual use of drug slang gave me the heebie-jeebies. What the heck was a "candy raver"? I hoped Rachel wasn't listening.

"Do you suppose she did it?" another voice asked.

The voices had dropped to little more than whispers and I couldn't tell who was speaking.

"Who? Did what?"

"You know. Whoever was going to get disqualified. Do you think she killed Miss Faye?"

Elise jerked her head up, pulling a section of her hair out of the curling iron. She winced but stayed silent.

I didn't hear an answer, but it was a darned good question. Did Agent Dillon know that Audrey had announced she was preparing to disqualify one of the contestants? And could a cheesy rhinestone tiara and a Miss Magnolia Blossom sash really be a motive for murder? Last week I'd have laughed at the idea. Now, having seen how serious some of the girls were about the pageant, how intent on winning, not just to add a crown to their collection at home, but to further their dreams and career ambitions, I couldn't dismiss the idea.

"That's just stupid," Elise said as if I'd spoken out loud. She kept her voice low. "No one would murder someone to win a silly pageant. It's ridiculous." Her voice was tight with emotion and she craned her head around to look at me. "Don't you think?"

"I think it's hard to know what drives people to murder," I said. I'd never given the subject much thought until Mom was accused of murder and I spent a couple of weeks investigating, tracking down the real murderer. A decades' old thirst for revenge and plain old-fashioned greed had prompted Constance's killing. But pride and the avoidance of humiliation or shame could also spark murder, I thought. As could anger or hatred. It wasn't a topic I wanted to spend time talking about, so I keyed on another part of Elise's comment. "Do you think the pageant's silly?"

She shrugged one shoulder slightly. "Not as silly as some things."

I wished I could see her face, but we didn't have a mirror in this corner of the changing room. "So how come you entered the pageant, then?"

"Mom."

The single word hung between us and the image of Mrs. Metzger floated into my mind. I could see where it would be easier to give in than stand up to her hectoring.

"I'm tired of watching every bite I eat and working out two hours a day and going to fittings and practicing that damn flute!" Elise said suddenly. The words rushed from her like shoppers pouring through the doors of a Walmart on Black Friday. "I'm sick of making nice with the judges and being sweet to the other girls even though some of them are total bitches, and never having pizza or chocolate and being in bed by nine so I don't look 'washed out' and—" She broke off, her chest heaving.

"Why don't you just quit?"

"My mom would kill me."

Hearing the words aloud, she gasped and slewed in the chair. She looked up at me, brown eyes pleading with me. "I didn't mean that. Mom wouldn't kill anyone. Sure, she's into the whole pageant thing, but not to where—I mean, she wouldn't—"

"Of course she wouldn't," I said reassuringly, spritzing her curls with hairspray. But I'd seen Mrs. Metzger backstage last night and I knew she had a temper. As Elise thanked me and hurried off to change into her swimsuit, I made a mental note to track down her mother and see what I could learn.

As I started to pack my combs and products away, someone knocked on a locker. "May I come in?" a husky voice asked.

I turned, surprised, to see the statuesque, dark-haired judge standing at the end of the bench, a questioning look on her smooth face. An ivory silk suit hugged her curves and a plum-colored blouse accented her coloring. Renata something, I remembered.

"I was hoping you might have a moment to fix my hair," she said, trying to run her fingers through the dark mane. It looked like she'd been standing behind a 747 at takeoff. "My car's AC quit on me this morning and I had to drive up from Jacksonville with the window down. I know you're really here for the contestants, but I was hoping . . . I heard there might be news cameras around . . ."

"Sure," I said, and she settled into the chair I'd purloined from an office across the hall.

"I really appreciate this," she said. "I'm Renata Schott."

"Right." I drew a comb through her thick hair. "You were a Miss American Blossom yourself."

"Runner-up," she corrected with a self-deprecating smile. Her lips were so pillowy under a slick of burgundy gloss that I wondered if she'd had collagen injections. "Audrey won. All the girls that year knew we didn't have a chance. She had 'winner' written all over her—everything she touched turned to gold. Up until last night, I guess."

Her voice was appropriately mournful, but I couldn't shake the feeling that she wasn't exactly grief stricken. "I guess you knew her pretty well?"

She winced as I pulled the comb through a stubborn snarl. "You could say that. We had a lot in common."

"Like what?" I worked styling product through her hair.

"Oh, we both came from small towns—her from down here, me from Minnesota. We both majored in communications. Of course, we both did the pageant thing for a few years. And we were both unlucky in love."

"How so? I thought she was married."

"Oh, Kevin's her second husband. Her first marriage only lasted a year. Mine imploded after nine months."

"Mine was over after a year," I offered, "although we dragged it out for another three before the divorce."

She turned to give me a commiserating smile. "Men. You can't live with 'em and you can't shoot 'em."

The sounds of toilets flushing and locker doors banging, plus the whirring of an industrial fan someone had dragged in to cool the changing room, took over as we lapsed into silence. I desperately wanted to ask Renata if she knew of anyone who hated Audrey or might have a motive to kill her (other than Stella or Darryl), but I couldn't think how to do it. I wished Mom were here; people naturally divulged everything to her. I think it had something to do with her calm, nonjudgmental air, or maybe the fact that she looked so darn motherly and wise. Maybe I should get glasses like hers. I decided to take the plunge.

"Who do you think did it?"

"One of her boyfriends, maybe," Renata offered immediately. "Or Kevin. Or it could be someone she trampled on her way to the top. Like Jodi. Jodi used to be in charge of this pageant until Audrey came along. Now she's playing second fiddle. Well, she was until Audrey died."

"I thought you said you were friends," I said, too astonished by the flood of vitriol to be tactful. I misted her now smooth hair with hairspray.

"I said we knew each other well," she corrected, rising from the chair in one elegant motion. "Audrey didn't 'do' friends. You were either the competition or someone who could help her. There was no in between. Thanks." She pressed a tip into my hand and glided from the room. I looked at the bill—a dollar.

Jodi Keen appeared just then to give the girls some last-minute instructions and I left the locker room, sneaking a look at Jodi as I passed her. I saw her with new eyes in the light of Renata's revelations. And the news that Audrey might have been involved with several men cheered me. It expanded the suspect pool beyond Stella and Darryl. I wondered if Renata would open up to the police. A moment's thought told me that of course she would; the woman was dying to trash Audrey Faye to whoever would listen. I wanted to share my discoveries with Stella, but she wasn't around. I wandered out of the yacht club to find a place to watch the swimsuit competition. The crowd had swelled and it seemed like half of St. Elizabeth had turned out to watch the contestants parade in their swimsuits. Wishing I'd had the forethought to bring a folding chair, I was looking for a place to watch from when I heard a voice.

"Grace! Over here!" I looked around and spied my best friend, Vonda Jamison, waving from the deck of her sailboat, *Wind Thief*.

I waved in return and slipped through the crowd to the dock. The scents of diesel fuel and brine floated up from the water as I stepped onto the deck, setting the small craft rocking. Vonda rose to hug me, blowing her platinum bangs out of her eyes with a huff of air. "I need a cut," she greeted me.

"Maybe this evening, if you bribe me with a glass of wine," I said, returning her hug. She wore a bikini top with a pair of Bermuda shorts and her bare skin was sticky with sunblock. "This is a good idea." I gestured to the boat. "We'll have a great view from here." The contestants were scheduled to sashay from the yacht club down the boardwalk to the gazebo where the judges would score them. They'd pass right by the dock. Glancing around, I noticed that other boat owners had the same idea; most of the nearby decks sported folding chairs and several people.

"Where are Ricky and RJ? No interest in beauty pageants?" Ricky was Vonda's former husband and her partner in the B&B they'd bought together ten years ago. They'd been on-again, off-again since high school and were currently pretty on—if Vonda's glow was anything to go by. RJ was their eight-year-old son.

"Visiting Ricky's folks in Fort Myers," Vonda said. "Ricky wanted to make sure they got some time with RJ before school starts up in a couple of weeks. So it's just us chicks. Soda?"

I accepted the diet A&W she held out and settled into a canvas chair. Reaching for the sunblock sitting on the deck, I slathered some on my forearms, bared by the airy sweater. If I sat cross-legged, pulling my legs up under my blue cotton skirt, I wouldn't have to goop them.

"So . . ." Vonda said, looking at me expectantly.

"So what?" I asked.

"The body. I heard you found Audrey Faye's mutilated body."

I shot her an exasperated look. "You've lived here long enough not to believe everything you hear through the small-town grapevine. She wasn't mutilated."

"But you found her?"

"Yes."

"I'm sorry." She put a hand on my arm. "It must have been ugly."

"Not much fun." I filled her in.

"So Special Agent Dillon's back, huh?" She gave me a sly look.

I tell her about finding a body and she zeroes in on the handsome detective? That's a best friend for you. "He's back. So what? He's only interested in me as a witness. Besides, I'm seeing Marty."

"It's not like you two are exclusive," Vonda said, flapping her hand. "You aren't even sleeping together."

I felt my face flush and looked around to see if the people on the other boats had heard her. "Sssh. If I wanted the entire town to know about my love life, I'd take out an ad in the *Gazette*," I said.

"What love life?" Vonda asked, unrepentant. "A few dates with a guy who lives four hours away hardly constitute a love life."

A cheer went up from the crowd so I didn't have to

come up with a response. The contestants had appeared at the yacht club entrance and were waving to the crowd. The emcee stood at the gazebo, mic in hand, but half his words got blown away by the gentle breeze. ". . . a hand . . . swim . . . Magnolia . . . contestants." Vonda and I joined in the applause.

The girls, led by Brooke Baker in a red bikini top and boy shorts, started down the boardwalk. Clearly, the pageant had left the choice of swimwear up to the contestants. I thought, and not for the first time, that you could learn more about a woman by watching her for thirty seconds in a bathing suit than you could in a half-hour conversation. I live in a beach community and see a lot of people in swimsuits. Women just move differently in bathing suits than they do in shorts or jeans. Some saunter, some hold their tummies in, some walk on tiptoe so their breasts don't bounce, some flaunt their best features with a gold chain at the waist or a backless one-piece or halter top. Almost all of them over the age of ten are self-conscious, tugging down bikini bottoms, readjusting straps, glancing around as they smooth sunblock onto their arms. The contestants were no exception.

Brooke strutted in her red suit, waving to the crowd, comfortable with her muscular, athletic body. Elise, right behind her, crept along in a skirted suit that a Victorian miss would find modest. Even her smile was strained, a flash of teeth quickly hidden. Contestants wearing suits in all the bright colors of a Skittles pack glided, tromped, and swayed down the boardwalk. Applause greeted each girl as she did a series of turns in the gazebo and then marched back to the yacht club. Rachel bounced along second to last, wearing a purple one-piece with cutouts at the sides and a ruffle on the asymmetrical neckline. She was barefoot—most of the contestants wore sandals of varying heights—and gave off the happy vibe of a teen planning to spend the day at the beach with friends. All she needed was a boogie board or a Frisbee. I cheered loudly as Rachel passed the boat. Vonda put two fingers in her mouth and blasted a shrill whistle. Rachel grinned.

Tabitha was last again—I wondered how she'd finagled it this time—in a shimmery white micro bikini that displayed every tanned, curvaceous inch. The sun struck gold sparks off her hair and she moved gracefully, even in four-inch heels. As she mounted the steps to the gazebo, the applause built to a crescendo and her smile edged toward smug. But then, as she twirled for the judges, the thin strap of her bikini top snapped and her breast popped out.

Chapter Eleven

"TAKE IT ALL OFF," A MAN YELLED. OTHER VOICES—
all male—turned it into a chant. Several guys who looked
like they were from the navy base removed their tee shirts
and twirled them in the air.

Gasps, giggles, and cheers bubbled up from the crowd
as Tabitha snatched at the tiny triangle of material and
yanked on it, crossing her arms over her chest.

The judge from channel nine's mouth hung open and I
was afraid he'd start drooling. I had to give Tabitha credit
for poise when she descended the stairs and sauntered back
toward the yacht club, still smiling for the crowd.

"Quite the Janet Jackson moment," Vonda observed.

"Embarrassing," I agreed.

"She didn't seem too embarrassed," Vonda said, watching as Tabitha turned for a final wave at the crowd. "She
didn't even blush."

"You just couldn't see it under all that makeup she had on."

"Look." Vonda nudged me.

I turned to see what she was pointing out and spotted the omnipresent Sam Barnes filming Tabitha's shapely rear view as she slipped into the yacht club.

"Whaddaya want to bet he sells that footage to one of the Jacksonville stations? And they'll air it with her boob tastefully fuzzed out?" Vonda said cynically.

Seeing Barnes had jarred loose a thought. "I've got to run." Vonda looked surprised as I jumped from the sailboat onto the dock. "I'll see you this evening. Don't forget the wine."

Leaving her sputtering behind me, I trotted toward Sam Barnes. The crowd had started to disperse and I threaded my way through the ambling mass of people. "Mr. Barnes!" I called.

He swung around, camera still held to his eye. Brown hair sprouted from around his head and curled to his collar. A photographer's vest with bulging pockets hung from broad shoulders. A worn plaid shirt was half tucked into designer jeans. He had a short beard a couple shades darker than his hair that hid his chin and jaw, maybe to cover old acne scars like the ones that showed faintly just above where the beard began on his cheeks. Leather sandals exposed grimy feet with long toenails. He wasn't wearing beads or a peace sign or smoking a joint, but something about him reminded me of photos I'd seen of Woodstock.

"Do you have a moment?"

He continued to focus on the camera, panning it up my body and zooming in on my face. "You're the hair lady."

"Right. Grace Terhune." I held out my hand and he shook it.

He smiled, crinkling the skin around his eyes and I put

him in his late thirties. "What can I do for you, hair lady? Hey, that rhymes with 'fair lady.' Hair lady, fair lady."

"You're filming the pageant for a documentary, right?"

He gave me a knowing look from the one eye I could see. The other was glued to the camera's eyepiece. "You want me to interview you. You're looking for your fifteen minutes of fame. Well, sure, you can say your piece. I can't promise it will end up in the finished film, though. Most of my footage ends up on the cutting room floor. Now, there's a saying that doesn't have much relevance in the digital age. Kind of like—"

I took a step back. "I don't want to be in the movie."

He frowned. "Why not?"

"It's just not me."

He walked around me like a buyer studying a heifer at a cattle auction. "You've got the kind of facial structure that the camera loves. Great cheekbones and love those green eyes. You could stand to lose a few pounds, though; the camera adds about ten."

I was half amused and half irritated by his assessment of my photogenic qualities. I turned so he was forced to face me. Tourists drifting by looked curiously at the camera, and one boy made silly faces. "Mr. Barnes—"

"Sam."

"Sam, I don't want to be in your documentary. I just wanted to know if you were filming backstage last night."

He lowered the camera to his side and met my gaze dead-on for the first time. "You want to know if I filmed Audrey's murder."

"I suppose you would have mentioned it if you'd caught the actual event on camera," I said, taken aback by the hostility in his voice. "But I thought you might have some film of who all was backstage. Maybe you even got some footage of Audrey with someone."

"And if I did?"

"Well, then, I'm sure the police would like to see it. The investigator is Special Agent Dillon. He—"

"I can speak for myself, thank you, Miss Terhune."

Dillon's voice came from behind me and I whipped around. He wore a blue blazer over charcoal slacks and a look that said he didn't appreciate my help. Showing his badge to Sam Barnes, he introduced himself. The two men sized each other up. The slight sneer on Barnes's face told me he either didn't like Dillon or he didn't like cops in general. He raised the camera again and looked through the viewfinder, shifting to the left in search of a better angle. It struck me that the camera made a pretty good shield.

"Miss Terhune beat me to the punch," Dillon said. "Ms. Keen told me about you filming the pageant. I'd like to see your film from last night. In fact, I'd appreciate it if I could see everything you've got that concerns the pageant or Mrs. Faye."

"Not without a court order," Barnes said, not looking up from the camera. He zoomed in on the annoyance stiffening Dillon's face.

"You have something to hide?" Dillon asked.

"Not at all," Barnes said with a little, irksome smile. "But I don't want to see pieces of my documentary on YouTube or the nightly news. It would undermine the impact of the finished piece. You understand." His voice plainly said he didn't care if Dillon understood or not.

"I understand you're not cooperating with a murder investigation," Dillon said tightly.

"Well, last I checked that's not a crime. Not yet. And no

possibility of terrorists involved here, so you can't water board me and hide behind the Patriot Act." Barnes's fleshy lips had thinned to a line almost hidden by his beard.

Whoa. Sam Barnes had some serious issues with the police. I stared at him wide-eyed. I could see Dillon wanted to come back with a harsh answer, but he bit his tongue, maybe because of the camera.

"I thought Audrey was your friend, that you went to college together," I put in, earning irritated glances from both men. "Don't you want to help catch her murderer?"

"Where'd you hear that?" Barnes asked. He lowered the camera again.

I couldn't remember. "But you did, right?"

"So we were at Berkeley at the same time. Big deal. Us and thirty thousand others. It's not like they're all getting invitations to my next birthday party."

"But you had a relationship with the deceased?" Dillon said.

"We weren't making the beast with two backs, if that's what you're asking," Barnes said, smiling at his own lewdness or maybe at the pleasure of making the interview difficult. "I wanted to do an exposé on beauty pageants. She wanted some free publicity. Tit for tat. She scratched my back . . . you get the picture."

"I'm not sure I do," Dillon said, unsmiling.

People milled around us, but it felt like we were on a small island, the tension crackling between Dillon and Barnes establishing a force field that kept us from getting bumped or interrupted.

"I had no reason to kill her, man," Barnes said forcefully. "This film"—he shook the camera gently—"is my ticket to the big leagues. It's going to be important. Think

Michael Moore. Audrey was giving me total access to the pageant and I was grateful. You wouldn't believe the restrictions I got in Atlantic City."

"You said 'exposé' just now, not 'documentary,'" I said, fed up with his air of pseudo-sixties rebellion married to his hunger for recognition. "Isn't that another word for hatchet job? Did Audrey know you were going to trash the pageant?"

Barnes's eyes narrowed and he stared at me for a long moment without saying anything. Finally, he looked down into the camera's viewfinder again and said in a stagy voice, "Voice-over: the cop and the stylist struggle to make sense of last night's murder, but flounder helplessly, reduced to harassing the photographer, the neutral observer determined to capture the truth in its many aspects on film." He began to walk backward, keeping the camera pointed at Dillon and me. "Fade to black." Without another word, he turned and walked away. The crowd swallowed him quickly.

I looked at Dillon but he shook his head. "I'll check him out before I talk to him again. And get a court order. I think the 'setting' for our next 'scene' might be an interview room." His gaze lingered on the spot where Barnes had disappeared.

"You didn't hit it off," I observed.

"Pretentious, self-serving opportunist hiding behind a camera and his contention that he's looking for the truth. All his type wants is a quick buck and a bucketful of accolades. He's not looking for the truth—he's already decided what 'truth' he wants to market and he's cherry-picking images and quotations that support his version."

A muscle worked in his jaw and the eyes he turned to me were a dark navy. His anger seemed out of proportion to Barnes's annoying evasiveness and I wondered what might lie behind it.

"Have you seen Mrs. Michaelson lately?" he asked, his tone still brusque.

"In the yacht club before the swimsuit competition. Why?"

"Has she heard from her husband yet?"

"I don't know. Why don't you ask her?" Dillon was dead wrong if he thought I'd inform on my friends.

"Audrey Faye's cell phone records show three calls to Darryl Michaelson's number round about the time she was killed. He's a person of interest in this investigation and I need to talk to him ASAP."

The news of the phone calls hit me like a bolster in the stomach. Did Stella know? I didn't think so. Which meant Darryl was lying to her. And if he was lying about that . . .

"If there were three calls, maybe it means she didn't get hold of him," I suggested weakly.

His look told me he didn't agree. "You'd be doing your friend a favor by persuading her to tell me where her husband is. He's got 'til the end of the day, then I'm issuing a BOLO, a be-on-the-lookout. Every cop in Georgia will be looking for him." A freshening breeze ruffled his gray-flecked brown hair. It was a bit longer than I remembered, not military-short like it was in the spring.

"I don't think she knows."

He met my gaze straight on. "If she finds out, make sure she doesn't try to meet him alone. Just have her call me."

I shivered at the seriousness in his voice. Did he really think Darryl was a danger to Stella? I couldn't see convincing her of that. He might have cheated on her, but I didn't think she'd believe he could harm her. "I'll do what I can," I finally said.

Chapter Twelve

✂

BACK IN THE YACHT CLUB LOCKER ROOM, TABITHA was seething. Wrapped in a white robe, she held the bikini top aloft. "The strap on my swimsuit was cut. Someone's trying to stop me from winning."

Only a couple of contestants were present, the others apparently having changed and left while I talked to Barnes and Agent Dillon. They ignored Tabitha's outburst. Jodi, dressed in an oatmeal-colored blouse and trousers set off with chunky silver jewelry, tried to calm her. "Now, Tabitha, I'm sure it just frayed. Accidents happen."

"It was cut," Tabitha insisted, her mouth set in a mulish line. "Look."

When no one took her up on her offer, I stepped forward. I examined the strap and the seam where it had joined the triangle of fabric. I was no expert, but the evenly severed threads looked like they'd been cut most of the way across. Only the last couple of threads looked like they'd pulled loose, still dangling from the strap. "Where did you keep the suit?"

Tabitha looked at me speculatively, as if deciding whether I was on her side or not. "All our outfits were in the Green Room at the theater."

"Were they labeled? I mean, would someone know this was your suit?"

After a moment, Tabitha shook her head. "Not necessarily. We all kept track of our own stuff, hung our talent costume and our evening gown and our bathing suit clumped together on the rack. So any of the other contestants could have figured this was mine, even without my name on it, because they all knew my dance costume, but I don't think someone who wasn't associated with the pageant would know."

"I'm sure it was an accident," Jodi said again, as if by repeating it authoritatively she could make it so.

Tabitha rounded on her in a swirl of righteous indignation and blond hair. "Yeah, like Kiley falling off the stage was an accident and the sprinkler ruining some of the girls' gowns was an accident. I suppose next you'll say that what happened to Ms. Faye was an accident." She snatched the bikini top from my hand and stomped out the door. The other two contestants scurried after her, not making eye contact with me or Jodi.

"Oh, dear," Jodi sighed.

"I think the suit was tampered with," I said. "Maybe you should tell the police."

She looked at me like I'd lost my mind. "Are you kidding? About a swimsuit that some contestant may or may not have fiddled with to embarrass Tabitha?"

"Maybe it's more than that. You've had a series of mishaps. Maybe someone's trying to stop the pageant."

"You think someone killed Audrey to sabotage the pageant? But that's insane!"

I was having second thoughts about having voiced my opinion. "I guess so."

She hesitated, pushing a lock of brown hair off her face. I longed to take my scissors to the lank hair and give it more body with some judicious layers. "There was a note . . ."

"A note. When? What did it say?"

Jodi flipped through the stack of papers on her clipboard and tugged at a folded paper tucked underneath the pile. "I found it this morning. In the Green Room when I went to pick up the swimsuits. It was on the counter."

I took it by one corner, not sure whether the police could get fingerprints from it or not. "STOP THE PAGEANT BEFORE SOMEONE ELSE DIES," I read. Black type on plain bond paper. A shiver traveled up my spine, like a beetle skittering under my shirt. I lifted my gaze to Jodi's sheepish face. "This is a death threat. Why in the world didn't you show it to the police?"

She snatched it back from me, clearly regretting showing it to me. "It's a prank. Some kid who thinks he's clever. It doesn't actually threaten anyone. We can't stop the pageant."

"It's a beauty pageant, not a G8 summit or something," I said. "Of course you can call a halt."

She shook her head. "No. I ran this pageant for the last four years without a hiccup. It was only when Audrey took over that things started going wrong. Everything will go smoothly now that—" She didn't need to finish the sentence.

"You've got to tell the police about the note, Jodi. If you won't, I will."

"It's none of your business!"

"Whoever wrote this note killed Audrey. It's evidence."

"They might make us stop the pageant."

The shock in her voice would have been more appropriate for a statement like, "They might amputate our legs."

"If that happens, I won't be asked to take over the state pageant when Fran retires next year. I won't ever get another job in the Miss American Blossom corporation." Before I could guess what she was going to do, she tore the note in half and then in half again.

I thought for a moment she was going to stuff the pieces of paper in her mouth, like some demented secret agent, but she spun on her heel and raced to the toilet stalls. I was half a step behind her when I heard the flush. I bent to pick up a scrap of paper. Palming it, I said nothing when Jodi reappeared, a triumphant look on her face. "Well," she said with an attempt at insouciance belied by a tic just below her left eye, "I guess I'll see you tomorrow."

I didn't say anything; I just stared at her until she flushed and turned away, letting the door bang shut behind her as she left. When I was sure she was gone, I uncurled my fingers from around the scrap. It contained a single word: DIES. I bit my lip, pretty sure Agent Dillon was not going to be happy when I presented it to him.

I PRACTICALLY TRIPPED OVER ELISE METZGER AND a young man in the hall, arms around each other's waists, when I left the locker room. They sprang apart like high schoolers afraid of detention for PDA when they saw me. Hurrying past them, I called the GBI office but had to leave a message for Agent Dillon to get in touch with me. Taking a deep breath, relieved not to have to tangle with Dillon immediately, I set out in search of Stella. She was nowhere in the yacht club building or immediately outside. I lifted my hair off the back of my neck, hoping for a cool breath of air on my damp skin as I scanned the dock and the park. No Stella. The protestors, though, were packing their signs, folding chairs, and loading coolers in the back of a tan Ford Voyager. Maybe they were returning to campus since the pageant action here was over for the day. I didn't see Kwasi Yarrow. About to walk past them on my way to my car, I noticed a familiar figure.

Althea crouched in the back of the van, accepting the placards as the protestors handed them in to her. Wearing a red tunic over loose black trousers, she was talking to Daphne, whose sandy hair straggled out of a loose braid. When she noticed me, Althea started and then waggled her eyebrows. I had no idea what she was trying to say, but when I took a step toward the van, she shook her head once and held up a finger in a "one minute" sign. I nodded and drifted to the nearby hot dog stand where I bought a lemonade and a foot-long dog. A spoonful of relish, a squirt of mustard—

"We can't talk here," Althea's voice said softly behind me.

I jumped and splattered mustard down my shirt. "What are you—" I started to turn but her voice stopped me.

"Sssh. Don't turn around. Give me a moment and then follow me."

I rolled my eyes, wondering if everyone in St. Elizabeth had been infected by a dangerous spy virus—first Jodi, now Althea. "Whatever," I muttered under my breath as Althea walked past the marina and down toward the river. Dabbing at the mustard stain with cheap napkins that shredded against the fabric, I bit into my hot dog and gulped some lemonade before trailing Althea.

I caught up with her at a kiosk that rented bicycles.

The Satilla River flowed past a few feet beyond the rental hut, its brownish water dappled by leaf shadows. Bikes in various sizes and colors were chained to tree trunks. A hand-printed sign on the kiosk window said, "Gone to lunch. Back at 1:15." Althea leaned against the far side of the hut, mostly hidden from the boardwalk.

"Why the Mata Hari routine?" I asked. I chucked my white hot dog tray into a trash can. Wasps buzzed in and out of a Coke bottle sticking out over the lip, getting woozy on the slurp of sugary liquid pooled in the bottom.

Althea made a show of looking in all directions, her dark eyes sparkling. "I can't be seen hobnobbing with you, baby-girl. You're with the enemy." Apparently satisfied that we were unobserved, she settled onto a bench that faced the river.

It was peaceful here, not crowded and frenetic like the beachfront. Birdcalls and insect whirrings sounded over the gentle murmurings of the water. A pair of mallards dabbled by the bank. It was still brutally hot, even with the cool breath of the water, but giant old trees trailing Spanish moss cast a welcome shade.

"The enemy?"

"The beauty pageant. You help exploit those young girls, keep them enslaved to ideals of beauty and utility perpetuated by white males." I couldn't tell from her tone if she was buying into the protestors' platform or making fun of it.

"I don't enslave anyone," I objected. "I style hair." Before she could expound on the slave theme, I added, "And you're an aesthetician whose paycheck comes from facials and skin care products, so don't be pointing any fingers."

She shrugged. "I know. And I enjoy it. And I like to think my clients feel better for my treatments. But I've got to admit that there's something to what Kwasi says. What woman in her right mind parades around in public, wearing nothing but a skimpy bikini and high heels, looking like a . . . well, you know what she looks like. Not respectable." She primmed her mouth. "No woman would do that of her own accord. They're only doing it because that's what the dominant culture tells her makes her valuable. Kwasi says that for women to become self-actualized, they have to see themselves as more than decorations."

Despite the pretentious academic-speak, that didn't sound totally loony. Then I thought of Brooke using the pageant to earn money for vet school. She didn't strike me as someone at the mercy of the "dominant culture." I didn't feel like debating, though, so I said, "I didn't see Kwasi."

She shifted on the bench. "He was there earlier, but he had to go back to the college for a meeting. He says meetings are the worst part of being an academic."

I could believe that. I told her about talking to Sam Barnes and about the note Jodi found. "Have you talked to anyone in the protestor group who might feel strongly enough to sabotage the pageant?"

Althea jutted her lower jaw forward. "They're college kids, Grace Ann. Only nineteen or twenty. They're protestors, not criminals. Kwasi teaches the ideals of civil protest in the tradition of Reverend King or Gandhi, not rioting or vandalism or anything."

News footage of abortion-clinic bombings and lab-animal rescues played in my head. Waving posters and chanting slogans wasn't enough for some protestors. I bent over to work a pebble out of my shoe. Straightening, I threw it toward the river and it disappeared with a little *plip*. "I'm worried about Stella," I said. "Agent Dillon thinks Darryl might be implicated in Audrey's murder somehow and I'm afraid she might do something stupid."

"He's a cheating skunk," Althea said. "Stella would do best to let him swing in the wind and reap the consequences of his actions."

Althea wasn't much of one for second chances.

"That said, he's been a good daddy to Jessica, and Stella always did have a soft heart. You better find that girl and ride herd on her so she doesn't do something *really* stupid like help him run off to Mexico." Althea pushed to her feet and rotated her shoulders. "I'll tell you what—protesting will get you in shape. Holding that placard up all morning sure did a number on my shoulder muscles. I'll leave first." Looking remarkably furtive—thank heavens there was no one in sight—she snuck back to the path and headed toward the marina.

Chapter Thirteen

I RETURNED TO VIOLETTA'S, THINKING MAYBE STELLA had gone back to the salon. Mom was doing highlights for an old customer and Beauty sat in the window, twitching her tail as she watched two squirrels chase each other around a tree, but Stella wasn't there.

"Seen Stella?" I asked Mom, slipping behind the counter to check the appointment book. A fairly light day. I didn't need to feel too guilty about leaving Mom in the lurch.

"Not since first thing this morning," she said. She shot me a look over her glasses. "Why?"

I hesitated, aware that her client was avidly soaking up every word. "No reason," I said.

Mom arched one brow, clearly aware there was more to it, but she let it go.

"If you see her, tell her that I—"

The door swinging open to let in a wave of humidity

stopped me. A man stood on the threshold, peering around uncertainly. In his early fifties, I guessed, he had thinning dishwater-colored hair slicked straight back, a la President Nixon, and a hint of jowls. A dime-sized mole marred his left temple. The crisp professionalism of a brown suit, white shirt, and shined loafers didn't mesh with his tentative expression and the almost timid way he stepped into the salon. Of course, many men felt self-conscious walking into a beauty parlor.

"I'm looking for Grace Terhune," he said. His voice was deeper than I'd thought it would be.

"That's me," I said, stepping forward with my hand out. His firm handshake made me reassess his seeming timidity. "How can I help you?"

"I'm Kevin Faye," he said.

I suppressed my surprise. He was clearly fifteen or twenty years older than Audrey had been and a very ordinary-looking man.

"Oh." Mom's client gasped. Her eyes rounded. "You poor man! I heard—"

His gaze flicked over her and he cut her off. "Is there somewhere we can talk? Privately?" He stared into my face, his brown eyes searching mine, and I realized he was only two or three inches taller than I was.

"Uh, sure," I said. "Let's go out on the veranda." I could have taken him back to Mom's air-conditioned kitchen, but I didn't feel comfortable leading him into her sanctum. Whatever he wanted, I figured he could tell me on the veranda.

He held the door for me as we exited and closed it firmly behind us. With a gesture, I invited him to take one of the Adirondack chairs that sat on either side of a plant stand we used as a table. Ignoring me, he walked to the rail and looked down into the yard as if studying the magnolia roots that broke through the grass in several places or contemplating how to get rid of the fire ant mound that had appeared after the last rain. His hands gripped the rail so his knuckles showed white. Without turning around, he said, "I understand you found her. Audrey. My wife."

"How did you—"

He turned. "The police told me." He hesitated. "I just want to know . . . did she . . . ? Was she suffering?" He blinked rapidly.

A wave of compassion brought me to his side. With a hand on his arm, I guided him to a chair. He sat on the edge of it, leaning toward me with his elbows on his knees. "She was already dead," I told him gently. "There was nothing I could do."

He raised his brows and the mole jumped. "Oh, I don't blame you. I'm sure there was nothing—" He kneaded his lips together. "Was she at peace?"

"I'm sure she was," I lied. "I overheard the coroner say it looked like she died instantly, that she never felt a thing." I figured a white lie in the name of kindness was okay.

"Thank you," he said. He sat up straighter and took a deep breath. "It's been so horrible. You can't imagine—"

I didn't even want to try.

"If only I'd been there like I was supposed to be. She really wanted me to come to the pageant and I'd told her I'd meet her at the theater. But then a client called and insisted on seeing a house—"

"You're a Realtor?"

He nodded and withdrew a card case from his pocket. He extracted a card and handed it to me with a gesture so automatic I knew he'd done it thousands of times before. "Broker and developer. With the economy like it's been, I didn't feel I could tell this client to pound sand, so I agreed to the showing. If only—"

He choked to a stop and dropped his face into his hands.

I felt both sorry for him and intensely uncomfortable. Part of me wanted to hug him and part of me was ill at ease with a stranger's grief. I shifted from foot to foot and felt perspiration drip down my lower back.

"Did she say anything?" He raised his gaze hopefully to my face where I stood in front of him. "Did she leave a message for me?"

I wished I could make up something to comfort him, but I couldn't go that far. I couldn't say Audrey had whispered, "Tell Kevin I love him," with her dying breath. "No," I said flatly.

He went very still and then a breath leaked out of him, like air from a deflating balloon. He pushed against his thighs to heave himself to his feet.

"Thank you for your time," he said.

"I'm very, very sorry for your loss. When is the funeral?"

He grimaced. "I'm not sure. The police . . . Whenever they finish with her. With the body."

From the agonized look on his face, I knew he was imagining the autopsy and the other indignities the police were inflicting on his wife's body. I winced inwardly, regretting bringing it up. "I'm sorry," I said again.

He mustered a sad smile. "Me, too. Do you believe in God?"

"Yes." It didn't seem like a strange question, not under the circumstances.

"I try to. I used to."

Before I could answer—he seemed to want a response— the salon door swung open with a tinkle and Mom's client, hair shining, crossed the veranda toward us with *click-*

*click*s from her kitten heels. Without another word, Kevin Faye trotted down the stairs.

"Well!" the client said, fists planted on her hips. "You'd think the man didn't want any condolences."

"Imagine that," I murmured, slipping back into the salon.

"THAT POOR, POOR MAN," MOM SAID WHEN I TOLD HER what Kevin Faye had wanted. "At least I didn't have to worry about what your daddy's last moments were like. He died right here in this house—reminded me to fertilize the azaleas and just slipped away. It was March fifth, a beautiful spring day with the sun shining like it would banish night forever and so many of our friends praying for us right here in this room." She looked around the salon that used to be the home's front parlor. Glancing out the window, she added, "That magnolia was only half as tall as it is now."

I'd heard the story so many times it was almost as though I remembered it, although I'd been only five when he died.

Audrey's death definitely wasn't that peaceful. "The killer and Audrey must have been fighting before she died, wouldn't you think?" I asked, trying to envision the scene in the small dressing room. "I mean, how likely is it that someone would walk in, snatch up Stella's file, and stab Audrey in the neck without some sort of argument?"

"Probably so," Mom agreed. She scooped up a handful of towels and soiled smocks to pop in the washer. "I just hope the folks that run the Ghost Tour don't fix on the idea of adding the theater to their shtick. It's one thing to tell tourists stories about a Civil War belle who pines away when her beau dies at Fort Delaware and slaves who died of yellow fever, but it's quite another to capitalize on a hideous crime."

"Agreed." Pushing away from the counter, I looked around for my purse. "I'm going to find Stella."

"Bring her back here when you do," Mom said. "She shouldn't be alone at a time like this. Oh, I know she's got Jess, but a woman needs her woman friends in time of trouble."

Chapter Fourteen

STELLA AND DARRYL'S RANCH HOUSE WAS A SINGLE-story, three-bedroom home with a red brick front. Its blocky design, small windows, and cement stoop suggested it was built in the seventies. Large sago palms sprawled on either side of the driveway and a live oak shaded the detached garage. A mockingbird squabbled with house finches and sparrows at a tray-style bird feeder positioned in the middle of the crabgrass- and dandelion-strewn yard. The house looked gloomy and empty, with darkened windows and no flutter of curtains or music from the oldies station Stella liked. Leaving my car at the curb, I walked up the pebbled sidewalk to the concrete stoop and rang the doorbell.

Just when I was wondering if Stella might be at her mom's house, the door swung open. Stella stood there, her eyes puffy and red.

"Still no word from Darryl?" I asked, giving her a hug.

She shook her head and invited me in with a gesture. "Nothing. I'm so worried about him, Grace. I've called and called but he doesn't call back. I suppose he could be camping out somewhere without cell service, but when he's on a hunting trip, he usually makes a point of stopping into a town every other day or so to give me a call."

"You think he's camping?" I followed Stella into the front room, a cheerful space with moss green walls and plaid upholstery on an overstuffed love seat and sofa combo. Stella was crafty and had cross-stitched the red accent pillows and made the dried flower and shell arrangements decorating the walls. She sat so she could look out the window and I got the feeling she'd been there since leaving the marina, watching for Darryl to pull into the driveway. I stood by the window and fiddled with the wand that opened and closed the blinds. The scent of ammonia stung my nostrils; Stella must have cleaned the windows while she kept her vigil.

"He likes to get up into the mountains when he's got stuff to think about," Stella answered. "And he did take the camper. His Chevy's in the garage so he must've come back last night after dropping me at Mom's and gotten the camper."

I remembered they had one of those pop-up campers that sits on a pickup bed. It was usually parked beside the garage.

"So you've known all along where he went?" I asked, disturbed by her lying to me and the police.

"But I don't know! Why do you think I'm so worried? Look." She held up her hands to show me fingernails, usually manicured to hand-model standards, now bitten to the quick. "He could be anywhere—the mountains, North Carolina, Florida, wherever."

Maybe she was more worried about Darryl's involvement with Audrey than about his whereabouts. "Does he have a place he likes to camp?"

"There's a spot in the Osceola National Forest," she admitted. "I thought about driving down there to find him. He took me there once and I think I could find it. Probably. But it's—what?—four hours from here, eight hours round-trip? I was thinking that if I left tonight, I could be home before Jess wakes up."

"Why don't you tell the police," I suggested, "and let them check it out? I'm sure they could call the Florida police and have them send an officer or ranger around to the campsite."

"I can't do that," she said, anger and fear tightening the skin around her eyes. "What if—"

I didn't get to hear what she would have said because at that moment a dark blue sedan and two marked police cars pulled to the curb and Stella broke off. "Something's happened to Darryl," she whispered.

Agent Dillon stepped from the car, his expression grim, and conferred with the uniformed officers clustered in the street. One of them was Hank. Great. Stella's hand groped for mine and I gave it a squeeze. Her fingers were icy. We both watched through the window as Hank and another officer headed toward the garage and the others started up the sidewalk.

"I'm sure it's just routine," I said. I mentally slapped myself for stupidity. What could be routine about having your husband disappear the night his mistress is murdered and then having a herd of police show up on your doorstep? "Why don't you get some hot tea?" I suggested to Stella. "I'll let them in." And let Agent Dillon have a piece of my mind for harassing my friend.

"No, I've got to deal with it," she said. Squaring her shoulders, she walked briskly down the hall and yanked open the front door just as the doorbell *bing-bong*ed. The officer who rang stepped back with a startled expression, bumping into Officer Qualls who had been at the theater with Hank. Agent Dillon stood a half step behind them and I got a good look at his strong profile, the slightly off-kilter nose—old sports injury? perp resisting arrest? fall from a horse?—and the square chin as he stared toward the garage.

"Tell me," Stella said without preamble. "It's Darryl, isn't it? Is he—"

Dillon followed her line of thought without difficulty. "We don't have any news about your husband, Mrs. Michaelson. As far as we know he's fine." He gentled her with his voice and I smiled at him, pleased he could allay her worst fear.

Her shoulders sagged with relief. "Thank God."

"What we do have is a search warrant." He produced a business-sized envelope and tried to hand it to Stella.

She stood with her arms at her sides, an uncomprehending look on her face. She glanced down at the envelope Dillon was holding out. "I don't understand."

"It's a search warrant, Mrs. Michaelson," Dillon said again. "A judge has given us permission to search your home for items related to the death of Audrey Faye."

"What items?" I asked. "You already have the murder weapon."

"Clothing," he said. Handing me the envelope, he motioned to the officers, who pushed past us and into the hallway.

"But you can't—" Stella said, reaching out a hand as if to grab Officer Qualls's sleeve.

Flipping through the warrant, I noted the judge's signature on the last page. I wasn't a lawyer or even a cop, but being married to one had taught me a few things about due process and suchlike, even more than I'd learned watching *Law & Order*. The original was still my favorite. "They can," I told Stella, putting a hand on her arm. "But you don't have to watch. C'mon in the kitchen."

"But I want to wa—Hey! That's my daughter's room. You can't go in there." She pulled away from me to confront Officer Qualls.

The dark-eyed cop was several inches shorter than Stella, but she didn't quail when Stella stepped in front of her. "I have to, ma'am," she said politely. "It's my job."

Stella whirled to jab an accusing glare at Dillon. "Surely you don't suspect a twelve-year-old of having anything to do with that woman's death, do you?"

Agent Dillon took her by the elbow and gently guided her back to the foyer, nodding at Officer Qualls to resume her search. "Of course not," he said. "Why don't you wait outside with Miss Terhune? We won't be long."

I wanted to challenge him, to ask what evidence he had that had persuaded a judge to grant a warrant, but I didn't want to upset Stella further. "Look, let's run down to Doralynn's and get a scone and some tea," I suggested.

"Good idea," Dillon said.

"Bad idea," Stella almost snarled. Fear and anger were taking a toll on her usually calm disposition. "I'm not going anywhere while these people are . . . are violating my home!" Crossing her arms over her chest, she plunked herself down on the top step of the stoop. I joined her, draping an arm over her slender shoulders.

"Where's Darryl?" she asked, eyes scanning the street, skimming over two teens on skateboards and the neighbors across the street who were staring, mesmerized by the prospect of scandal or tragedy the police cars promised. "He should be here."

I couldn't argue with that.

"Look at this!" The cry of triumph came from the garage.

I recognized both the voice and the tone and winced. Hank had crowed just like that when he found the Civil War sword that killed Constance DuBois in my mom's hall closet. So either he'd just discovered a winning lottery ticket in his pocket, or his find might rock Stella's world.

She had started to her feet and now took a few steps toward the garage. I caught up with her as Hank ducked under the three-quarters open overhead door and headed our way, something black draped over his arms. The other officer followed him.

"What's that?" Stella asked, staring.

"Evidence," Hank said tersely. He had his self-important look on as he marched past us.

A breeze twitched at a corner of the fabric and I recognized it. My heart thudded against my rib cage. I'd last seen the garment swishing around a corner in the Oglethorpe.

"It's a cape," I told Stella. "The murderer wore it when he left the theater."

Stella gasped.

Hank pouted his lower lip, peeved with me for spoiling his game of "I've got a secret." "You civilians wouldn't understand," he said. "But I'll bet blood transfer from the murderer's clothes to this cape will give us all we need to get this guy the needle."

"I've never seen it before," Stella said, looking from Hank to me. "It's not mine or Darryl's. What was it doing in our garage?"

"In the pickup bed," Hank corrected smugly.

I wanted to belt him, but Agent Dillon spoke from behind me.

"Good work, Officer Parker. Put that in an evidence bag and log it properly. Officer—Kharitonoff, is it? Finish searching the garage."

Officer Kharitonoff turned without a word and reentered the garage. Hank looked like he was going to resume his forensics lecture, thought better of it, and trudged toward the patrol car.

"Is that your husband's truck, Mrs. Michaelson?" Dillon asked, nodding his head toward the red Chevy S-10 in the garage.

"Yes, but—"

"Was he driving it last night?"

Stella hesitated.

"We'll find witnesses who saw him," Dillon said.

"Yes, he was driving it. But—"

"Anyone could have put something into the bed of his truck," I pointed out. "Just because the cape was in there doesn't mean Darryl had anything to do with Audrey's murder."

"I'm sure the defense attorney will be very interested in your theories," Dillon said, implying that he wasn't. "I'm sorry, Mrs. Michaelson." He walked back to his car and reached in for the radio.

I didn't tell Stella, but I was pretty sure he was arranging for an arrest warrant and putting out the word to pick up Darryl Michaelson. I had to admit it didn't look good. Sure, anyone could have put the cape in Darryl's truck, but what would be the point?

"He didn't do it, Grace," Stella said, desperate to convince someone of her husband's innocence. Maybe she was really trying to convince herself. "How stupid would it be to put the cape in the truck and leave it here if he killed Audrey?"

Darn stupid, I had to admit. Which didn't mean he hadn't done it. From some of the stories Hank told, and others I'd seen on the news, most criminals ended up in jail because they weren't exactly rocket-scientist material. If Darryl had killed Audrey in a fit of passion, he could have stuffed the cape in the truck bed and been so frantic to get away that he forgot it when he got home and took off in the camper.

"Darryl!"

I thought Stella's cry was a generalized shout of despair until she took off running toward the street. Turning, I saw her almost collide with a dented pickup capped by a camper. Brakes squealed and the driver's-side door opened simultaneously. Darryl's wiry figure jumped into the street. He gathered Stella into his arms.

"What do you think you're doing, honey? I almost hit you." Clad in grubby jeans and an equally grimy blue tee shirt with a picture of a buck's head in a scope, Darryl had a couple days' growth of reddish beard scruffing his jawline. Darker red hair had the outline of a ball cap pressed in at the temples. He looked exhausted but not nervous or scared, as you might expect a hunted fugitive to look when returning to home base.

"Where . . . been?" Stella gasped out between sobs.

"I'm sorry if I worried you," he said, stroking her hair. "I was down to Osceola. I'd've called you when I started back, but my damn phone was out of juice. I left here so quick last night I forgot to take the charger. What's all this?"

His only answer was more hiccupping sobs from Stella.

"What's going on?" He looked at the police and at me, having given up on getting anything intelligible out of Stella.

Agent Dillon had emerged from his car when the truck pulled up. Now, he advanced on Darryl, handcuffs in hand. "Darryl Michaelson, you're under arrest for the murder of Audrey Faye."

Darryl's eyes widened and his jaw sagged as Agent Dillon read him his rights. He moved his mouth but no sound came out. "Audrey's dead?" he finally managed to gasp. "Oh my God."

Stella reared back at his sorrowful tone. "Don't you dare cry for her," she said fiercely. "Don't you dare." She thumped a fist on his chest for emphasis.

An audience had gathered. Two women with babies in strollers, a yard-care guy with a fertilizer tank strapped to his back, a loose border collie, and miscellaneous neighbors crowded the sidewalk and spilled into the street. A man in a silver Mustang honked to goose a bicycler to keep pedaling.

"Mrs. Michaelson." Dillon nudged her away from Darryl. "Grace—"

I responded to the request in his voice, even though I was mad that Darryl's arrest was becoming a public spectacle. I grasped her wrist to stop her from following as one of the officers led Darryl to a squad car and urged him into the backseat. "Stella, let's go call Simone."

"Simone?" She sounded like the syllables didn't make sense, like she'd never heard the name before. Her eyes followed the police car as it gave a whoop of its siren to clear a path and edged away from the curb.

"DuBois. She's a lawyer, remember?"

Stella trailed me to my car, seeming oblivious to her neighbors gawking like we were filming an episode of *One Life to Live*. "Do you think—"

"No." I answered before she could complete the question. Any doubts I'd had about Darryl's guilt were resolved by the look of total incomprehension on his face when he heard Audrey was dead. No way was he putting it on. Tom Hanks wasn't that good an actor.

Chapter Fifteen

✂

I DRAGGED STELLA TO VIOLETTA'S. MOM WAS THE calmest, most sensible person I knew; if anyone could help Stella stay sane while the police carted her husband off to jail, it was Mom. Me, I'm an organizer. I would call Simone and find out about getting Darryl out on bail while Mom dealt with Stella.

"Jessie!" Stella gasped as we pulled up in front of the salon. She slewed in the seat to face me, her green eyes sunken. "I've got to get Jess. Someone will tell her her daddy's been taken to prison. Oh!"

I didn't think seeing Stella in this state would reassure her daughter. "Can you just call your mom?" I suggested. "Maybe she could take Jess some place for a few days." Although Jess would have to know at some point—especially if Darryl went to trial—it might be better if she didn't find out until Stella knew more about the situation and had her own emotions under control.

Stella raked her fingers through her already disordered hair. "Maybe. Mom was talking about visiting a friend of hers up Savannah way."

"Good," I said, thrusting my cell phone at her. "Call her."

I went into the salon to give her some privacy and filled my mom in.

"We've got to help her," she said immediately, her brows knitted. She found a pen and marker, scribbled "Closed for Family Emergency" on a half sheet of paper, and was taping it to the door when Stella came onto the veranda. She promptly burst into tears at sight of the sign.

"You're family, dear," Mom said, hugging her tightly, "and we take care of family. Come in and let me get you some tea."

Tea. Mom's go-to for any emotional emergency. I knew she thought things were really in a bad way when she added a tablespoon of honey as she did today. The coziest room in the house, the kitchen was where Mom and Althea originally started doing hair and facials for friends, back after their husbands died. Cheery yellow paint and a brick wall gave the kitchen a warm feeling. The appliances dated back to my childhood, as did the well-used copper pots hanging from a ceiling rack that reflected our faces in fun-house ways.

Stella took the mug in shaking hands and drank deeply. "Oh, Violetta," she said. "How did things come to such a pass? One minute, my life is good—not perfect, but really good—and the next my husband tells me he's sleeping with another woman and then he gets arrested for murder."

"Being thrown in prison is just what he deserves for cheating on a good woman like you," Althea said tartly, letting the screen door bang shut. She helped herself to tea and sat at the kitchen table. "You weren't going to have this confab without me, were you? I was at Doralynn's when I heard about Darryl having his ass hauled off to the pokey and I came right over."

"He doesn't really deserve to be in jail," I said. "He didn't kill Audrey."

"A couple of days won't hurt him." Althea stuck her jaw out. "Maybe it'll give him pause next time he thinks about unzipping his jeans anywhere but in his own bedroom. How do you know he didn't kill Audrey?" She shot a sharp glance my way.

"He didn't know she was dead," I said. "I'm sure of it. When Agent Dillon arrested him for her murder, he was flabbergasted."

"He did seem surprised," Stella said, taking another sip of tea.

"Surprised he got caught," Althea muttered.

Mom gave her a minatory stare.

"Okay, okay, I'm done. If y'all think he's innocent, that's good enough for me. Have you made any progress in figuring out who really did it, Grace?"

"Not really." I filled them in on the note Jodi found and destroyed, on the bikini sabotage, and on Sam Barnes.

"Sounds to me like someone wants to stop the pageant," Mom said, "and maybe went too far."

"Could be," I agreed. An ugly thought struck me. "Since killing Audrey didn't get the pageant cancelled, you don't think whoever it is will try anything worse, do you?"

An uneasy silence clouded the kitchen. "What would be worse than killing someone?" Stella asked.

I didn't verbalize any of the ideas that popped into my head, superstitiously not wanting to give them more power. "Not knowing whether it's someone with a grudge against Audrey personally or a thing for pageants makes it almost impossible to narrow down the suspects," I said.

"First things first," Mom said. "Oughtn't you to call Simone? Then it seems to me a good idea for someone to touch base with Rachel and see what she thinks. She's closer to that pageant than any of us."

"Good thinking," I said. I called Simone DuBois and explained the situation. She promised to get over to the jail to interview Darryl and see when they were having the arraignment. "She wants to talk to you, too," I told Stella when I hung up. "At her office as soon as you can get there."

Stella scrambled to her feet. "Oh! I don't know how we'll pay her," she said, trying to smooth her hair with her hand. "And I left my car—"

"You're not in that much of a hurry," Mom said. "C'mon upstairs and tidy yourself up a bit. I'll drive you to Simone's and go with you to pick up your car and an overnight bag. You're staying here tonight. With your mama and Jess off to Savannah, you shouldn't be alone."

Without giving Stella a chance to argue, she nudged her up the stairs that lay behind a door near the pantry. Mom followed, turning back to make shooing motions at me and Althea. "You two go do something to sort this mess out. The answers aren't going to come marching up to you in my kitchen."

ALTHEA DECIDED TO GO WITH MOM AND STELLA AND I called Rachel's house only to have her mother tell me the girl was at the St. Elizabeth high school rehearsing a dance number for the pageant's finale. Jodi Keen, Rachel's mom said, had managed to borrow the high school's stage until the police let the pageant back into the Oglethorpe. I thanked her and headed out, pulling into the high school parking lot just as the bells from the Catholic church across the street bonged the half hour. Four thirty. The day's heat had sunk into the asphalt of the parking lot and radiated up in shimmering waves. My sandals stuck to the tarry surface and made *phlupp* noises with each step. I figured I knew how a hapless dino mired in a tar pit felt. The protestors, minus Althea, clustered around an ice cream truck parked at the curb across the street. They were too intent on scoring Push Ups and Drumsticks to notice me.

Two stories of sixties-era red brick, the high school had less character than a Lego project. Glass doors with a chain hanging off the metal handle opened onto halls of worn linoleum lined with metal lockers. I went in. Bracing air-conditioning scented with eau de high school—a mix of steamed broccoli from the cafeteria, sweaty gym clothes, lip gloss, and musty books—swept me back to my days as a St. Elizabeth Sabertooth. A fifteen-foot-tall version of the school's mascot, painted by someone in the class of 1973, leered at me from the side wall. I assumed that the muralist had not gone on to a career as an artist. The sabertooth tiger was an orangey shade, spotted here and there with pale green where the paint had flaked off to show the color beneath. One of his fangs was longer than the other and his slightly cross-eyed expression was more reminiscent of a drugged kitten than a fierce predator. Which might explain our football team's perennially dismal performance.

Although it was summer vacation and the school was deserted, I heard the ghostly echoes of lockers clanging shut. I hadn't set foot in these halls since graduation and it was eerie how the intervening twelve years seemed to melt away. Vonda and I had recoiled from dissecting a fetal pig together, made fun of students making out in the halls (while secretly envying them), and dared each other to speak to boys we were crushing on. A rousing rock beat leaked out of a door halfway down the hall and pulled me out of my nostalgia.

"No, Morgan. Left-shimmy, right-shimmy, *then* kick," Jodi called as I pushed open the door of the auditorium, home of pep rallies where cheerleaders stumbled over the awkward syllables of "St. Elizabeth Sabertooths" as they shook their pom-poms. The contestants all wore electric blue shorts with halter tops and had their eyes glued to Jodi as she demonstrated a dance sequence, clipboard held high in one hand while she shimmied. Sam Barnes was filming from the orchestra pit, an angle guaranteed to net him flashes of undies as the girls high-kicked above him. Pervert. Another man stood in the middle of the aisle, watching the rehearsal, and I recognized the set of his shoulders and the way his head cocked a bit to one side as he concentrated.

I snuck up behind him. "Done flogging Darryl Michaelson with a rubber hose already?"

Showing no surprise, Agent Dillon looked at me over his shoulder. He'd shucked his coat and rolled up the sleeves of his pale yellow shirt, showing tanned forearms. "Wore out my whipping arm." He flexed an impressive bicep. "His lawyer showed up and shut us down."

"So you decided to come watch beauty contestants practice dance moves?"

"So I decided to interview possible murder witnesses," he corrected. "Why'd you call?"

His question startled me and it was a moment before

I remembered I still hadn't told him about the note Jodi found. I pulled the scrap out of my pocket and filled him in. His gaze fixed on Jodi when I got to the part where she tore up the note. "I guess I'll have to chat with Ms. Keen about destroying evidence," he said.

"She'll say I'm lying," I warned him.

"But I know you're not."

I felt a surprising tingle of happiness at his faith in me. "How?"

He gave me an amused smile that set my blood thrumming. "You're not a liar, Grace. You may be the most straightforward person I know." His smile broadened at my confusion.

I tried to cover it with a question. "I don't suppose you know where Kevin Faye was last night?"

"Not cutting up bikinis and leaving threatening notes. He was with me or one of my agents either at the morgue or at headquarters until almost nine this morning."

After the swimsuit competition had started. Scratch Kevin as a suspect. Alibis didn't get much better than that. And obviously the murderer left the note because it referred to "someone else" dying. Only the murderer and a handful of cops knew about the murder this morning, which was when Jodi said she found the note. It was pretty ballsy of the murderer to sneak back into the crime scene and leave the note right under the cops' noses, as it were. I wondered how he got into the theater.

"Did you go to high school here?" Dillon interrupted my thoughts.

"Yep. I'm a proud St. Elizabeth Sabertooth." I growled our pep rally growl.

"Seems you enjoyed it."

"High school?"

He nodded. The girls on stage formed two lines and began marching to a Sousa-like number.

"It was okay. I wasn't the most popular girl, but I had friends. I made decent grades and was the photo editor for the yearbook my senior year. And, of course, there was Hank."

"True love." His smile was twisted and I got the feeling he was thinking about something in his own past and not my high school romance that outlived its sell-by date.

"For a while. What about you? Did you like high school?"

"Hated it," he said. He didn't seem inclined to expand his answer.

"Because . . . ?"

"My best friend committed suicide when we were juniors," he said. He faced the stage, not looking at me, his profile inscrutable.

I put a hand on his arm. "I'm sorry," I said, feeling incredibly awkward at having forced such a confidence.

"It was a long time ago."

No doubt. But that didn't mean the pain and the aftereffects were gone. The music stopped before I could say anything else—probably just as well—and Jodi dismissed the girls, reminding them of rehearsal the next morning. Barnes sidled through a row of chairs and disappeared through a side entrance.

"The police say we can use the Oglethorpe again," Jodi said. "Nine o'clock. We have to be out of there by eleven so the *Phantom* group can rehearse, so don't be late."

"Just a minute, please," Agent Dillon said, starting forward. He took the stairs beside the stage two at a time and joined a startled Jodi and the contestants on stage. He introduced himself and asked anyone who had noticed anything out of place or unusual yesterday, no matter how minor it had seemed at the time, to talk to him. He paused, making sure he had their attention, and then said, "I also have to tell you that we're doing background checks on each of you."

Gasps and widened eyes greeted his announcement. "That's unconstitutional," someone muttered.

"Given that Ms. Faye was contemplating expelling one of you from this competition for some infraction, I have to check it out, in case it has any bearing on her death."

"My girls would never—" Jodi began.

"It was me!" The girl's voice cracked and I couldn't tell who it was.

Chapter Sixteen

THE CONTESTANTS PULLED AWAY FROM THE GIRL who had spoken as if afraid they'd catch swine flu from her. They formed a deep semicircle around her, as perfect as if it had been choreographed. Left alone in the center of the stage, Hayley of flaming-baton fame stood with her head bowed. Flax-colored hair curtained her face. From the way her shoulders shook, I thought she was crying.

Murmurs of "murder" and "Miss Faye" swirled up from the girls surrounding her. Their mood reeked of mingled fear, excitement, and relief.

"She killed Miss Faye," someone muttered.

My money was on Tabitha.

"And cut my swimsuit strap," the same someone said louder.

Yep, Tabitha.

A new voice said, "She ruined my evening gown with

that sprinkler 'accident.' And it was only on loan from Filomena's Fashion Cove."

"She sabotaged Kiley's mats."

The accusations kept coming as the gaggle of young women morphed disturbingly quickly into a mob. If Hayley had been a witch tied to a stake, one of them would have tossed a match.

"I didn't!" Hayley jerked her head up, eyes wide with astonishment. "Of course I didn't kill Miss Faye. Or any of the rest of it."

Agent Dillon started to say something, but Rachel broke out of the pack and threw her arms around Hayley. "It's okay," she said. She glared at the other girls. "I'm sure you didn't do anything very bad."

Dillon stepped forward then. "I need to speak with Miss . . . ?"

"Hayley Greenfield," she said, talking to the floor. "I didn't kill her. But when she said she'd found out about the photos—"

"Told you it was photos," a girl said in a satisfied tone.

"Let's talk in private, Miss Greenfield," Dillon said as the girls pelted her with questions.

"It's none of your beeswax," Rachel told the other contestants. "Leave her alone."

"But she—"

"That's enough," Agent Dillon said. His voice was no louder than usual, but the contempt and anger in it silenced the contestants. His gaze traveled around the semicircle but most of the girls refused to meet his eyes. "Right, then." He gave Rachel a small smile and then guided Hayley toward the stairs at stage right.

The other girls broke into clumps of two and three and straggled toward the stairs at stage left, muttering.

"Remember, tomorrow at nine," Jodi called, shooting a look at Agent Dillon as if daring him to contradict her.

"Rachel," I called, waving a hand.

Catching sight of me, she skipped the stairs and jumped down from the middle of the stage, landing with knees bent. As she straightened, her mouth formed an O and she pointed. I whirled around to see Sam Barnes stumbling toward me, one hand clutching the back of his head. Blood dripped from between his fingers and stained his collar.

"Attacked . . . camera," he croaked. He crumpled to his knees four feet in front of me and I sprang forward to catch his shoulders before he could plant his face in the carpet.

AGENT DILLON WAS ALREADY CALLING FOR AN ambulance and backup by the time I lowered Barnes as gently as I could to the floor. He groaned. Rachel darted away and returned in a minute with a purple bathing suit soaked in cold water.

"Where'd you get this?" I asked, pressing it gently against the bloody knot on the back of Barnes's head.

"My gym bag. It was still there from this morning's competition. I sweated in it, though. You don't, like, think that will give him an infection or anything, do you?" She looked down at me anxiously where I squatted beside the injured man.

"The crud in this carpet poses more of a threat than your suit." From my low vantage point I could see years' worth of chewing gum bumps sprouting from the undersides of the seats. Ick. Barnes's eyes fluttered open. "What—" he asked. He seemed to have trouble focusing for a minute, then recognition sparked in his eyes. "The hair lady."

"What happened, Barnes?" Agent Dillon's voice came

from above me. Uniformed officers had arrived and corralled the contestants and Jodi. Rachel joined them at a nod
from Dillon.

"My head." Barnes reached around and fingered the
lump. "Ow."

"I think it's stopped bleeding," I said, pulling the swimsuit away.

"Doesn't look too serious," Dillon said, "but it's best to
have the EMTs examine you. They're on their way. Can
you tell me what happened?"

"I damn well can." Barnes's voice grew stronger and a
healthier color flushed his face. With my help, he pushed
to a sitting position, resting his back against the side of a
chair. "I was attacked in the men's room."

"Attacked? By whom?" Dillon had his notebook out,
but he hadn't written anything yet.

"How the hell should I know? Someone who wanted my
camera. He stole it." His eyebrows slammed together.

"You saw him?"

"No, the coward snuck up on me. I was at the urinal. I
heard the door open—didn't think anything of it—and the
next thing I know . . . wham! He clocked me with something. He must have snatched my camera while I was out.
I came around and found my way back here. That's all I
know. What kinda creep takes advantage of a man with his
johnson in his hand? That's low."

Penciling a couple of notes, Dillon looked back at
Barnes, not reacting to his vulgarity. "If you didn't see the
attacker, you don't know for sure it was a man, right?"

"I was in the men's room!"

He said it like the room had a force field that kept anyone with two X chromosomes out.

"It didn't surprise you to hear the door open when you

and I are the only men in the building?" He gestured toward the contestants being interviewed by the uniformed officers near the stage.

"I didn't think about it," Barnes said. "I wasn't thinking about anything except an editing problem I'm having with the film. Next thing I know, I'm on the floor with my head split open. Hey, you got an aspirin?"

"The EMTs will be here in a minute. You have any enemies who might have done this?"

"Everyone's got enemies, right?" Barnes shrugged.

I gave him a thoughtful glance. What a sad statement. I didn't have any enemies as far as I knew, nor did Mom. At least, not since Constance died. And even Constance wasn't an enemy. Not the kind who plotted to do you harm. She was more a pain in the butt, a thorn in the side, a cross to bear . . .

"But I've figured out who did it!" Barnes said, surprising me and, to judge from the expression on his face, Agent Dillon.

Dillon raised his brows, inviting Barnes to continue.

Barnes paused dramatically. "It had to be the killer. The one who offed Audrey. He was afraid I had something incriminating on my camera, so he stole it." He looked from me to Dillon, eager to have us praise his reasoning.

"That's a possibility," Agent Dillon said. "Did you?"

"If it's true, that means Darryl didn't kill Audrey," I said.

"Who's this Darryl?" Barnes asked. "If he took my camera, I want him arrested. The camera is worth thousands, but the intellectual property on it—my film—is worth hundreds of thousands. Maybe more."

"I'm sure you have insurance," Dillon said unsympathetically. "If you'd turned the camera over to me when I asked, you wouldn't have a broken head and you'd still have your blockbuster."

I detected the sneer in the last word and bit back a grin.

"Oh, I've still got that," Barnes said slyly. "I've been in this business too long not to have a backup. I downloaded it last night, as soon as I got back to the hotel."

"Great," Dillon said. "I'll send a patrol officer over to get a copy."

"You got that court order?" Hostility simmered in Barnes's eyes, replacing the pain. "It's worth even more now. Think of the publicity this will generate."

Dillon snapped his notebook closed. He looked like he wanted to thwap it up against Barnes's thick skull. "If you turned it over to us, the killer would have no reason to try to steal it, if, in fact, that's what happened. You'd be safe."

"I'll take my chances," Barnes said as the EMTs trotted toward us.

AGENT DILLON MOVED OFF IN DISGUST AND I followed him, still clutching Rachel's damp bathing suit. He took long, angry strides and I'm not even sure he realized I was with him until he reached the door of the men's room two corridors away from the auditorium. Pulling plastic gloves from his pocket, he slipped them on before pulling the door open. "You stay here," he told me.

Obediently, I stood at the door, propping it open with my back, while he moved into the white and blue tiled space. A bank of urinals marched across the right side of the bathroom and three stalls with graffiti scratched into the doors lined the left side. Sinks with soap dispensers sat under a small window set high on the wall. The fresh scent of pine cleanser spoke of a conscientious janitor and the two-month absence of teenage boys. Three or four small drops of blood glistened red on the tile beneath one of the sinks.

Standing just inside the door, Dillon surveyed the scene without moving. I tried to see what he did, but my brain didn't work the same way. Nothing seemed out of place to me except the string mop propped in a corner. There was no sign of a struggle that I could see: no cracked mirrors, no blunt instrument left conveniently on the floor, no broken tiles. Only the small drops of blood.

"If Barnes was at the urinal when he got clobbered, why is the blood by the sink?" I asked.

Dillon didn't answer; he just moved into the room and pulled a slim digital camera out of his pocket. He took several photos of the blood and more of the room from different angles. He peered into each of the urinals and then bent to examine the underside of the sinks.

"Maybe someone was hiding in one of the stalls," I suggested as he tapped each door open and looked inside.

"What would be the point? No one could know for sure that Barnes would have to take a whiz, so why hide in here?"

"Maybe the robber wasn't after Barnes specifically. Maybe Barnes was just a target of opportunity—wrong place, wrong time."

"Possible," Dillon said in a voice that told me he wasn't convinced. "But if it was a simple robbery, why didn't the thief take Barnes's wallet and watch?"

He had me there.

While I tried to construct another scenario, Dillon moved to the silver trash can under the paper towel dispenser. He reached in—yuck—and pulled out a crumpled paper towel. He studied it for a moment and then said, "Blood."

"Barnes probably cleaned himself up a bit before he came back to the auditorium. That would explain why the blood drops are by the sink, too," I said.

"He didn't mention it."

"Confused? Rattled by the attack? Didn't think it mattered?"

"I'm sure that's what he'll say." Without explaining his own thinking about the incident, Agent Dillon flipped open his cell phone and asked for a crime scene tech to bring some luminol.

"What's that for?" I asked when he hung up.

"Showing blood. Even minute traces left after someone thinks he's cleaned up." Tucking the paper towel into a Baggie he pulled from an inner pocket, Agent Dillon swept past me into the hall. "Coming?"

I scooted after him, letting the bathroom door bang shut behind me. We hadn't gone three steps when a clamor from the front entrance quickened Dillon's pace. Sam Barnes, a bandage around his head, stood under the sabertooth mural, one hand uplifted to silence a small crowd of reporters, some with microphones, some with notebooks, who were shooting questions at him.

"What the hell does he think he's doing?" Dillon muttered. We stood shoulder to shoulder just inside the hall, out of Barnes's line of sight.

"No one can steal the truth, or quash it, or keep it from coming out," he proclaimed as the group quieted. "Today, someone thought he could bury the truth about my wife's death by attacking me and stealing my camera. Well, he was wrong. The camera might be gone, but not the truth. I will not be cowed by attempts on my life!" He lifted his chin and struck a noble pose.

Whoa. His wife? Was he still talking about Audrey? I looked at Dillon and he shook his head, anger tightening the muscles in his jaw.

"You and Audrey Faye were married?" A young woman

with ginger curls corkscrewing around her face wrote furiously in her notebook.

"We divorced many years ago," Barnes said, "but our spiritual connection was still intact. She was the love of my life. And I will see her death avenged."

"What are you talking about?" a reporter in too-short chinos and a short-sleeved shirt asked. "Do you have film of the murder?"

"Not of the actual murder," Barnes admitted. "But when my documentary *Ugly: The Other Side of Beauty Pageants* is released, a lot of people will see truths they'd rather stayed hidden."

Talk about ambiguous. Barnes had clearly gone to the politician's school of How to Answer Questions without Answering Them. "How did the Jacksonville station get here so soon?" I asked, nodding at a cameraman with the familiar News9 logo on his camera.

"Good question," Dillon said. "A very good question." He simmered beside me, his mouth thinned into a line. I didn't envy Sam Barnes his next interview with Agent Dillon.

One of the reporters spotted him and called out, "Special Agent Dillon, can you update us on the investigation into Audrey Faye's death. Is today's attack related?"

"The GBI is following a variety of leads," Dillon said. "Other than that, I have no comment on an ongoing investigation. Mr. Barnes, when you've finished here, I have a few more questions for you."

Barnes looked from the pack of reporters to Dillon, clearly annoyed with Dillon for ripping him away from the limelight but unwilling to look obstructive in front of the media. "Absolutely, Agent Dillon," he finally said. "Anything I can do to help catch Audrey's killer."

"Great!" Dillon said with a smile as false as Barnes's. "Then I'm sure you'll be happy to loan the GBI your film so we can analyze it and put your *wife's* murderer behind bars."

Checkmate. Barnes couldn't refuse without looking like a self-promoting, lying fraud. I underestimated him, though. Turning back to the media, he said, "That's it for today, folks. I've got to help the police with their investigation. I hope you all will come to the premier of *Ugly*."

Barnes walked toward us, a triumphant smile on his face. Before he could say anything, Agent Dillon said, "I think this conversation will go better at headquarters. If you'll excuse us, Miss Terhune?" Avoiding the journalists milling in the lobby, he escorted Barnes to a side door.

"Freedom of the press . . . unlawful search and seizure . . . lawyer . . ." Barnes was sputtering as the door wheezed closed.

Chapter Seventeen

✂

I FOUND RACHEL WAITING FOR ME IN THE AUDITO-rium. Everyone else had gone. She stuffed the bathing suit I handed her into a blue gym bag after examining it for blood.

"No biggie," she said when I apologized for ruining it. "It's not like I was ever going to wear it again. It had, like, a *ruffle*. My friend Willow said it would work for the pageant, though, so I bought it. She wants to be a stylist. You know, one of those people who put together outfits for stars so they don't look like they're color blind and two months behind the latest trend."

Emerging into the parking lot, I blinked as the sun assaulted my eyes.

"Ice cream," Rachel said, beelining for the Good Humor truck still parked across the street.

When we each had a treat—a cup of chocolate ice

cream for me and a Heath ice cream bar for Rachel—we wandered into a small park and sat on the swings. No kids were out in this heat so we had the place to ourselves. I told Rachel about Darryl's arrest and asked if she could think of anyone associated with the pageant who might have wanted to harm Audrey Faye.

"Elise's mother," she said promptly, biting off a corner of her ice cream bar. "Mrs. Metzger."

"What did she have against Audrey?"

Rolling her eyes, Rachel said, "Like, everything. She was in there arguing with Ms. Faye at least six times a day. To hear her talk, you'd think Ms. Faye was doing everything she could to make sure Elise didn't win: choreographing dance numbers that didn't show Elise at her best, giving Elise a less advantageous spot in the talent show lineup, letting Elise's evening gown get ruined by the sprinklers. She, like, never let up. She threatened to sue."

"How did Audrey react?" I pushed off with one foot and let the swing arc gently.

"She banned her from rehearsals," Rachel said.

"Did that upset Elise?"

"Heck no. I think she was relieved. I get the feeling Elise isn't too into the pageant scene."

I'd gotten the same feeling.

"And she fought with that Dr. Yarrow, you know, the guy who organized the protestors."

"Mrs. Metzger did?"

"No, Ms. Faye."

I stilled my swing and faced her. A dot of chocolate lurked beside her mouth and I pointed to the same spot on my face. She swiped her tongue out. "What did they fight about?"

Rachel shrugged. "Don't know. I was late leaving after rehearsal on Monday night and I heard Dr. Yarrow shout something about 'hold you responsible' and Ms. Faye came back with something like, 'does the college know about Berkeley?' Whatever the heck that means. But she sounded all 'I'll tell on you' when she said it."

I had no idea what it meant, either, but it made me uneasy. Yarrow was easily twenty years older than Audrey Faye, so it was unlikely they'd been classmates. Had he taught at Berkeley before coming to St. Elizabeth? It seemed unlikely that a professor would willingly trade a berth at one of the most prestigious universities in California for a job at a Georgia community college. Unless he was forced to. I swung silently for a moment. This promised to be a sticky wicket. If Althea's new beau had a shady past, did she know about it? If not, how would she react if I dug up some dirt on him? Worse, if he did have something to do with Audrey's death, was Althea in danger?

"Anything else, Rachel? Who do the contestants think killed her?"

"Whoever she was going to toss out of the contest," Rachel said promptly.

"Hayley, right?"

"Maybe. But no one thought it was Hayley until she confessed today. Most of the girls thought it was Tabitha, but that's probably just because they don't like her very much," she said shrewdly. "I was thinking it might be Brooke."

"Really? Why?" I thought Brooke was one of the more together girls in the pageant.

Rachel shrugged. "Don't know. She just seems like the kind of person who would have a secret."

Interesting. A slight breeze kicked the scent of cypress toward us. I looked up to see dark clouds scudding the sky. Hallelujah. Rain would cool things down, at least temporarily.

As if reading my mind, Rachel said, "We should do a rain dance." A huge grin split her face. She leaped from the swing and grabbed my hands. Over my weak protests, she started around in a circle, dragging me with her.

"Rain, rain, make us wet. We're so tired of our sweat," she sang to the tune of "Rain, Rain, Go Away."

"Rachel and Grace want lots of rain; the heat is driving us insane." My improvised verse set Rachel laughing so hard she plopped down in the mulch cushioning the playground. I pulled her to her feet and offered her a ride home as the first fat drops splatted into the mulch, sending up little poofs of dust.

I PULLED UP AT MY APARTMENT HOPING FOR PEACE and quiet, but got my landlady. Genevieve Jones was in her mid-eighties but had more get-up-and-go than your average teenager. On a normal day, she might start off with tai chi in the park, serve lunch to housebound people with Meals on Wheels, and play four hours of bridge before dining with a crony or one of her many nieces or nephews. With a frill of white hair that made her look like a crowned crane, she was thin and long-legged, which only enhanced the resemblance.

I lived in the one-bedroom carriage house that was her son's. He'd never married and had died of cancer the day before he turned sixty. She rented the place to me when I came back from Atlanta. Living with Mom wasn't an option and I liked the cozy apartment and Mrs. Jones. I checked up on her and did some gardening in return for a break on the rent. Lately, though, I'd been thinking a place of my very own—a house—would be nice.

"Yoo-hoo! Grace." Mrs. Jones waved from her veranda, which protected her from the rain. "Did I hear you've entered a beauty pageant? You're a lovely girl, but aren't you a teensy bit long in the tooth?"

Closing my car door a bit harder than necessary, I started toward her, not caring that I was getting wet. It felt good. I noted that the forsythia bushes were encroaching on the sidewalk again. I'd trim them back this weekend.

"I'm not a contestant, Mrs. Jones," I said. "I'm doing the girls' hair. And Stella's doing their nails." I climbed the steps to the veranda and ran my fingers through rain-tangled hair.

Mrs. Jones shook her head, setting her pouf of hair dancing. "Such a shame about her husband. It just goes to show that you never know, doesn't it?"

"What does?" I asked, wary of what the local gossips might have relayed to her. They took one part fact and mixed in three parts imagination or wishful thinking or spite and came up with a tale that didn't bear much resemblance to actual happenings.

"Why, about him fathering that woman's baby and then killing her when she told him about the pregnancy. Wine cooler? The sun's well over the yard arm, as my father used to say."

"What!"

"Peach or strawberry?" she asked, dipping her hand into the cooler beside her rocking chair. She held up a dripping green bottle.

"Uh, peach, thanks," I said, sinking reluctantly into the rocker. I hadn't meant to stay—hopefully Vonda was on her way over—but I had to learn what Mrs. Jones had heard, even if it was no closer to the truth than Chicago to London. Rain drummed on the veranda's roof and I had to lean in to hear Mrs. Jones.

"Well, you know that my niece Karen works at the coroner's office over to Kingsland. And she heard that nice Dr. Butler mention that the autopsy showed a fetus, not but two and a half or three months along." She sat back in her chair with an expectant air.

Doing mental math, I realized that the baby very well could be Darryl's from what Stella had said about the affair. The thought made me sick. Or maybe it was the wine cooler. I put down my half-drunk bottle. "Are they doing tests to establish paternity?" I asked.

She shrugged her bony shoulders. "As to that, I couldn't say."

Of course they were. If they were going to prosecute Darryl, it would be nice to have a clear-cut motive like a pregnancy to explain why he jabbed Audrey with his wife's nail file. Things were looking grim for Stella's husband. I held on to my conviction that he hadn't murdered Audrey even if he fathered her baby and said diplomatically, "I hope this rumor doesn't get around. Think how hurtful it would be for Jessica to hear about from one of her friends."

Mrs. Jones nodded wisely. "Little pitchers have big ears. It never ceases to amaze me what parents will say in front of their children these days. And what they let them watch on television or at the movie theater. Heavens! You don't need to worry about me, dear. Mum's the word."

"Thanks." I stood and gave her wrinkled cheek a kiss. "And thanks for the wine cooler. I've got to go—there's Vonda."

Vonda pulled to the curb in her ancient Volvo station wagon. She and Ricky had bought it when they took on the B&B. "It might not be sporty," she had said with a rueful look, "but it hauls enough groceries and linens to make life as an innkeeper a bit easier."

"I heard she and Ricky Warren are tying the knot again,"

Mrs. Jones said, watching as Vonda got out of the car and waved.

"Where did you hear that?" I looked at her, astonished. Vonda hadn't even hinted as much to me.

"My great-niece who works at the courthouse said Ricky was in a couple days ago, hanging out in the marriage license office." She winked at me. "And that little gal sure looks all lit up."

Vonda *did* look happy. I hustled down the stairs to meet her, giving her a big hug.

"I'm here for my haircut," Vonda said, holding a bottle of wine aloft. "Payment to be drunk after the cutting so I don't end up looking like you went after me with a hacksaw again."

"Unfair." I led her around the side of the house and across the driveway to my apartment and unlocked the door. The carriage house coughed the accumulated day's heat at us and I left the door open as I punched on the window air conditioner. "Phew." I headed into the kitchen and opened the window over the sink. Ever since someone had dumped a water moccasin in through the screen, I locked up tight when I left. "The only time I botched your hair even a little bit was when we were seventeen and you were dancing in the chair to that tape we bought. It was like trying to clip a Lhasa apso on speed. What *was* that tape?"

"Bowie's *Earthling*. Not his best, but still great." She hummed the opening to "Seven Years in Tibet," plopping down in the orange and cream floral easy chair I'd found at a garage sale. The price was right, so the fact that the orange wasn't ideal with the pale taupe walls didn't faze me.

"So," I said, ultra casually. "What's this I hear about you and Ricky getting remarried?"

"You're not coming near me with the scissors; you've

already had too much to drink," Vonda said. She made a show of tucking the wine bottle back in her tote.

"Half a wine cooler," I protested. "And don't change the subject."

"Been there, done that," Vonda said. "You were maid of honor, remember? And you were counselor and comforter in chief when we split. Whatever makes you think I'd do it again?" She looked half annoyed, half amused.

"I heard Ricky was seen in the marriage license office," I mumbled, embarrassed that I'd let myself think even for one minute that an unverified rumor from the St. Elizabeth's gossip mill might be accurate.

Vonda laughed. "Which is also the place to get copies of birth certificates. We needed RJ's for his baseball team. They're mental about kids being in the right age bracket."

"I'm an idiot," I apologized. Maybe Mrs. Jones's rumor about Audrey being pregnant had no more basis in fact than this one. For Stella's sake, I hoped so.

AFTER I TRIMMED VONDA'S PLATINUM HAIR, KEEPING it in the modified pixie cut she'd been sporting all summer, we opened the bottle of pinot grigio and settled on the front stoop. The rain had stopped, but water dripped from the eaves. It was still twilight but the crickets were chirring and a bullfrog croaked loudly. I told her everything I'd learned that day, except for Mrs. Jones's news that Audrey was pregnant when she died.

"I think that Sam Barnes must have done it," Vonda said.

Worked for me—I didn't much like Mr. Barnes. I sipped my wine. "Why?"

"Could be anything. He was married to her. No one has

more reason to kill a woman than her husband. At least, that's what Ricky says."

"Then what about Kevin?"

"He's a good choice, too." Vonda nodded approvingly. "His brokerage business has really been on the skids since the economy nosedived. Maybe he needs the life insurance payout."

"Is there one?"

Vonda shrugged. "How would I know? It's my job to brainstorm suspects and your job to come up with some proof."

"He knew about the affair," I said. A vision of the grief-stricken man on Mom's veranda this morning gave me pause. "He did seem genuinely upset about her death, though. But if he knew about—" I almost said "the baby" but stopped myself in time. "But he couldn't have done it." I explained about Faye being with the GBI when someone left the death threat.

"Maybe he's got an accomplice," Vonda said.

"Maybe." That didn't feel right to me, but it wouldn't hurt to learn more about Faye. And I knew just how I'd do it. He was a Realtor and I was interested in buying a house . . .

"And this professor guy that Althea's dating," Vonda put in. "I don't like it that he apparently had history with Audrey, too."

"Me neither."

"I suppose Althea might take offense if you start investigating him, huh?"

I gave her a speaking look.

She nodded. "That's what I thought. Maybe you can get someone else to do a background check on him. How about

Marty? He could get one of his researchers to plug him into a database and see what pops out."

"Not a bad idea," I said. "I already tried to get Marty to write a story and he passed, but maybe he could wangle a few days in St. Elizabeth if I pushed a bit harder."

"Who else do we need to investigate?" Vonda asked.

I counted on my fingers. "Mrs. Metzger, the pushy mama."

"The lioness defending her cub."

"Something like that. The contestants." I lumped them all together on one finger.

"All of them?"

"Well, not Rachel," I conceded. "Maybe they're not suspects anymore, now that we know it was Hayley that Audrey was going to toss out of the pageant."

"Skip the contestants," Vonda advised.

"The protestors." I held up a third finger.

"What you need to look into," Vonda said, "is access. Who had access to the theater to pull off the pranks, the sprinkler thing, and the mat thing?"

"Excellent question." I hadn't thought about that. "All of the contestants, obviously, and their parents. The judges. Sam Barnes. Kevin Faye, if he was coming to see Audrey. The theater staff and crew. The community theater people rehearsing *Phantom*. Half the town apparently." I took a healthy sip of wine.

Vonda stood and dumped the dregs of her wine into the grass. "I guess that doesn't narrow the suspect pool too much then, does it? And, unless they've fixed it, the back door from the parking lot doesn't latch right. Anyone could walk in. Ricky and I used to sneak in to watch movies when we were dating. Our first kiss was in the back row of that theater watching *Jerry Maguire*. Maybe I *would* marry him again if he'd say, 'you complete me,' with that soulful Tom Cruise vibe. I've got to get home, sweetie. We have a full house so I'll be up early cooking biscuits and grits for twenty-two people. Remind me why I thought I wanted to own a B&B?" She hugged me. "Thanks for the hair."

After Vonda left, I stayed on the stoop for a while until night surrounded me and my fanny went to sleep. No revelations about the murderer's identity struck me, so I went to bed.

Chapter Eighteen

✄

I APPROACHED THE OGLETHORPE THEATER THE next morning at an unusually early hour. Vonda's remarks about access must have played in my dreams, because I awoke determined to find out how secure the theater was. I wanted to check rear and side exits and windows without anyone asking me what I was doing. The sun had barely begun its assault when I pulled up across from the theater, and the air was crisp after the night's rain. Worms wiggled on the sidewalk. Mockingbirds sang and early-morning exercise nuts were the only other people out, their faces serious as they pounded the pavement.

I tugged on the front doors—locked—then took the sidewalk along the left side of the building that led to the parking lot in the back. A door I assumed was an emergency exit from the theater proper sat at the top of a short flight of stairs, three-quarters of the way down the building.

I climbed up and tried it. Locked. Several narrow windows looked down on me, but they were set too high to give access without a ladder. I continued around to the parking lot. No cars at this hour. A Dumpster, lid open, squatted at the rear of the lot where it connected with Yew Street.

Two more doors opened onto the lot, one at either corner of the building. And a window well, covered by a grate, let light into the theater's basement, I presumed. I turned the knob on the first door. Also locked. Maybe they'd fixed it since Vonda's time. I walked toward the window well, thinking someone needed to get back here with a Weedeater. Rank weeds grew a foot high against the back of the building, trapping discarded ticket stubs, plastic grocery bags, and other trash. *Clang!* Something banged against metal and I whirled. A black-and-white tomcat half the size of a puma glared at me from atop the Dumpster, daring me to interrupt his breakfast. "It's all yours, kitty," I murmured.

I hadn't been nervous before—it was broad daylight, for heaven's sake—but the butterflies in my tummy riled up by the cat refused to settle down. I rattled the grate on the window well after checking for spiders, but it didn't budge. This was silly, I told myself. Even if I found an open door or window, what would it prove? Hurrying to the second door, I grasped the knob, expecting to meet resistance. Instead, it turned easily and the door creaked toward me, knocking me a little off balance. Drat. I would much prefer to have found the building secure against all invaders except mice and cockroaches because that would have given me a finite number of suspects for the murder. This way, anyone in the tri-county area could have snuck in.

A strange odor drifted from the open door and I sniffed. It was too faint for me to identify. Probably just musty

basement smell aggravated by the damp from the rain. I
started to shut the door when a low growl made me freeze.
Turning my head, I saw the tomcat from the Dumpster
crouched ten feet away. His tail lashed. Sticky matter clot-
ted the corners of his eyes and he listed to one side. This
was one sick kitty. He made a menacing noise again deep
in his throat and inched closer to me. I retreated a step.
Rabies is unfortunately fairly common in the county, and
feral cats were carriers. I did not need to tangle with a po-
tentially rabid feline. Reaching a hand behind me, I pulled
the door wider and jumped through it backward, yanking
it closed as I fell onto my derrière. The cat thudded against
the door and yowled. The eerie sound made me shiver.

Pushing to my feet, I brushed off the seat of my khaki
slacks and looked around. Dim light ghosting in from the
window well showed me a storage room. Labeled boxes
were piled high against two walls, and I spotted a spinning
wheel, what looked like a church spire, and a stack of boul-
ders. I poked one. Styrofoam. Old props. *Sleeping Beauty*,
I guessed for the spinning wheel. I couldn't figure out what
play the church spire came from. I tried to orient myself
and decided I must be under the backstage area. If I made
my way upstairs, I could go out the front doors and avoid
Cujo cat. I'd call Animal Control when I got to my car. A
flight of stairs beckoned from the far corner and I made
my way to them, keeping my arms close to avoid brushing against the spiderwebs that draped props that probably
hadn't been moved since the Nixon era.

As I climbed the stairs, the odor I'd smelled earlier
grew stronger. There was something familiar about it . . .
I pushed open the door at the top of the stairs, dismayed to
step into almost total dark. Blinking my eyes, I stood still
until I could make out vague shapes. I was pleased to dis-

cover I was right about my location; I was in a narrow hall, an alcove really, just behind the stage area. Behind me, a wider hall led to the Green Room and the small rooms where Stella and I had beautified the pageant contestants. Crossing the stage would be the quick route into the auditorium. From there, I could make my way to the foyer and escape into the fresh air.

The stink was almost overpowering as I fumbled my way through a gauzy scrim and onto the empty stage. I finally identified it: dead skunk. Anyone who has driven on Georgia's roads has encountered that smell. But what was it doing here? With rabies on my mind, I wondered if a sick skunk had found a way into the theater and died in a vent or something. Pee-yew. Breathing shallowly, arms extended to keep from bumping into anything, I crossed the stage. The open feeling, the lack of walls or anything to anchor myself with, disturbed me. I could imagine the openness going on forever, a vast Arctic wasteland or a stretch of empty sea. Don't be a doofus, I chided myself. A creaking noise on my right stopped me. I stood still, listening. Nothing. Hadn't Marv said something about rats in the theater? I stepped forward again, tripped over something bulky, and fell flat.

I knew without thinking about it that I was draped over a some*one*, not a some*thing*. And the someone's total lack of response at having my hundred and thirty pounds crash down on him or her scared me more than an outraged, "Get off of me!" would have. Trying not to disturb the body, I pushed hard with my hands on the stage so my torso lifted off what felt like a pair of legs. I stayed on my knees for a moment before pushing to my feet. My knees wobbled so badly I could hardly stand. I couldn't bring myself to search for a pulse and I would've paid a week's wages to know where the light switch was.

Tears straggled down my cheeks as I half ran, half stumbled toward where I thought the stairs would be at stage left. I didn't even much care if I fell off the stage. At least I'd be that much closer to getting out of the theater. My right foot suddenly met no resistance when it came down and I thudded onto the stairs. Grateful to have a wall to guide me, I kept my hand against it as I sprinted up the aisle. I was gasping for breath by the time I burst through the swinging doors and into the sunlit foyer. Holding the door open to illuminate the auditorium, I peered back toward the stage and thought I saw a smudge of beard and a flash of plaid shirt on the crumpled figure. He could have been an actor playing Romeo, Oedipus, the Hunchback of Notre Dame, or any number of other tragic heroes dead at the end of the fifth act.

But Sam Barnes wouldn't be reviving for curtain calls.

Chapter Nineteen

I WAS TOO FAMILIAR WITH THE PARADE OF OFFICIALS who show up at a murder scene: EMTs, police, firefighters, coroner, crime scene technicians, and others. After making the 911 call from my cell phone, I huddled in my car, waiting for the parade to begin, and tried to scrub a smear of blood off the front of my sage green blouse with a fast-food napkin I'd found under the seat. It just spread the stain. A rap on the window made me jump and look up.

Agent Dillon stood there, his face full of concern. He pulled open the door. "Are you okay, Grace?"

I shook my head mutely and he reached in and pulled me out of the car, wrapping his arms around me. I clung to the solid warmth of him, conscious of a faintly spicy after-shave and the ironed cotton of his shirt beneath my cheek.

"Are you hurt? Is that your blood?"

I shook my head against his chest, slightly comforted by the strength in his arms and the *tha-thump* of his heartbeat.

"Tell me what happened," he said to the top of my head. "Dispatch said something about a rabid cat and a dead man. Were you attacked?"

Okay, so I hadn't been a model of coherence when I called 911. I pushed away, suddenly shy about being snuggled against him. He let me go easily. "No. I found Sam Barnes. On the stage. I think he's dead." And I explained how I came to be in the Oglethorpe.

"God damn it, Grace! Would you just let us do our jobs?" he exploded when I finished.

I stepped back, feeling like he'd slapped me. "I'm not—I can't—"

"I'm sorry," he said, running a hand down his face. "It's just that I'm worried you're going to *be* the body one of these days and not just find one."

The real concern in his voice almost made me cry again. Before I could say anything, though, the rest of the parade showed up, lights flashing and sirens wailing.

"I've got to check out the scene," he said, moving away from me. "Wait here. We'll need a formal statement." He signaled to a uniformed officer, who came to keep me company. Or keep me from leaving, I wasn't sure which.

The cop turned out to be Officer Qualls, the dark-haired woman who'd helped secure the scene after Audrey's death. The one who had the hots for Hank. She looked trim and competent in her dark blue uniform. "You okay?" she asked as I rubbed at the bloodstain again. "Want some coffee? We just stopped by the Perk-Up and I haven't even touched mine yet. You're welcome to it."

"Thanks," I said with real gratitude. I trailed her to the patrol car, where she reached in for the mega-sized cup in the holder. Why can't coffee shops just have small, medium, and large cups anymore? Starbucks uses tall, venti, and grande and the Perk-Up went them one better with mega, giga, and tera, apparently catering to the computer-savvy crowd.

"So, you found another body?" Officer Qualls asked a bit too casually, leaning back against the cruiser, arms crossed over her chest.

I sipped the coffee: too sweet, too milky, and with a hint of hazelnut, but comforting nonetheless. "Looks that way."

"What were you doing in an empty theater at seven in the morning?"

Clearly, her interrogation style ran to blunt. "Escaping a rabid cat."

Her dark brows drew together. "Come again?"

I told her about Cujo kitty and she called dispatch and asked that an Animal Control officer be sent out. "I had a cousin who was attacked by a rabid raccoon when we were in third grade," she said. "It came right up to us on the playground. I had nightmares for years."

"Was your cousin okay?" I gulped more coffee.

"Yeah, but the injections were no fun. That was back when you had to take them in the abdomen. I don't think they do that anymore. So, you and Hank used to be married?"

I was glad she'd given up interrogating me, so I answered. "Four years."

"He seems like a really sweet man," she observed, shooting me a sidelong look. Her eyes were her best feature, a warm brown with tawny flecks, fringed by thick lashes.

"He has his moments." Few and far between by the time we divorced.

The Animal Control vehicle showed up and a stocky,

gray-uniformed woman got out holding a stick with a noose on the end. She pulled on heavy gloves that covered her arms to the elbow. "Rabid cat?" she asked.

"Around back," I told her. "Black and white."

With a nod, she trudged around the building, apparently uninterested in the collection of emergency vehicles blocking Pecan Street. I could tell Officer Qualls wanted to follow her, but her mission was to keep tabs on me. Moments later, an unearthly yowl split the air, startling one patrol officer so he dumped coffee on himself. "What the hell was that?" he asked, eyeing the Oglethorpe as if afraid the real phantom of the opera would come floating out.

Suddenly, I couldn't face seeing the sick cat dragged around the building and bundled into one of the bins opening out of the Animal Control vehicle. Bound for euthanasia. "Tell Agent Dillon he can get hold of me at my mom's," I said, dashing toward my car.

"But you can't—" Officer Qualls started, only to be drowned out by the squeal of my tires as I pulled away from the curb.

IT FELT LIKE HALF THE DAY HAD ELAPSED, BUT IT was still shy of eight o'clock when I slipped into Mom's kitchen through the screen door. Mom and Stella sat at the table in their robes, syrup-smeared plates in front of them and the smell of pancakes in the air. Mom took one look at me and rose to hug me. "What's wrong?" she asked.

For a moment I just hugged her hard, snuffling back tears. Her soft bosom and the smell of the Jean Naté powder she'd used forever gave me comfort, and the feeling of Barnes's body under mine receded. I sat. As I started to tell what had happened, she slid a mug of tea in front of me and started mixing another batch of pancakes. I didn't even try to stop her.

"At least," I finished, dousing my pancakes with syrup, "this should put Darryl in the clear. No way he could've murdered Sam Barnes from jail."

Silence greeted my silver-lining pronouncement. I looked up to see Mom and Stella staring at me, identical expression of dismay on their faces. "What?" I asked.

"Simone got Darryl out on bail late yesterday afternoon," Stella said.

"The judge granted bail?" That surprised me, given the nature of the crime and Darryl's disappearance afterward.

"Simone's good," Mom said simply.

Too good, maybe, I thought.

"I've got to call Darryl," Stella said. "Excuse me." Dabbing her lips with a napkin, she rose and hurried up the stairs by the pantry.

Rapping on the screen door grabbed our attention. Agent Dillon stood there, white shirt sleeves rolled to his elbows, looking hot and tired.

"Good morning, Mrs. Terhune," he said as Mom let him in.

"Good morning, Agent Dillon." She gave him a lovely smile, not one whit discomposed at having him drop by while she was wearing her robe and slipper socks.

"Please, call me John."

I stifled my surprise. That was new. During last May's investigation of Constance DuBois's murder, he kept things very formal. Maybe you got to call him John if you weren't a murder suspect.

He turned to me. "You ran off." He sounded exasperated rather than mad.

"You found me." I didn't want to tell him about feeling sorry for the cat and overwhelmed by the whole finding-a-body thing, but something in his face told me he understood at least part of it.

"Those pancakes sure smell good," he told Mom with a hopeful look.

"Coming right up," she said. "Violetta's short-order service, at your beck and call." She said it good-naturedly and I knew she was happy to cook for anyone who appreciated her food. She ladled batter on the griddle and the yummy aroma filled the kitchen. "So, was it really Mr. Barnes that Grace found?"

He nodded, washing his hands at the sink. "Yes."

"Dead?" I asked, even though I knew the answer.

"Very. Shot twice at close range."

I shuddered and warmed my palms on my tea mug. "When?"

"We won't know until after the autopsy. Analysis of his stomach contents should give us a more definitive time, assuming we can find someone who knows when he ate last. Probably after eleven, though."

I was glad I'd already finished breakfast because the thought of analyzing stomach contents made me queasy.

"Do you think it was the same person who attacked him yesterday?" Mom asked, sliding a plate of pancakes in front of Agent Dillon.

"Definitely not," he said. He forked up a bite and chewed slowly, enjoying our impatience.

"Why not?" I asked before he could take another bite.

"No one attacked him yesterday. He staged it."

"However could he do that? Why ever would he?" Mom wondered.

I sat back in my chair, studying the men's restroom again in my mind's eye. Dillon watched me with a hint of a smile, prompting me to figure it out.

"He banged his head underneath the sink, didn't he?" I said. "To make it look like someone hit him. That's why the blood was near the sink and on the paper towel—he'd wiped it off the sink."

Dillon nodded his approval. "Exactly. The luminol showed traces of blood on the underside of the sink. He must have crouched beneath it and stood up hard."

"Ouch." I winced just thinking about it.

"But why?" Mom asked again.

"For the publicity, I should think," Dillon said. "That's how the reporters got there so fast. He called them before he staged his little attack. He was trying to drum up more of an audience for his film; instead, he spooked a killer."

"You think his bragging on TV yesterday about his film prompted the murderer to go after him?"

Dillon nodded. "Yep. Tying up loose ends. The murderer didn't know what was or wasn't on the film, but he—or she—obviously isn't one to take chances. He's dangerous. The skunk makes it look like he's got a real thing against beauty pageants."

"Skunk?" Mom asked. "You lost me."

I remembered the odor in the theater. "What about the skunk?"

"It was left on a counter in the Green Room with a note that said, 'Beauty pageants stink. Stop the killing.'"

Mom looked horrified. "How sick. Well! I'm sure they'll cancel the pageant."

Dillon was shaking his head before she finished. He clicked his fork rhythmically against the plate. "I talked to Jodi Keen and then to the folks responsible for the Miss Georgia Blossom pageant at the state level and no one is willing to shut it down. A couple of the girls have withdrawn, though. I had my team contact all of them to make sure they were aware of the danger. Best I could do." He looked at me. "Keen denied there was a threatening note until I showed her the scrap you saved. Then she tried to laugh it off as a prank."

"Big surprise," I muttered.

"Grace Ann, I think you should quit the pageant," Mom said. "And Stella, too. They can get along without a hair stylist and manicurist."

"Good idea," Dillon approved.

I wasn't so sure. First, I couldn't see the killer fixing on me or Stella as targets—we were pretty peripheral to the whole pageant thing, not like the contestants or the coordinator. Second, if I quit, I'd lose my best chance of finding out who killed Audrey. I needed to be on the inside.

Stella agreed with me when she came downstairs moments later, dressed in a navy blue blouse and with her hair French braided. She hesitated at the sight of Dillon but said a civil good morning. "I don't want to quit," she said when we told her what was going on. "We're going to need the money for Darryl's defense if it comes to a trial."

Mom had on her stubborn look, peering at me over her glasses. "I can't stop you from staying with the pageant, Stella, although I think it's foolish. But Grace—"

"You can't stop me, either," I pointed out evenly.

She gripped her lips tightly together but said nothing. "Thank you for breakfast," I said to her back as she began to stack the dishes in the sink.

The dishes clanked against each other, making me fear chips. She turned on the spigot and water gushed over them.

"I'll stop by later," I said.

"Suit yourself."

Mom didn't often get mad, but when she did it was a quiet, freeze-you-out mad. I'd talk to her later, without an audience. Stella and Dillon thanked her for breakfast, earning a curt "You're welcome," and we left by the screen door.

Chapter Twenty

AGENT DILLON TOOK OFF BEFORE I COULD PULL HIM aside and ask if the news about Audrey's pregnancy was true. Stella looked more resolute than yesterday, so I figured she hadn't heard the rumor. Stella gave me a lift to the nursing home where the contestants and judges had their first "community photo op" of the day. They'd go from there to the humane society and finish up at the marina. The point of the exercise was to assemble one of those video montages that show the contestants interacting happily in the host community, the way Miss America contestants cavort on the Atlantic City boardwalk and some other pageant's contestants throw craps in a Las Vegas casino.

"What did Simone think of Darryl's case?" I asked as we pulled up in front of Happy Meadows Retirement Community. Talk about being put out to pasture. The main building had a faux historical front, with pillars I was pretty sure would collapse if you leaned against them, and happy yellow paint. The "happy" theme continued inside with all the staffers wearing smiley-face buttons with their names on them, and a Disney medley playing softly over speakers. The smells of bleach and incontinence took the cheery right out of the atmosphere, however. I saw no residents; maybe they were all at breakfast.

"She thinks the prosecutor has a weak case. It's all circumstantial. Nothing pins Darryl to the scene—no fingerprints or hair or fibers or anything. I didn't understand all the technical details, but she said that's good. And he doesn't really have a motive. Affairs end all the time, Simone said, without anyone getting killed. She said *I* had a better motive than Darryl."

Stella tried to smile and I could tell that talking about the affair hurt her.

"And she said that Kevin Faye is coming into a five-hundred-thousand-dollar life insurance policy."

I whistled softly. "That sounds like a real motive."

"Exactly! Anyone could see that, don't you think? Simone says we can use that to cast reasonable doubt."

Ted Gaines, the weatherman judge from channel nine, all gelled hair and white teeth, brushed past us, deep in conversation with Renata Schott, her hair in an elegant chignon and her makeup flawless. Guess she wouldn't be asking for my help today. A cameraman trotted after them, reminding me of Sam Barnes. Five or six contestants straggled in and I saw more getting off a van that had pulled into the circular drive. I guessed Jodi was making sure all her charges stuck together by ferrying them to their various appointments. Marv, the theater owner, climbed out of the van last, awkwardly maneuvering a large, wheeled cooler.

"What are you doing here?" I asked as he pulled the red

cooler into the lobby, biceps and tattoos bulging from a sleeveless shirt. "And what have you got there?"

He hitched up his worn jeans. "With the theater closed by the cops again, I didn't have much else to do today," he said. "Ms. Keen was looking for a driver and I volunteered— for a nice hourly wage. These"—he nodded toward the cooler—"are just bottled waters and snacks for the 'celebrity' judges." He hooked his meaty fingers in the air. Looking back toward the parking area, he sighed. "I'm also supposed to be security and keep them away."

"Them" were the protestors, jumping out of a large van driven by Kwasi Yarrow. The college kids looked vigorous and rested, ready for a fun-filled day of placard waving. Whatever happened to disc golf and binge drinking as student entertainment? Those had been the big things when I was at UGA. Althea climbed down stiffly from the front passenger seat wearing a yellow caftan with black zigzags and a red and yellow patterned scarf wrapped around her head.

"What's Althea doing here?" Stella asked, watching the newcomers set up under a tamarind tree.

"Dr. Yarrow is her new boy toy." I immediately felt ashamed of myself for joking about the age difference. "He's her significant other," I amended.

"Get out," Stella said, wide-eyed. "I would never have pictured them together."

"Why not?"

"Well . . ." She thought about it. "Althea's always cracking jokes and laughing. I haven't seen that guy so much as smile all week."

She had a point. Dr. Yarrow did come across a bit on the serious side. But maybe he was a bundle of laughs when he was "off duty," as it were—out of the classroom and away from his students.

"Grace, Stella!" Jodi beckoned from a linoleum-lined hallway. "We're on a tight schedule today."

WE'D BEEN ALLOTTED AN EMPTY BEDROOM AS OUR temporary beauty parlor, and although it was disconcerting working next to a hospital bed with a stainless steel bedpan on the unmade mattress, we cycled the girls through in record time. Of course, only eight girls remained in the pageant after Sam Barnes's murder, including Rachel, Elise, Brooke, Morgan, Tabitha, and three others whose names I couldn't keep in my head. Hayley wasn't there and I wondered what Agent Dillon had learned from her and whether she was still a suspect. I couldn't see her luring Sam Barnes to the theater and shooting him.

When the contestants were all beautified and dressed in their casual resort wear, graciously supplied by Filomena's Fashion Cove (as a large sign in the dayroom announced), they trooped down to the dayroom where the Happy Meadows residents were gathered for their visit. Elderly men and women sat on couches or in wheelchairs, some with an air of eager expectancy and others with dazed or zoned-out expressions. A couple were sleeping. The judges, sipping designer water and making nice with the patients, were already in the room when the contestants arrived. A feisty nonagenarian with no teeth was whupping Renata Schott at checkers, cackling as his king jumped six of her pieces in a row. She looked happy to excuse herself when the contestants filed into the room, followed by the cameraman.

"Mingle, girls, mingle," Jodi urged, throwing up both hands.

As the contestants began making conversation with the residents, another girl and a young man slipped into the room. It took me a minute to recognize the sandy-haired protestor, Daphne, and her friend Seth. The poster gave them away. "We've come to visit my grandma," she said when Marv, at a frantic sign from Jodi, tried to hustle them out. "I've got a perfect right to visit her."

Marv hesitated and she slid past him, advancing on the most out-of-it-looking resident in the room, a frail woman with thinning white hair wearing a blue cotton dressing gown. "Grandma!" Daphne said, swooping down on her and hugging her.

The woman smiled uncertainly and the suspicion that she'd never laid eyes on Daphne crossed my mind. Daphne settled beside her, patting her clawlike hand, making sure her anti-pageant poster was angled so it was almost impossible for the cameraman not to include it in his shots. Seth stood behind them. Pretty clever, I thought, semi-admiring their tactics.

I leaned back against a wall, out of camera range, and watched the girls work the room. Rachel settled beside a pleasant-looking woman in a wheelchair and chatted with her. From her hand gestures, I thought she was talking about cutting hair. Tabitha moved from resident to resident, doing little more than smiling and letting them admire her. Brooke advanced on a pair of African American women playing cards and they dealt her in. The others, including the judges, eased into conversations. After a few awkward moments, the residents seemed to be enjoying themselves and I thought it was a nice idea—Jodi's?—to visit the nursing home. The cameraman circled the room, recording it all.

Just as Jodi clapped her hands and asked the contestants to gather around and sing a couple of songs, the weatherman lurched to his feet. His face was a sickly green color. "I feel sick," he announced.

A nursing aide moved toward him with a glass of water, but he brushed her aside and threw up on the floor.

"My tummy's very sensitive, too," a woman piped up in the loud tones of the hard-of-hearing. "Can't abide cabbage or brussels sprouts or—"

"I'm afraid—" Renata Schott began, putting her hand to her mouth. She dashed toward the door and barely made it to the hall before she upchucked. The third judge sank to his knees and vomited into the container holding a potted palm tree.

Jodi, the contestants, and the residents gazed at each other with bewilderment turning to fear. The stench was unbearable.

"Gross. I'm out of here," Tabitha announced, wrinkling her nose and heading for the door.

Gaines, on his knees, raised his head weakly after another round of vomiting. "Get a doctor," he croaked. "I've been poisoned."

Chapter Twenty-one

✂

AN HOUR LATER, SOMETHING RESEMBLING ORDER
had been restored. Jodi had the contestants corralled in the
cafeteria at the far end of the Happy Meadows complex.
Aides had escorted the residents to their rooms. The retirement home's on-call doctor was treating the judges and
they were recovering. Crime scene technicians were col-
lecting samples—double ick—to determine what caused
the judges' sudden illness. One of them had carted off the
cooler and the empty bottles. The protestors were waving
their signs and chanting "Ban beauty pageants! Ban beauty
pageants!" probably in hopes of getting some airtime from
the cameraman who had tired of recording his sick col-
league. He was roaming the grounds, camera pointed at the
police, the protestors, and random visitors who came to see
Pop-Pop or Great-aunt Nellie and almost stroked out at the
sight of the police vehicles and crowded courtyard.

I had snagged a bench under a bougainvillea bush in front of the residence and was waiting for Stella to appear. Where had she wandered off to? I had a clear view of the activities in the courtyard and sat up a bit straighter as a Volvo station wagon skidded to a stop just inches from a police car's bumper and Mrs. Metzger leaped out. The startled officer, having jumped back to avoid being peppered with gravel, advanced on her. At six feet tall and over two hundred pounds, her bulk overwhelmed the officer, a wiry-looking five-nine or so. My money was on him, though; he had a gun.

"My baby! Is she okay? Was she poisoned, too?" She tried to brush past the officer blocking her way.

"Settle down, ma'am," he said. He looked like a grizzled veteran, his hair cropped short and graying, his voice no-nonsense firm. "No one's in any danger."

"How do you know? I'll hold the police department and Happy Meadows and the pageant responsible if any harm has come to her."

The officer eyed her with distaste. "The young ladies will be out in a moment. You can talk to your daughter then."

"I'll sue!" she threatened.

Those seemed to be her favorite words. She looked like she was debating an end-run around the officer when a cream-colored Volkswagen pulled up and the young man I'd seen with Elise at the yacht club got out. He swept his light brown hair off his forehead. Mrs. Metzger whirled to face him, her arms slightly spread as if she'd tackle him if he tried to get by.

"Jason Loudermilk, what are you doing here?"

"Elise called me," he said calmly. "She wants out of this pageant. I'm here to take her back to the dorm."

"Out of the pageant!" Mrs. Metzger's voice startled a flock of starlings that took to the air, cawing. "Don't think you can make a fool out of me!"

"You don't appear to need any help," he responded.

His manner was so quiet that for a moment no one quite grasped what he'd said. When it penetrated, Mrs. Metzger advanced on him, swinging her hefty purse like a mace. "Why you rude, obnoxious, no good—"

"We don't need any of that," the policeman said, stepping between them. He got a purse in his midsection for his pains and doubled over. "Ungh!"

Mrs. Metzger made as if to plow through him, but he straightened and caught her arm by the wrist before she could swing the purse again. "That's assault with a deadly weapon," he said as another cop hastened to his assistance. Mrs. Metzger pulled away and ran for the door, sprinting pretty good for a woman her size. "Elise," she called.

By this time, the Happy Meadows residents had gathered at their windows to watch the entertainment in the courtyard. I heard windows sliding up.

"You go, girl," a woman's voice called.

"Are they filming that wrestling show?" a man asked. "Is this a smack down? I don't think much of their costumes. Give me Awesome Kong and her Kongtourage any day. Now, that gal's got a costume."

The purse-whacked officer, a determined look on his face—I guess he didn't want to be the laughingstock of the station house for letting himself get sidelined by an irate mother with a handbag—launched himself through the air and tackled Mrs. Metzger around the ankles. She thudded to the ground two feet in front of my bench. While she was gasping for breath, huffing air on my ankles, he sat on her rear end and pulled her arms behind her back, cuffing them.

He was hauling her to her feet when Elise hurried out the main entrance.

"Mom! Oh, Jason." She threw herself into the young man's arms and he hugged her. "I don't want to do this anymore," she told him.

"Sssh. You don't have to." He stroked her hair back from her face. "Look, don't you think it's time for the truth?"

She nodded. They turned to face Mrs. Metzger, their fingers entwined. "Mom, I'm the one Ms. Faye was going to disqualify. Jason and I got married a month ago."

Jodi Keen came through the door in time to hear Elise's announcement. "Married! Then you're not eligible to be Miss Magnolia Blossom." She clutched the clipboard to her chest.

Elise hung her head. "I know. But Mom wanted it so much—"

"It's not true," Mrs. Metzger said. Her face was stony. "My daughter is not married. Don't you think I'd know if my own daughter were married?" She looked at me, then the cop holding her arm, hoping for agreement.

"I *am* married," Elise said.

"We'll have it annulled. You can still finish the pageant—"

"No." Elise set her lips firmly. "I should have told you no before, but I didn't want to disappoint you."

Mrs. Metzger thrust her head toward her daughter, her lips curling back from slightly yellowed teeth. "You've been a disappointment since the day you were born. You—"

"That's enough." Jason's voice cracked through her abuse. He put his arms around the weeping Elise's shoulders. "My wife and I are leaving. If you need to talk to her"—he looked at the cops—"we'll come to the station later." He brushed his hair out of his eyes.

He was probably only in his early twenties, but he had the good sense and dignity of an older man. I felt like cheering as he led Elise to the Volkswagen. Several of the watching senior citizens applauded. "Bravo," called one. "Encore."

"I wanted to see the Kongtourage," a disappointed voice muttered before a window slammed down.

I WENT LOOKING FOR STELLA A FEW MINUTES LATER and couldn't find her anywhere at Happy Meadows. Perplexed, I wandered out to the parking area and realized her car was gone. Annoyance and worry warred within me. I was about to call her and ask how she expected me to get home when the contestants, Marv, and Jodi trooped tiredly out to the van. Jodi agreed to give me a lift and I sat beside her as Marv gunned the engine.

"Where am I going to find another celebrity judge at this late date?" Jodi Keen asked, slumping back against the plaid cloth seat. "That Ted Gaines absolutely refuses to go on. It doesn't surprise me—his forecasts are wrong at least seventy percent of the time."

I wasn't sure what one thing had to do with the other, but I let it go. "I might know someone," I said.

"Really?" She brightened.

"A good friend of mine writes for the *Atlanta Journal-Constitution*. He's a pretty famous political reporter. He won a Pulitzer a couple years back."

"Really?" Jodi sounded less enthused now; clearly she'd rather have someone who had won a reality show or a beauty contest than a writing award.

"Up to you," I said, leaning back and crossing my arms over my chest.

"What's his name?"

"Martin Shears."

"I think I might have heard of him." She chewed on her lower lip. "Sure, give him a call. At this late date, we can't afford to be picky."

Marty agreed to do it, asking hopefully if I thought any of the contestants might try to bribe him.

"It's certainly possible," I said. "Several of them lied about their eligibility to compete, so why should they draw the line at bribery?"

He laughed. "Sounds promising. I'm looking forward to seeing you."

"Me, too. Maybe we can go out with Vonda and Ricky after the pageant."

"I was thinking more along the lines of a quiet dinner for two on the deck at that riverfront seafood place, a bottle of nice wine . . ."

"I'll make a reservation," I said. "I don't think the pageant should take too long—at this rate, there'll only be two or three contestants by the time we get to Saturday."

I hung up and told Jodi she had herself a new judge. When the van dropped me at the salon—Jodi said they didn't need me at the animal rescue since the girls were already coiffed—I called Vonda and made Marty a reservation at her B&B. When I told her about the judges getting sick and about Elise's revelation, she asked, "Do you think she had anything to do with Audrey's death?"

"No way. First, she's so timid she probably doesn't even squish mosquitoes. Second, she probably would've been *elated* if Audrey had kicked her out of the contest."

"But her mother wouldn't have been."

I hadn't thought about that, but of course it was true. Mrs. Metzger would have frothed at the mouth if Audrey

threatened to kick Elise out of the pageant. And she did
have anger-control issues, as today's incident had amply
demonstrated. I wondered how much time you got for
beaning a policeman with a purse. "But Mrs. Metzger
didn't know about Elise's marriage," I said. "So she
wouldn't have thought Audrey was referring to Elise when
she talked about disqualifying someone."

"True enough," Vonda said.

We said our good-byes and I flipped the phone closed,
staring at the pale purple façade of Mom's house. I'd told
her I'd drop by, but I didn't want to continue this morning's
argument. Maybe I should just walk back to my apartment.
As I was debating, Mom appeared at the salon door and
beckoned.

"Are you going to stand there all day or are you going
to come in?" Her tone and smile seemed to indicate she
wanted to make up.

I climbed the stairs and crossed the veranda to where
she was standing. "I'm sorry," she said. "About this morning. It wasn't my place to get huffy with you. You're thirty
years old—you can make your own decisions. I just worry
about you."

I hugged her. "I love you. I hope you'll always care
enough to get huffy when I'm doing something you think
is stupid or dangerous."

"You can count on that," she said. "Now, tell me you can
come for dinner tonight. Althea called to say that tonight
works better than Friday for her and Kwasi. I was going to
do gumbo, but then I remembered he's a vegetarian, so I'm
making a salad of roast vegetables and barley that I found
online. I thought I'd make a peach cobbler for dessert."

"Sounds delish," I said. "You haven't seen Stella, have
you?"

"No, why?"

"She ditched me at the old folks' home." I told her what had happened at Happy Meadows.

"She probably just forgot she'd given you a lift," Mom said. "You know Jess calls here a couple times a month when Stella forgets to pick her up after band practice or chess club."

"True enough." Still, I wanted to find Stella.

As it happened, it wasn't hard: Stella appeared two minutes later as I was helping Mom pick out new smocks from a supply catalog. She burst through the door, auburn hair wisping around her face, apologies spilling from her mouth. "Oh, Grace, I am *so* sorry! Darryl called and wanted to talk and I just took off, completely forgetting about you. I'm so sorry."

"It's okay," I said. "Jodi gave me a lift in the van."

"What did Darryl want to talk about?" Mom asked. "Does he have an alibi for last night?"

"No," Stella said mournfully, sinking into one of the easy chairs in the waiting area. She folded her arms around a throw pillow and hugged it. "He was home alone. We didn't even talk on the phone. He wanted to discuss us. You know, where we go from here?"

"And where do you go?" Mom asked.

I tidied the counter, which didn't need tidying, giving Stella a moment to collect her thoughts without me staring at her. She watched my mom turn down corners in the catalog, then blew her breath out hard.

"I just don't know," she said. "The choices seem to be move back into the house, file for divorce, stay with my Mom, find an apartment for me and Jess, go to counseling, or some combination of the above. Darryl wants us to move back in. He says he's sorrier than sorry about the affair and that it'll never happen again. He says he'll go to counseling. But, honestly, Vi, I can't look at the man without seeing red! And bawling my eyes out. That he could do that—lie to me, sleep with another woman. How do I forgive that?"

"It would take time and counseling and wanting to," Mom said.

"Well, I guess I'm just not sure I want to," Stella said. She punched the pillow in her lap.

All this talk of infidelity was making me light-headed; it brought back the arguments Hank and I used to have about his womanizing. I remembered forgiving Hank the first time he cheated on me and apologized, swearing it would never happen again. Well, it had. Again and again until I finally got some self-respect and guts and called it quits. I hoped Stella wasn't letting herself in for the same grief if she stayed with Darryl. Of course, they'd been married sixteen years and this was apparently the first time he'd strayed. Hank hadn't made it eight months.

"You don't have to decide now," Mom pointed out. "Give it some time."

See what happens with his trial, I thought but didn't say. Moving back in together might not be an option if Darryl's new residence was a state penitentiary.

Chapter Twenty-two

WITH NO COMMITMENTS FOR THE REST OF THE DAY,
I returned to my apartment and changed into scruffy clothes
to do some yard work. I also called Kevin Faye and made
an appointment to talk about houses with him on Friday
morning. Brightened by the prospect of taking the first step
toward buying a house, I attacked the overgrown forsythia
with gusto. By the time I had a stack of pruned branches on
the sidewalk, I was sweating like a horse in the backstretch
of the Kentucky Derby. I probably smelled like one, too.
I added some oleander branches from the bushes behind
my carriage house to the pile, and dug up a few dandelions
for good measure. I was folding the branches and pushing them into yard bags when Agent Dillon's car pulled to
the curb. Great. I looked like I'd been doing yard work for
two hours on the hottest day of the year. My hair clung in
sweaty tendrils to my neck and a fire ant bite had raised an

ugly welt on my ankle. I was probably spattered with dirt and sap.

Agent Dillon looked crisp and almost cool in a short-sleeved shirt and chinos. His navy eyes scanned me and a slight smile curved his lips.

"Casual Thursday?" I asked as he approached.

"Qualifying on the range," he said. "I heard you were involved in the excitement out at Happy Meadows this morning."

"'Involved' is a strong word. I was there."

"I was hoping you'd tell me what happened."

"I told the officer who interviewed me what I saw—nothing. Other than the three judges throwing up."

"I know. I read the reports. I'm after the intangibles you wouldn't mention to the cops—your impressions of the people who were there, of the events. I trust your instincts."

I was pleased but didn't want to show it. "Here, make yourself useful. Hold the bag open," I said, thrusting it at him. His hands were strong and work-roughened, with long fingers and nails trimmed short. For a brief second, I imagined what they'd feel like against my skin, then jerked my mind back into line. I told him as much as I could remember while scooping armfuls of branches into the bag.

He was quiet for a moment when I'd finished, yanking the tie closed around the bag's neck. "What about the protestors who came in? Did you see them anywhere near the cooler with the drinks?"

I thought about it. "No. They came into the dayroom and sat beside a woman she said was her grandmother."

"She wasn't," he said.

No surprise there. "So you think someone poisoned the stuff in the cooler? That means Darryl is in the clear, right?"

"Ipecac," he said. "Someone doctored the water bottles with ipecac—the berry and papaya flavors hid the taste. Easy to get, impossible to trace. Problem is, they came from the fridge in the judges' room at the theater—anyone with access to the theater could've put the ipecac in any time during the past week, which leaves Michaelson squarely in the picture." He hoisted the yard bag to his shoulder. "Where do you want this?"

I led him around the side of the house to the garbage cans in the back. He put the bag into a galvanized aluminum can and clanged on the lid. "I keep meaning to start a compost heap," I said, "but somehow I never get around to it."

He smiled, his teeth very white against his tanned skin. "If you get one going, I can let you have some manure."

I wondered where he boarded his horses. "You really know how to wow a girl with gifts, don't you?"

"Flowers and candy are so commonplace," he said. "I like to be original." His smile grew and the look in his eyes made my tummy flutter. "Why don't you come out to the stables with me Sunday afternoon? We can ride, then stop for dinner on the way back. I know an inn that doesn't mind if we smell like horses."

My mouth opened slightly. He was asking me for a date. And I surprised myself with how much I wanted to go. Then I remembered. "Marty's coming this weekend," I said. My tummy twisted in the kind of knots it hadn't experienced since Jeff Albright asked me to the prom my junior year after I'd already told Hank I'd go with him—our first date. I sometimes wondered how things might have turned out if Jeff had asked first. Maybe Hank and I would never have ended up as a couple. No way to know.

Dillon froze for a moment, then said lightly, "Ah. Well, maybe another time."

"He's replacing Ted Gaines as a pageant judge." Why was I trying to make it seem like Marty wasn't coming to see me?

"Tell him to be careful," Dillon said.

I hadn't even thought about Marty being in danger as a judge. I was a world-class idiot.

Agent Dillon started back around the house. I trotted after him. "Is it true that Audrey was pregnant?" I asked as we stopped by his car.

He banged his palm on the hood. "Damn it! Where did you hear that?" His eyes were the cold blue of the deepest sea now, not the sun-flecked navy of earlier. He waited for my answer.

"Around." I didn't want to get Mrs. Jones's niece in trouble.

A muscle in his jaw worked but he didn't pursue it. "Don't repeat it," he said. "We're trying to keep that piece of information confidential."

"Was it Darryl's?" My voice came out as a whisper.

"We're running DNA tests," he said.

His tone said they wouldn't be sharing the results with nosy civilians. I wanted to ask if he really thought Darryl was guilty. I wanted to ask for a rain check on the horse-back riding. I wanted the easy camaraderie of just a few moments earlier that had disappeared with my question about the pregnancy. I wanted . . . I didn't know exactly what I wanted. The grim set of his mouth intimidated me. "Thanks for helping with the yard," I said feebly.

He hesitated a moment, as if he wanted to say something, but then nodded and climbed into the car. I watched until he was out of sight.

I WALKED OVER TO MOM'S A FEW MINUTES BEFORE six, letting myself into the kitchen. Balsamic vinegar and olive oil scented the air. Peach cobbler cooled on the counter. Mom had set the kitchen table for five with a white tablecloth patterned with deep red picnickers in rural scenes and white cloth napkins. She was pulling a cookie sheet with two loaves of French bread from the oven when I came in. Her cheeks were flushed and a hint of perspiration fogged her glasses.

"You've been working too hard," I said, shutting the oven door.

"I wanted Althea to know I'd made an effort," she said. Wearing pale blue linen slacks, a striped shirt, and sandals with seashells glued to the straps, she looked attractive and pulled together. Her gray and white hair spiked softly around her head and she'd put on a bit more makeup than usual. She was going all-out to impress Althea's new guy. I'd done my best by putting on a halter-neck sundress patterned with leaves and pulling my blond-highlighted hair back from my face with a sparkly comb.

"Am I early, Miss Violetta?" Walter Highsmith came through the door carrying a bottle of wine. "Good evening, Grace."

"Right on time." Mom smiled and he kissed her cheek, stepping back quickly as if afraid he'd been presumptuous. A short, plump man with a goatee and a mustache waxed into loops, Walter usually wore a Confederate uniform, especially when working in his Civil War memorabilia shop. Tonight, though, he had on tan slacks and a short-sleeved yellow shirt. In a weird way, the modern clothes seemed out of place on him with his courtly airs and formal speech patterns. The tip of his nose quivered as he sniffed the air. "Smells heavenly," he said. "The pinot grigio I brought should enhance the flavors nicely."

A pro forma knock heralded the entrance of Althea and

Kwasi Yarrow. She wore a cream-colored caftan embroidered with brown, and wooden bangles on both arms. He was dressed in a tunic-style top and baggy pants in a rough-woven green cotton. He had one of those pillbox sort of hats on his head, green with a band of gold and cream fabric. Cultural statement or bald spot cover-up? He carried a bouquet of grasses and seed pods with one large, red bloom I didn't recognize and handed them to my mother. Kind of classy.

"Thank you for inviting me this evening, Violetta," he said as Althea performed the introductions. "Althea has told me so much about you and your daughter that I was anxious to meet you."

"We've already met, sort of," I said, extending my hand. "Grace."

"Yes. Outside the theater. Perhaps you will let me explain why beauty pageants are so objectionable? I am quite certain that you would not lend your talents to one if you understood the evil they do." His light brown eyes fixed on mine and I could see how he convinced college students to participate in the protests: he had a faint shimmer of charisma. He wasn't JFK or Princess Di, but he had something.

What could I say? He was a guest in my mother's house. "Uh, sure. I'd like to hear your position."

"Would you like something to drink?" Mom asked. "Beer, wine?"

"I don't drink alcohol," Kwasi said. "Perhaps just a glass of water?"

It's fine with me if someone doesn't drink—I prefer tea or diet root beer to alcohol more often than not—but there was just a hint of rebuke in Kwasi's voice that ruffled my feathers. Walter put down the bottle he'd brought with a crestfallen air.

"Just water for me, too, Vi," Althea said.

I stared at her. Althea loved wine. I studied her from under my lashes for a moment. She seemed unusually subdued; she'd hardly said anything. Normally by now she'd have insulted me at least twice and had us laughing or arguing so hard we forgot all about food. I let Walter pour me a glass of his wine and fetched waters for Althea and Kwasi. Mom already had a beer going.

"I'll help you put those in water, Vi," Althea said. She tugged the bouquet from Mom's grasp. "You two go out on the veranda. We'll call when dinner's ready. We don't need you underfoot while we're trying to get food on the table." She made shooing motions, looking and sounding much more like the pre-Kwasi Althea.

"Walter, will you help me with the rice?" Mom asked her friend, sparing him the need to decide which group to join.

"We've got our marching orders," I told Kwasi, gesturing toward the door that would lead us through the salon to the veranda.

He looked with interest at the salon as we passed through it. "I very much admire your mother for making a success of this business when her husband died," he said, running a hand over the glass brick half wall separating the shampoo sink from the styling stations.

"Althea played a big part," I said.

He nodded. "When I was in Kenya and Rwanda last year, I was interested to see how many women are starting cottage industries, not even on this scale, to earn some money. They get micro-loans and purchase a loom or a sewing machine. They are quite successful with textiles. I try to support them by purchasing as much of my clothing as is practical from them, including my kufi." He patted the hat.

"Mom started out with just a chair and some shears in her kitchen," I said. "Do you get to Africa often?"

We pushed through the door to the veranda. I indicated the Adirondack chairs, but he wandered to the rail and stood looking out at the yard and the street beyond, where a fair number of tourists still wandered, looking for pre-dinner watering holes. He took a swallow of water and the ice clinked. "Since I first went there with the Peace Corps just after college, I try to get back at least every other year."

"You were with the Peace Corps?"

He nodded. "Before I became interested in the politics of oppression, I got a degree in civil engineering. It came in most useful in small villages without indoor plumbing or sewage-treatment facilities."

Despite myself, I found a lot to admire in what Kwasi had accomplished. "Did you get your CE degree from Berkeley, or is that where you went for your PhD?" Maybe he and Audrey *had* been students together if he'd gone back to grad school some years after his Peace Corps experiences.

He stilled. "What makes you think I went to Berkeley?"

"You didn't?"

"As it happens, that's where I got my PhD. I was just curious how you knew." His voice was insistent and I knew he wouldn't let me duck the question.

"I heard someone mention it. Maybe one of your students? It caught my attention because that's where Audrey Faye went, too. And Sam Barnes."

"Really? I wonder if we ever crossed paths? I hope they were not killed by someone with a vendetta against Berkeley grads. Perhaps even now an assassin has me in his scope." He threw his arms wide as if to embrace a bullet.

Now, there was a new thought. I dismissed it after

a nanosecond. Audrey and Barnes weren't killed by a Berkeley hater. "Don't you think it's more likely they died because of something to do with the pageant?" I asked. I noticed he hadn't denied knowing either Audrey or Barnes.

"Absolutely." He set his glass on the railing and turned to face me. "Beauty contests proliferate evil in many different ways—in undermining self-esteem, in promoting unrealistic images of women, in encouraging eating disorders, yes, even in killing."

I slapped at a mosquito on my neck. "I think you'd have to admit that deaths related to beauty pageants are pretty rare," I said skeptically.

Steepling his fingers together, he pressed them against his pursed lips. "Not so rare as you might assume. Especially not if one extends the definition of 'beauty contest' to such activities as cheerleading, modeling, and other so-called sports or careers that exploit a woman's appearance. There was that cheerleading murder in Texas and a woman died competing in the Miss Magnolia Blossom pageant just three or four years ago."

"I heard about that—she had a heart attack. That's hardly the pageant's fault."

Kwasi shook his head as if I were a slow student missing the point. "Her name was Leda Wissing. She was twenty. Yes, the official cause of death was a heart attack, but who knows how she might have abused diet pills or over-exercised in her drive to win. The unrealistic standard of beauty propagated in this society is what killed her."

"How sad."

"Exactly," Kwasi said in a softer voice. "It's tragic. And everyone who promotes a pageant or participates in one in any way, or spectates at one, contributes to the tragedy."

I expected him to level a forefinger at me and proclaim: "You, Grace Terhune, are guilty!"

I preempted him by asking, "Do the students know before they sign up for your class that they'll be protesting at beauty pageants? How does that work into their grades?"

He looked at me like I'd lost my mind. "Protesting is not a matter of grades; it's a matter of conscience. I don't prearrange protests for the students. As the conversation develops in the classroom, sometimes one or another of the students will speak up and suggest we protest a particular event or organization. Only those students whose consciences push them to it participate. This is the first time someone's suggested protesting at a pageant."

An ambulance siren *whee-whoo*ed in the distance and a heron glided overhead. I was about to ask him which student had suggested protesting at the Miss Magnolia Blossom pageant when Althea appeared at the door and told us dinner was ready and to get our butts to the table before it got cold.

The meal went off pleasantly enough. I'd take a piece of fried chicken over roast vegetables any day, but the portabellas, zucchini, onions, and tomatoes were tasty with the marinade Mom had found online. Kwasi talked a lot about his multicultural and oppression studies program. "Althea says she may even sign up for a course in the spring semester," he said, smiling at her.

She thrust her jaw out a tad. "Maybe," she said. "It's been a long darn time since I went to school and I'm not sure I'm up for having homework assignments at my age."

A tiny frown puckered Mom's brow and I wondered if she shared my concern: Althea sure seemed to be doing a lot of things—changing her clothes, thinking about going back to school—because it was important to Kwasi. I hoped it was important to her, too.

"Well, I've been thinking about going back to school, too," I said, surprising everyone. I drained my wineglass. "I could finish off my business degree in a little more than a year and a half at night school. If I focus on accounting, I could do the books, Mom."

"That's a great idea, Grace," she said, beaming.

I rose to clear the table, motioning Mom back down when she started to stand. "You cooked. I'll clean up."

Mom is constitutionally unable to sit while someone else putters in her kitchen, so she rose and made coffee, prompting a lecture from Kwasi about the superiority of African coffee over the Kona blend she served. He promised to give some of his favorite Ugandan Gold Rukoki coffee to Althea to pass along to Mom.

"I'm sure it's very good," Mom said, a little tight-lipped.

Althea caught the note of restraint in Mom's voice and turned the subject, talking about how robust the tourist season had been in St. Elizabeth this summer. "Thank the good Lord we didn't end up with that Morestuf on the west side of town," she said. "That would really have cut into our business."

The Morestuf organization had wanted to erect one of its big box stores last spring, but the town had voted it down. Preserving our reputation for Southern charm and hospitality trumped convenience.

"My sales are down overall," Walter said, chewing on a corner of his mustache, "but my Internet sales are up."

"There's a fund-raiser tomorrow night at the college," Kwasi said, pushing aside his mostly undrunk coffee. "It's to raise money for a team of students visiting Africa over Thanksgiving to get in touch with their heritage. I have extra tickets if you'd like to come." He looked expectantly from Mom and Walter to me and Althea.

"Thank you, but I'm going to the pageant tomorrow night," Mom said. "To cheer for Rachel. They'll announce the finalists after the evening gown competition."

"Me, too," I said.

"I'm visiting my sister in Fort Lauderdale for the weekend," Walter said.

Everyone looked at Althea. She got a cross look on her face—peeved at being put on the spot, I assumed—and tossed her napkin on the table. "I don't know what I'm doing tomorrow night," she said. "I'll have to check with my social secretary."

And on that note, Althea and Kwasi said their goodbyes. Walter left soon after, saying he had to pack. Mom and I finished cleaning up, carefully not talking about Althea and Kwasi, and I hugged her before heading back to my apartment. "Althea's a strong woman," Mom said, apropos of nothing we'd been talking about. "I'm sure she'll find her way."

I wasn't sure if she was trying to convince me or herself.

Chapter Twenty-three

[Friday]

HANGING OUT WITH BEAUTIFUL, FIT WOMEN ALL
week prompted me to hie my fanny off to the gym Friday
morning for the first time in . . . well, at least a month. I
wasn't what you'd call a regular exerciser. I relied on walking and doing isometric exercises while standing in line at
the Piggly Wiggly and taking stairs instead of elevators to
keep me in reasonable shape. After hanging out with the
beauty queen wannabes, though, my definition of "reasonable shape" was a bit skinnier and buffer than it had been
on Monday.

With my hair in a ponytail, I joined a step class minutes
before it started. Someone waved at me from the back corner and I lugged my step over to a free space beside Brooke
Baker. She had three blocks stacked under her step. I was
debating whether to use one or lay the step flat on the floor.

"I didn't know you worked out here," she greeted me.

She looked svelte and buff in a yellow spandex top and matching shorts. Her chocolate skin glowed with good health and she bounced from foot to foot as we waited for the instructor. I was getting worn out just watching her.

"I don't," I said. "This is an aberration. You and the other contestants inspired me."

"Really?" She giggled. "I can tell those protestors that something good *does* come from pageants. Who knows how many women and girls decide to work out more because they saw a pageant or know someone in one?"

Not a bad point. "Do the protestors bother you?"

"Nah, not really. It just pisses me off that they think they know the right answer for everyone. Until they've walked a mile in my shoes, they don't have any right to belittle the choices I make. That Dr. Yarrow dude gives me the creeps, going on about women's body-image issues. Where does he get off thinking he knows anything about how women feel about their bodies?"

The instructor appeared, a whippet-thin woman in her forties wearing a leotard combo that looked very Jane Fonda. She cranked up the Village People—as if this weren't already painful enough—and adjusted her head mic. "Ready, ladies?"

"You don't think the protestors have a point?" I asked as we swung our arms to warm up. Some of what Kwasi had said last night actually made me question whether or not beauty contests were as benign as I'd always thought.

"Maybe for some women." She shrugged as if to say it takes all kinds. "I just don't accept that you have to give in to marketing messages like what toothpaste to use or what car to buy or how to look. Am I using my body to get ahead, to make money for school? Absolutely. But isn't that exactly what a scholarship athlete is doing?"

I was breathing hard and hoped it was a rhetorical question. We quit talking as the routine got more complicated. An hour later, limp as a soggy toaster waffle, I hobbled from the room beside Brooke, who still looked disgustingly energetic.

"I'm going to do a quick circuit," she said, nodding toward the room full of weight machines I was pretty sure were designed by Torquemada and his henchmen from the Spanish Inquisition. "Want to work out with me?"

"Thanks," I said, deciding to be flattered that she thought I'd even be able to stagger to the locker room, never mind push some weights around. "But I've got to get going."

"See you this evening." She waved and bounced into the weight room.

THE EUCALYPTUS-SCENTED BODY WASH IN THE showers revived me so I arrived for my appointment with Kevin Faye looking reasonably perky in a khaki skirt topped with an emerald tank top. I felt leaner already and resisted the urge to flex my biceps as I passed the plate glass window in the store beside Faye's office. It was located in an upscale strip mall slightly west of the downtown area. Nearby businesses included a day spa, an independent bookstore specializing in Southern fiction and guide books, and an adventure travel agency. Laughing at myself for thinking one aerobics class had made any difference in my fitness, I pushed open the door and found myself in an expensively decorated office foyer that didn't show signs of being hit by the recession. Plush blue carpet, handsomely framed oil paintings, and heavy walnut furniture upholstered in tan leather set the tone. On the other hand, the receptionist's

desk was empty—out to lunch or laid off?—and Kevin
Faye hurried from an interior office to greet me himself.

His dishwater hair was slicked back and his hand was
out. A summer-weight suit and a tie with a fish pattern on
a maroon background made him look every inch the successful businessman. "Grace," he said. "It's good to see
you again." His broad smile revealed large upper teeth and
cramped and misaligned lowers. I realized he hadn't smiled
once during his visit to the salon. No surprise there . . . his
wife was murdered just three days ago.

"We can do this another time," I said, suddenly feeling awkward about wanting to buy a house so soon after
Audrey died.

"Why—Oh, no, it's better for me to stay busy." Grief
flitted across his face and was replaced by professional so-
licitude. He led me into his inner office. "How about you
tell me what you're looking for?" He grabbed two waters
from the small fridge behind his desk and handed me one
before seating himself.

I glanced around the office, tastefully decorated in warm
earth tones. A sixteen- by twenty-inch portrait of Audrey
accepting the Miss American Blossom crown dominated
one wall. A smaller photo on the desk showed three tow-
headed kids with gap-toothed grins.

Following my glance, Kevin said, "My nephews."

"They're adorable."

"Audrey and I wanted children," he said, unscrewing his
bottle cap. "We tried, but it just wasn't to be." He glugged
water like he was washing away a bad taste.

Little did he know. It certainly didn't sound as if he were
aware of Audrey's pregnancy. And did the fact that he and
Audrey had tried without success mean that the baby wasn't
his?

"When will Audrey's service be?" I asked.

Without the smile, he looked older, his face sagging into lines that dragged at his eyes and mouth. He fingered the mole on his temple. "There won't be one."

I must have looked startled, because he added, "It'll be a private cremation and interment. I don't want a media spectacle."

I could respect that, although here in the South we like to show our respect and love for those who have passed on with music and flowers and a little hoopla. "Can I send flowers somewhere?"

"That's kind of you. I'll have Stephanie—my assistant— let you know. Now, what is it you're looking for? You're a first-time buyer, right? There's a new condo community going up a couple miles south of here—Delta Bayou—and the properties are very affordable if you get in now."

"I don't really think I'm the condo type," I said.

He listened attentively as I described the small bungalow I wanted with its two or three bedrooms, eat-in kitchen, and yard big enough for a couple of bird feeders and flowering shrubs. "A couple of big shade trees would be nice, too," I added as he took notes.

"I don't think we'll have any problem finding something that will suit you," he said.

I mentioned the paltry sum I thought I could afford to pay.

"Hm, well, there are plenty of starter homes out there, and quite a few handyman's delights."

I didn't consider myself "handy," but I could read up on painting and tiling and give it a try. I drew the line at plumbing, though.

"I'm busy this afternoon, but we could set up a couple of showings for tomorrow morning, if you like. Say, eleven o'clock?" He rose and came around the desk to usher me out. Still no sign of a receptionist. Maybe she was out sick for the day.

"Sounds good," I said. "But I have to be at the Oglethorpe by three to help the girls get ready for the finals." I bit my lip, hoping mention of the pageant didn't grieve him. Apparently not.

"It's a date," he said.

MY CELL PHONE BUZZED AS I WALKED OUT OF THE cool office.

"I'm here," Marty said.

A smile spread over my whole body. "Already?"

"I left Atlanta at six. I was supposed to meet the Keen woman at the theater so she could show me around, but she's not here."

"On my way," I said.

I saw Marty's yellow and white MINI Cooper parked on the curb across from the Oglethorpe. Pulling up behind it, I got out and crossed the street. Marty came around the side of the building as I reached the sidewalk and I smiled at the sight of him. He just has that effect on me. Six-foot-five, with sandy hair that flops across his forehead and brushes his collar in the back, he had a lanky elegance that a crisply ironed shirt, red-patterned bow tie, dark slacks, and shiny loafers played up. I could see him swinging a croquet mallet with Jay Gatsby at an early-twentieth-century lawn party. His sensibilities are all modern day, though. He eats, drinks, and lives politics, especially Georgia politics, and his condo in the Buckhead section of Atlanta hums with leather and granite and sleek lines.

He caught sight of me and smiled in return. He picked

up his pace and swept me into a big hug when he reached me. Kissing me lightly on the lips, he let me go.

"What were you doing back there?" I nodded toward the rear of the theater.

"Just checking out the scene of the rabid cat attack. There's a shiny new padlock on the door now."

"He didn't really attack me—just chased me into the building. Want a tour?"

"Sure. I left a voice message for Jodi Keen. Hopefully, she'll show up before long and explain my judging duties."

"I think you'll be able to handle it," I said drily.

Leading the way up the steps, I pushed through the doors and into the foyer. Rhythmic sounds of something rasping against wood filtered from the auditorium.

"What the hell is that?" Marty asked as I bumped open the door with my hip. He crowded behind me to see over my shoulder.

Marv, the theater owner, hunched on all fours on the stage, his right arm scrubbing back and forth. He looked up at the sounds we made or the light we let in.

"Come on in," he called. "I'm almost done." He stood and let something thud to the floor.

As we got closer to the stage, I saw that the tool he had dropped was a sanding block. A fine grit coated the stage for several feet around Marv, who wore rubber gloves, pads around the knees of his faded jeans, and a paper face mask, which he pulled down.

He followed the direction of my glance. "The whole stage needs refinishing," he said. "Maybe this will get me motivated."

I gathered that by "this" he meant having to clean up after Barnes's murder. "Aren't there companies that do this sort of thing? Biohazard cleanup and stuff?" I asked.

"They cost money," he said simply. He looked at Marty and I introduced them. "You wouldn't happen to want to buy a theater, would you?" he asked.

"Sorry, no," Marty said, clearly tickled by Marv's lugubriousness. "Not my line."

"Not mine, either," Marv said glumly. "It's a goddamned millstone around my neck."

"Burn it down for the insurance," Marty suggested.

I punched his arm. "Not funny."

"I think Aunt Nan tried that back in the eighties, but the only thing that burned before the fire department got here was the set for a production of *Mame*. Kitty Carlisle was going to be in it. Remember her from *What's My Line*? The investigator said there was a short in the lighting, so maybe Aunt Nan didn't really have anything to do with it. I'm around if you need me. A couple of the contestants are here, doing something with their gowns." He wandered offstage, stripping off his gloves as he went.

"Is it kosher for me to meet the contestants?" Marty asked as we followed Marv.

"I don't know why not. The other judges have been hanging out with them at photo shoots and whatnot all week."

"Lead on, then."

As we rounded the corner near the Green Room, angry voices bounced off the walls.

"I don't effing believe this! You're trying to sabotage me because you know I'm going to win."

"I didn't do it! You so need to get over yourself. There are other girls in this pageant, you know."

Marty and I exchanged a look and hurried toward the Green Room. We paused on the threshold to see Tabitha and Rachel glaring at each other, a cloud of white chiffon on the floor between them.

"Look what she did to my dress!" Tabitha said, swinging around to face us. She wore low-cut jeans that fit like skin and a cropped top that displayed her tanned and toned abdomen. I noticed Marty noticing.

"She's, like, off her meds," Rachel said, looking as angry as I'd ever seen her. "Someone cut up my dress, too." She held up a handful of blue taffeta, fluffing it out to show where quarter-sized holes and bigger gouges rent the material. Either a moth on speed or a very disturbed person with scissors had had a field day.

"Are they all like this?" Marty asked.

"I don't know. We didn't check," Rachel said. She crossed to the rack that held plastic-swathed evening gowns and lifted the plastic away from a red number. "Yep. This one's chopped up, too," she said. "It's Brooke's, I think."

Marty and I watched as she and Tabitha inspected the other girls' dresses. "All of them," Tabitha said, frowning.

"You might say 'sorry,'" Rachel prompted the other girl.

"Hmph."

I didn't get the feeling that "sorry" was a word Tabitha bothered with often. "Someone didn't want you to see the damage until it was too late," I said. "That's why she put the plastic back over them and cleaned up all the fabric bits." I gestured at the clean floor.

Marty nodded. "Yeah. If you'd come in to dress for the competition tonight and found the gowns like this, it would've been too late to do anything about it."

"Why 'she'?" Rachel asked.

I knit my brows. "I don't know why I said that. It just

feels like something a woman would do, cut bits and pieces out. But it could've been a man."

"We need to call the other contestants," Rachel said.

"I don't have time," Tabitha said breezily. "I've got to go shopping for a new dress." She sashayed out, casting Marty a speculative look on her way.

"Witch," Rachel muttered.

"I'll help you make the calls," I said. "And we should let Jodi know."

"And the police," Marty put in.

Chapter Twenty-four

✂

TWO HOURS LATER, I FOUND MYSELF ALONE WITH Rachel, the ruined dress draped over her lap. The police and other contestants had come and gone. Jodi had shown up, wrung her hands, implored the police or Marv to post a guard, and hustled Marty off for a "pageant briefing."

"I can't afford another evening dress," Rachel said, looking forlorn. "I got this one at the Goodwill store for twenty-five bucks. Willow helped me pick it out."

"Let me think." I wished I had the cash on hand to buy Rachel a new gown, but I didn't. I eyed Rachel closely. "You're not too much shorter than Stella. I have an idea."

I got hold of Stella at her mother's house and explained the problem. "Maybe I can help," she said. "Meet me at my house in fifteen minutes."

Darryl answered the door when Rachel and I knocked. He looked bleary-eyed and surprised to see us. No more

surprised than I was to see him; I'd forgotten he was staying there. "Stella asked us to meet her here," I explained.

"Sure," he said dully, pulling the door wider. "C'mon in.
Is she coming over?" A flicker of hope lit his eyes.

Stella's car pulling up answered his question. He stood
at the door, watching her come up the sidewalk, hunger
and remorse and hope roiling in his expression. He leaned
forward as if to kiss Stella's cheek when she reached the
stoop, but she ducked away.

"We'll just be here a minute, Darryl," she said coolly.
"We won't bother you."

"It's no bother," he said. "This is your home."

Stella didn't respond. She turned right down the hall and
pushed open the door to a small bedroom. "In here," she
called. Rachel and I followed her. I, at least, felt the tension
between Stella and Darryl like something that congealed
the air, making it hard to reach the bedroom, a guest room
with a double bed covered with a crazy quilt and a small
chest of drawers. Stella was on tiptoe in front of a closet,
hauling down a long, rectangular box.

"I haven't looked at this in ages," she said, laying it gently on the bed. At the puzzled look in Rachel's eyes, she
asked, "Didn't Grace tell you? This is the evening gown
I bought for my one and only pageant appearance. If we
shorten it, I think it will work on you." She lifted the lid
and unfolded a layer of tissue paper. A pink dress with a
sweetheart neckline and padded shoulders—very '80s—
shimmered in the box. Stella lifted it out and the satin skirt
cascaded to the carpet. "We could maybe cut out the pads,
too," Stella said, "and make it look more 'now.' Want to
try it on?"

Rachel nodded. I closed the door, catching a glimpse of
Darryl still hovering in the foyer, and Rachel stripped down

to bra and panties before slipping the dress over her head. Stella zipped it for her and stepped back.

"Oh, Rachel," she breathed. "You look just lovely."

She did look beautiful. The pink gave a pearly sheen to her skin and set off her dark hair dramatically. The expression on her face, though, detracted from the effect.

"What?" I asked.

She screwed up her face, staring at her reflection in the full-length mirror on the back of the door. "It's awfully *sweet.*"

"It *is* sweet on you," Stella said, apparently not understanding that Rachel didn't mean it as a compliment. She dropped to her knees and fussed with the hem. "If you have a pair of three- or four-inch heels, I don't even think we'll need to hem it. Just be careful when you walk."

Indecision clouded Rachel's face and I could see she didn't want to hurt Stella's feelings by telling her she didn't like the dress. But the way she tugged at the bodice and ran a finger under the sleeve where it ended at her wrist told me she wasn't comfortable in it.

"I feel like Cinderella after the fairy godmother has, like, bippity-boppity-booed her," she complained.

"Exactly!" Stella said, clasping her hands together and gazing up at Rachel with admiring eyes.

"What if Cinderella wanted a black dress?" Rachel asked.

"She knew better than to look a gift horse in the mouth," I said warningly. I appreciated Rachel's dilemma, but it was giving Stella pleasure to do something kind for the girl and to relive her own pageant days. Stella needed a lift, and I didn't think it would kill Rachel to pretend she loved the dress.

"You don't like it?" Stella asked, hurt crumpling her face.

"It's fab," Rachel said quickly. "I just, like, needed to get used to all the pink. I can absolutely win in this dress."

Stella's face cleared and I gave Rachel an approving nod. She shrugged and gave me a half smile. "You're a good kid," I whispered as I unzipped the dress.

We carefully refolded the gown and put it in the box. "Be careful when you iron it, or you might want to hang it in a steamy bathroom for a bit," Stella suggested as we trooped back down the hall.

Darryl appeared from the direction of the kitchen; he'd clearly been listening for us. He wiped his hands down his jeaned thighs. "Stel, can we talk?"

"I don't think so," she said with a brittle smile. "I promised my mom I'd do the grocery shopping while she was gone and then I've got to get over to the theater."

"We need to talk," he said, an edge creeping into his voice.

"Actions speak louder than words," she said sadly. She held up a hand to cut him off when he would have responded. "I've got to go. Come on, Rach, Grace." She shepherded us out the door, carrying the dress box as if it were full of Ming dynasty porcelain.

I PICKED UP MARTY OUTSIDE THE OGLETHORPE and drove to The Pirate for lunch. At the far south end of the boardwalk, The Roving Pirate had a deck with beautiful sea views and the marsh stretching out behind it. It's too far from the center of town to be a real tourist haunt, so locals tend to congregate there. At one o'clock on a Friday afternoon, we had the place to ourselves except for two men in work clothes and boots watching a Braves game at the bar.

We sat by the windows—it was way too hot to eat on the deck—and I ordered a tuna salad sandwich while Marty got crab patties.

"So, what did you think?" I asked around a mouthful of sandwich.

"About?"

"The pageant. Jodi. Everything."

He watched a pair of gulls wheeling outside the window. "That Jodi's a piece of work. Talk about organized! But she is wound way too tight over this pageant—she seems to think that if anything bad happens on her watch—"

"Like more murders?"

"—that her career with the Miss American Blossom organization will be kaput. She's bound and determined to earn a spot on the national board. If I were the prankster—whoever it is ripping up gowns and leaving roadkill around—I'd be watching my back. I get the feeling Ms. Jodi Keen takes no prisoners when it comes to climbing the career ladder." He ripped a bite from his crab patty and chewed, possibly to demonstrate what would happen to anyone who got in Jodi's way.

"You said 'prankster,' not murderer. You don't think they're the same person?"

He shook his head, still chewing. "Hell, no," he mumbled.

I waited, thinking about it, until he swallowed. "Audrey's murder is way out of line in terms of seriousness with the sabotage incidents, isn't it?" I asked. "There was the screwup with the advertising materials, then the sprinkler ruining a few dresses, then Kiley's mats being cut."

"I just can't see someone leaping from those penny-ante acts to murder," Marty agreed.

"Unless maybe Audrey caught whoever in the act? And he or she overreacted and stabbed her with Stella's file?"

"I suppose that's possible, but then why go back to tricks like booby-trapping the swimsuit—pun intended— and hacking up the dresses? Personally, if I'd murdered someone without meaning to, I'd be lying low. Like in Honduras, say."

"It'd be even hotter and muggier there than it is here. If I become a fugitive, I'm heading north."

"Noted." He grinned and leaned over the table to wipe a crumb from the corner of my mouth.

His touch distracted me for a moment, but I got back on track. "So, maybe what we're dealing with is a saboteur who has a grudge against beauty pageants and a murderer with a grudge against Audrey Faye."

"That's my best guess," Marty said. "But it feels to me like the saboteur is escalating. The way those dresses were hacked up was kind of scary. He or she has gone from relatively benign things like sprinklers to poisoning the judges and going after things with scissors."

I shifted uneasily in my chair, wondering what the saboteur would come up with next. "You don't think he'll give up?"

"Not unless or until the pageant gets shut down. I think the fact that he's continuing with the sabotage even after Audrey got killed is proof of that. Any sane person would've backed off."

"You don't think whoever it is is sane?" The thought of a lunatic wandering around gave me the creeps. Maybe I'd seen too many *Friday the 13th* movies as a teen.

He shrugged one shoulder. "Well, they're not thinking rationally. I'd say that whoever it is has a personal stake in this. It's not just a generalized hatred of beauty pageants. If so, why pick on a rinky-dink pageant like Miss Magnolia Blossom?"

"Rinky-dink!" I tried to sound affronted but couldn't suppress a smile. "But you've got a point. Who could hate a beauty contest this much? The protestors? Maybe they're all in on it."

"Doubtful. But you might want to have a word with that Dr. Yarrow you asked me to research. Real name Charles Alfred Yarrow, by the way. He came up with the Kwasi about fifteen years ago after a trip to Africa."

Clanging metal from the kitchen and a loud "Shit!" told me someone had dropped pots and pans. The guys at the bar didn't even look up from their baseball game.

"What else did you find out about him?" Changing one's name from Chuck to Kwasi wasn't too heinous.

"He allegedly plagiarized part of his dissertation, so Berkeley never granted him his PhD."

Ooh. Now we were getting into murkier territory. "So he's not really *Dr.* Yarrow?"

"Not unless he picked up the degree online or someplace."

"So how'd he get the job at Georgia Coastal College?"

"Inflating one's résumé is not exactly unheard of," Marty said cynically. "And HR folks don't always take time to cross their t's and dot their i's when they hire someone." He looked at his watch. "I've got about two hours' work to get done on a story before I do the judging shtick, so I've got to run. Don't go poking your pretty nose"—he kissed the nose in question—"into any dark corners until we've had a chance to hash through this a bit more. There's a murderer and a potential psycho running around. I don't want you pissing either of them off."

I had no intention of pissing anyone off, but I also had no intention of sitting on my hands while Stella's husband got convicted for a murder he didn't commit or a whack-job with a grudge against beauty pageants laid plans that might end up hurting Rachel or Marty. I had to admit I was coming over to Mom's way of thinking . . . cancelling the pageant might be the best move.

I said as much to Jodi when I ran her to earth at the theater, supervising Marv as he rehearsed the lighting for the night's contest.

"Absolutely not." She barely spared me a glance as we stood in the middle of the stage looking up toward the lighting booth. "Aim that spot a bit left," she called to Marv.

"Someone could get seriously hurt," I said. "Look what happened to the judges—we're just lucky that it was ipecac and not cyanide and no one died."

She gave me a scathing look. "Cyanide? Get real. This isn't *Arsenic and Old Lace*. The pranks are just someone's warped idea of a joke."

"Whoever's doing this won't stop until the pageant gets cancelled."

"Or until we crown the new Miss Magnolia Blossom," Jodi said triumphantly. "Then what will they do? Try blue."

"You got it," Marv said.

A haze of purply blue lighting turned the stage to twilight. "I don't know. Shoot the winner?"

The words leaped out of my mouth and gave us both pause.

"No way," Jodi said, shaking her head. "What would be the point?"

To discourage girls and young women from entering pageants? To get revenge for some wrong—real or imagined—in the past? I didn't know and I didn't want to find out. "Look, you've been involved with this pageant—"

"I've run it."

"—for several years. Can you think of anyone who

thought they were a shoo-in but lost, or anyone who had a really bad experience?"

"They all think they're going to win, honey, and most of them lose," Jodi said. "Some of them take it harder than others. And sometimes the girls can be mean to each other. There was one girl a couple of years ago who was a bit heavyset. The other girls were vicious about her weight and she ended up withdrawing. Her parents tried to sue the pageant, but nothing came of it. It's not our fault if their daughter ate too many donuts and couldn't find her way to the gym with a GPS." Her story and the condemnation in her voice made me wonder if Kwasi Yarrow didn't have a point: maybe pageants were evil.

"What's her name?"

"You expect me to remember?" Her brows arched up. "Erin or Erica . . . something like that. I have no clue what her last name was."

"Do you have records?"

"Yes, but I'm not going to dig them out for you." She gave me her full attention for a moment, shaking the clipboard for emphasis. "Look, just leave it alone. The girls have all picked up their gowns and costumes and are keeping them at their homes. There's nothing left here for the practical joker to get at. We'll crown the winner tomorrow night and we'll move on. Don't go looking for trouble."

Chapter Twenty-five

I WASN'T LOOKING FOR TROUBLE; I WAS LOOKING for answers. Jodi's story about the overweight girl getting run out of the pageant haunted me. If she wouldn't give me a list of the contestants, how could I get the girl's name? Maybe the newspaper? They usually published a story or two about the pageant. I didn't want to trek down to the *Gazette*'s offices and burrow through the morgue so I sat on the steps outside the theater and called my friend Addie McGowan. In her mid-sixties, Addie had been a reporter for the *Gazette* but now spent most of her time running the newspaper's morgue, only returning to reporting if a story caught her fancy.

"McGowan," she answered on the first ring, her raspy voice testifying to her years as a smoker.

"Addie! It's Grace. You busy?" I explained what I was after.

"Shouldn't be a problem," she said. An audible exhalation told me she was sneaking cigarettes at her basement desk again. "Back issues that recent are actually online. Hold a mo and I'll pull them up."

I listened to keyboard clickings for several minutes. A thin green caterpillar inched past me on the concrete and I wondered why nature made him move in such an awkward way: hunch up, stretch out.

"Okay," she finally said, just when I was going to suggest I call her back later. "There were no Ericas or Erins in last year's pageant or the year before's, but here's a group photo on the first day of the pageant three years ago and one of the girls is called Eryca M. Smith. Eryca with a Y."

"Does she look a little chubby?"

"More Rubens than Modigliani."

Her name would have to be Smith. How was I supposed to find someone named Smith? "I don't suppose there's anything else about her?" I asked.

"Daughter of Ezekiel and Carol Smith of Harriets Bluff. Wanted to major in fine arts at Florida State when she graduated. Which should have been"—she paused to calculate—"two years ago."

The Ezekiel cheered me. Smith was common but Ezekiel stood out. "Thanks, Addie," I said.

"Is there a story in this?" Addie asked. I could almost see her pointed nose quivering.

"You mean beyond the fact two people have been killed?"

A long, indrawn breath told me she was lighting a cigarette. "Murder by itself doesn't get my storytelling juices flowing anymore," she said. "It's the whys and wherefores that make a good story. Someone kills her cheating hubby—hell, it happens every day. Some gangbanger shoots a 7-Eleven clerk to rob the till—ditto. Now, some overambitious mama kills a cheerleader so her daughter can make the squad or does away with a pageant contestant that stands in her daughter's way, now that's a story. Or a drug lord infiltrates a beauty pageant to sneak more coke into the country—"

"How would a beauty pageant help a drug smuggler?" I interrupted.

"I'm just making this up as I go along," Addie said with a laugh that turned into a cough. "But you get my drift?"

I got it. And as I hung up, I wondered if there might well be an Addie-type story behind the Miss Magnolia Blossom murders.

A COUNTY PHONE BOOK SHOWED NO EZEKIEL SMITHS. On impulse, I ran my finger down all the Smiths and came across Zeke at the end. Good enough. I dialed the number and, when a woman answered, asked for Eryca.

"Why, bless you, Eryca doesn't live here anymore," the woman said. "Not for going on three years. She and her brother share an apartment up in Brunswick." She obligingly rattled off an address. "One-two-three Tara Street—like in *Gone with the Wind*. Apartment one-two-three. Isn't that the easiest? I can't remember her cell phone number to save my life. If you see her, you tell her her mama's going to forget what her pretty face looks like if she doesn't come visit soon."

I promised I would. Brunswick was twenty minutes north. Doable.

HALF AN HOUR LATER I WAS KNOCKING ON A DOOR IN a pretty apartment complex on the southern edge of

Brunswick. The buildings were two story, with tiny balconies or porches. Many had grills or bicycles chained to the rails, and flowers spilling out of window boxes. Set in a rectangle, the apartments ringed an aquamarine pool with a slide. Eight or ten kids splashed and Marco Poloed in the pool while a small group of mothers huddled around the one table with an umbrella and chatted. A lone man lay prone on a lounger, baking his skin to a mahogany shade that promised carcinomas as he aged.

I knocked again when no one answered and tried to peer in the narrow window beside the door. Mini blinds blocked my view. I wiped sweat off my forehead and lifted my hair off my neck. It was too dang hot. Pawing in my purse for a pen and a scrap of paper—an old receipt would do—to leave a note with, I jumped when a voice spoke behind me.

"Looking for Mick?"

I turned to see a young woman of twenty-two or so with long blond hair in a braid over her shoulder and a basket of folded laundry in her arms. The scent of fabric softener wafted off it. Boy, was I glad my days of popping quarters in a dryer at a Laundromat or pulling someone else's wet jockstraps out of a washer to run a load were over. My carriage-house apartment had a stackable washer and dryer just off the kitchen. The young woman stood behind me on the sidewalk, balancing the basket on her hip while she pulled keys from her cutoff jeans pocket.

"His sister, actually," I said as she fitted the key into the door of the neighboring apartment.

"I don't know about her," the woman said, "but Mick's over there." She nodded sideways toward the pool.

"Great. Thanks."

I had to walk to the far side of the pool to find the gate. It protested when I pushed it open and a couple of the mothers looked over at the squeal. Mick Smith didn't so much as wince. Chlorine fumes burned my nostrils and eyes and I wondered how the kids swam without goggles. When I got close to the lounger where the man lay, I called, "Mick Smith?"

Nothing. I took another couple of steps until I was looming over him. "Mr. Smith? Can I talk to you for a moment?"

His arms hung off the sides of the lounger, hands limp on the broiling concrete. A Stephen King paperback lay close to his right hand and a bottle of Corona was within reaching distance of his left, in clear violation of at least two rules posted not a foot away: "No glass containers in pool area" and "No alcoholic beverages allowed." Two o'clock seemed early to be knocking back the brewskis, but maybe he worked a night shift or something. He was thin enough I could see the suggestion of ribs, and fine dark hairs led from the small of his back into the elasticized waist of his forest green swim trunks.

"You're blocking my sun," he said without opening his eyes.

I hopped back, startled. "Sorry."

His hand groped for the beer bottle and he brought it to his lips, swallowing awkwardly with his face still mashed against the lounger.

"I'm looking for your sister," I said. "Eryca. Do you know where I can find her?"

One eyelid peeled back a hair and a green eye scanned me lazily. "What do you want her for?" His eye drifted shut again.

It didn't seem polite to say I thought his sister might be sabotaging the Miss Magnolia Blossom pageant to get revenge for being ridiculed out of it. "I just want to meet her, okay? Your mom gave me this address." I hoped that invoking the power of mom would prompt his cooperation.

"Shit."

Apparently not.

"I need another beer." He slipped his hand into the scruffy deck shoes aligned under the lounger and pulled out a key ring. He tossed it in my direction and it clattered to the ground. "In the fridge. Bottom shelf."

I stared at him uncomprehendingly for a moment and then anger wormed its way through me, flushing my skin. Did he think I was a cocktail waitress? I opened my mouth to tell him to get his own beer, but shut it without saying anything. Something about his air of entitlement tickled my funny bone. If fetching a beer would get me the info I needed, I could hike back to his apartment and grab a beer. I stooped to retrieve the keys and headed for the gate. Mick Smith appeared to have dozed off again.

The lock opened easily and the apartment breathed out cool air scented with old pizza when I pushed the door open. I found myself in a room with a sofa and big-screen television on one end and a dinette with two chairs at the other. Textbooks stacked on the table suggested either Mick or Eryca was taking a class or two. A pair of ladies' running shoes stuck out from beneath the sofa and a basketball huddled under the coffee table. Other than that, the place was empty of personal belongings. I didn't bother locating a light switch; I just marched through the dimness to the kitchen attached to the tiny dining area. A pizza box, lid up, contained a single piece of pepperoni pizza, dried up and curling at the tip. Someone had balanced empty Corona bottles atop each other on the counter to form a huge triangle against the wall. All in all, the place wasn't as gross as I expected—Eryca's influence, maybe.

I opened the fridge door and yanked out a Corona. Opening it with a church key magneted to the fridge door, I locked the apartment behind me as I left. The cold bottle felt wonderful and I held it between both hands as I returned to the pool enclosure. This time, I deliberately blocked Mick's sun. "I've got your beer," I said.

He held out his arm sideways.

"Uh-uh," I said, holding the beer aloft. I shuddered to think what the women at the other end of the pool thought was going on. One of the kids cannonballed into the pool behind me and water splashed my ankles and shins. "Not until you tell me where to find your sister."

He opened one eye, decided I was serious, and said, "She's practicing." The eye closed.

"What? Where?"

He heaved a huge sigh. "D'you know St. Elizabeth?"

"I'm from there."

"Great. Well, on the way into town—about two miles off the interstate—there's a dirt road on your left. Follow it down almost to the river. You'll hear her. I mean see her. Beer." He waggled his fingers.

I debated pouring the cold liquid over his back but let my better self win out. I thrust the bottle into his hand. He drank half of it in a noisy sideways guzzle, burped, and said, "She doesn't go by Eryca anymore, y'know. She's using her middle name. Tell her her half of the utilities bill is sixty-eight dollars." He set the beer carefully on the concrete and relaxed into the lounge chair's webbing again.

"What name?"

No response and a delicate snore suggested he'd fallen asleep. Whether or not he was sleeping or just pretending, I'd gotten everything I was going to get from Mick Smith. I moved the beer three feet away so he'd have to get off the lounger to grab it, and left.

*   *   *

MAKING THE TURNOFF MICK MENTIONED, I BUMPED
down a dirt road under an arch of trees that fanned from
either side of the road and met in the middle. Old pines and
deciduous trees labored under the burden of kudzu vines
trying to bend them down to the forest floor. The leaves
blocked most of the sunlight and only a forceful beam or two
penetrated to the ground, where ferns and ivies—including
poison ivy and poison oak, I was sure—provided a breeding
ground for ticks and other creepy-crawlies. The Satilla River
flowed just out of sight, giving the air a water scent I loved.

About three-quarters of a mile in, I saw a newish white
pickup parked in a small lay-by. I pulled in beside it, unsure
where to start looking for Eryca. Could she be hiking by the
river? A faint path led off in that direction. I started down
the path, wishing I were wearing hiking boots instead of
sandals. Red dirt scuffed under my toes and I was bending
to dislodge a pebble when a shot startled me. I ducked even
lower. Three more shots rang out in quick succession.

My heart beat faster and I stayed in a crouch, feeling
particularly foolish when a squirrel scampered down a tree
and eyed me contemptuously before grabbing an acorn.
I straightened and continued down the path in the direction of the gunshots. Mick had said Eryca was "practicing," right? And that I'd hear her. I wasn't surprised when
I rounded a bend and found myself looking at a makeshift
shooting range with targets nailed to trees at varying dis-
tances and a woman standing with her back to me, level-
ing a rifle at a silhouette of a deer. She was tall and trim
from the back, wearing camouflaged pants and boots that
could've come from a military surplus store and a pink tee
shirt that showed off slim but muscular arms. Dark hair
spilled from beneath a ball cap held down by ear defenders.
She fired and the target jerked.

Before she could bring the rifle to her shoulder again, I called loudly, "Eryca Smith?"

She spun, automatically pointing the rifle at the ground, and I found myself looking at M16 Morgan, the Miss Magnolia Blossom contestant. Her dark hair set off light olive skin and full red lips. Not an ounce of fat blurred the lines of her fit body; no one would believe she'd ever been chubby.

We stared at each other incredulously for a second until I blurted, "Morgan?"

"I don't go by Eryca anymore," she said at the same time, pulling off the ear defenders.

I couldn't think what to say. She had easy access to the theater and all the things that were sabotaged: sprinkler system, Kylie's mats, judges' water bottles. And she had a gun. That fact, even more than my surprise and confusion, kept me silent.

"What are you doing here?" Morgan asked, regaining her equilibrium quicker than I had. Her dark brows drew together in a suspicious frown.

"Your mother says she'd like you to visit," I said. "And your brother says you owe him sixty-eight dollars for the electric bill."

Her mouth dropped open a half inch. "What?" Her frown turned to a look of total confusion. "How do you know my mom and Mick?"

"I don't really know your mom—we just talked on the phone. Look, could you put the gun down?"

Morgan looked at the rifle like she'd forgotten it was there. "Sure. Let's walk back to the truck. I'm done for the day."

I made a gesture for her to precede me down the path like I was polite or something; really, I didn't want her behind me with the gun. "What are you practicing for?" I asked, stopping a thin branch from slashing into my face.

"There's a marksmanship competition at Fort Benning," she said.

We reached the lay-by and Morgan retrieved a gun case from the back of the cab. Walking around to the tailgate, she lowered it, sat on it, and began to wipe the rifle with a cloth. "So," she said, looking at me from under the bill of her ball cap, "tell me why you tracked me down. And how you knew my first name."

"Well . . ." I wished I'd thought this through a little further. "A friend of mine told me she thought you'd been in the pageant before. I was curious, so I looked through some back issues of the *Gazette* and found your photo. I almost didn't recognize you."

"I've lost some weight," Morgan acknowledged. Her hand stroked the stock of the rifle absently as she fixed her dark gaze on me. "But your story is total bullshit."

She had me there. Maybe honesty was the best policy. "Okay, I heard from Jodi that an overweight girl got laughed out of the pageant a few years back. It struck me that she—you—might have a good reason for wanting to . . . to get back at the pageant."

"You think I murdered Miss Faye?" Shock slammed her features. Her grip tightened convulsively on the gun, making me nervous.

"No, no," I said. "I thought you might be responsible for the sabotage, though. For revenge."

"Oh, I'm out for revenge, all right," Morgan said with a humorless bark of laughter. "But my idea of revenge is to win this candy-ass pageant and throw their trinkety crown into the nearest Dumpster. Or crush it under my boot on the stage. Can't you just see Tabitha's and Miss Keen's faces?"

Actually, I could, and the image made me laugh. Morgan joined me and our mirth startled a dozen sparrows taking a dust bath in the roadway. They fluttered to the safety of nearby branches.

"You can sit," Morgan said, patting the tailgate. She laid the rifle in its case and closed it up.

"So, how did you lose all that weight?" I asked. I hopped backward onto the warm metal of the tailgate.

"The abuse I took from the girls in the pageant was the last straw," she said. "They were cruel and mean and hateful, but they were right. I was a blimp. I joined Weight Watchers. When I'd lost twenty pounds, I joined a gym. When I started working out, the weight just melted off. I was within fifteen pounds of my goal weight when I graduated and talked to an army recruiter. I signed up for the U.S. Reserves and went off to boot camp. Twelve-mile marches with thirty-pound packs, running, obstacle courses . . . if you want to slim down, I'm here to recommend boot camp." She laughed. "That's where I discovered I could shoot, too."

"Why take another stab at the pageant, then?"

Her eyes drifted to the right and she stared into the woods as she thought. One leg kicked out and swung back and forth. "Well, the guys in my unit thought it would be funny and . . . I don't know. I guess I just wanted to prove to those girls—the ones who made fun of me—that I could do it. Maybe I needed to prove it to myself. That I'm not Fat Eryca anymore. I'm Lean Mean Fightin' Machine Morgan. And I don't take crap from anyone."

Chapter Twenty-six

✂

DRIVING BACK TO MOM'S AFTER TALKING TO MORGAN, I pondered the girl's answers. She'd seemed confident and she'd had reasonable answers to my questions, but I wasn't sure she hadn't been the saboteur. She admitted she wanted revenge, and even though she made a joke of it, I'd seen the hurt in her eyes. Embarrassing a girl like Tabitha by sawing through her bathing suit strap must be almost irresistible to someone who'd been the butt of fat jokes from pageant princesses just like her. A disturbing thought niggled at me: Morgan was comfortable—and proficient—with guns. And Barnes had been shot. Could Morgan be a murderer? I shook my head and my hair whisked the back of my neck.

My cell phone rang as I was pulling up in front of the salon. Addie McGowan started talking before I even said hello.

"Grace, listen up. After we talked, I thumbed through a

couple more issues, looking for articles about the pageant. I found one that talked about that poor girl who died. When I saw her photo, I remembered the story. And I got to thinking about what you said about someone having it in for the pageant."

Electricity tingled through me. "Leda something, right?"

"Leda Wissing. Says here she died of a heart attack. Survived by her parents, Thad and Stacy Wissing of Kingsland, three grandparents, two sisters, one brother, and a niece. And a partridge in a pear tree. How do you ever come to terms with that as a parent?" she wondered rhetorically. "With your child dying so young and in such a freaky way."

"I don't know."

Maybe you don't. Maybe you look for someone or something to blame.

MAPQUEST GOT ME TO THE WISSINGS' HOUSE IN Kingsland half an hour later. Their address was in the phone book and Stacy Wissing had told me to come on over when I called and said I wanted to talk about Leda. She didn't even hesitate; I got the feeling that she welcomed any excuse to talk about her daughter. Now, I sat in my car in front of their two-story brick house wondering what I was going to say. "Hello. Poisoned any beauty pageant judges lately?" Somehow, I didn't think that would work.

I got out of the car, smoothing my khaki skirt over my hips, and walked to the door. A weeping willow draped over the portico, its shadow making it feel like dusk rather than mid-afternoon. They're such beautiful trees, but their name is so melancholy; I don't like thinking of their leaves as tears.

A woman opened the door. "You must be Grace," she

said. "I'm Stacy." Still under fifty, I'd guess, with expertly dyed blond hair and a complexion beginning to show signs of sun damage, she offered a friendly smile and a firm handshake. She was tall and still slim. "Do you mind if we talk on the patio? I'm deadheading the roses." That explained the dirt stains on her white tee shirt and the secateurs pulling down the pocket of her shorts.

"It should've been done a couple months ago," she said, leading me down a wide, carpeted hallway to a kitchen with maple cabinetry, an island, and French doors leading to the backyard. We stepped over the sill and onto a brick and sand patio surrounded by flower beds. A fountain dribbled gently in the middle of the yard and the scent of cedar mulch and mown grass perfumed the air. "But we were traveling some this summer—my son and his wife just had their second baby—and what with one thing and another I haven't gotten round to it."

"Congratulations on your new grandbaby," I said. "Boy or girl?"

"A precious little girl. They named her Leda Elizabeth."

She actually smiled when she said it, so I assumed she had gone on with her life. Not that she was over her daughter's death, but that she had tucked the grief away somewhere and didn't let it color her every waking moment. She certainly didn't come across as a psychotic, revenge-seeking lunatic. I told her about my role in the pageant and about talking to the protestors and their poster of her daughter.

She pulled the clippers out and snipped at the brown clumps of petals, letting them drop to the mulch. "I read about Audrey Faye's death, of course," she said. "And that other man. I didn't know either of them. A woman named Keen was running the pageant the year Leda entered it."

"She's taken it over again since Audrey died," I said.

Moving to another rosebush, Stacy snipped at more dead blooms. "Are you thinking there's some connection between their deaths and Leda's? I just can't see it. Leda's heart gave out—a tragic consequence of her eating disorders. There was nothing criminal about it."

"She had eating disorders?" I hadn't heard that.

"Anorexia and bulimia both. We had her in a residential treatment facility when she was just fourteen, and she seemed to be getting better for a few years after that. But when she went off to college, we think she fell back into old habits. We tried desperately to talk her out of entering the pageant—even threatened to quit paying her tuition— but she was over eighteen. We couldn't stop her."

I thought about a woman throwing her body so out of kilter through starvation and vomiting that her heart seized up. Tragic. "So you think being in the pageant killed her?" I tried to read Stacy Wissing's face, but her back was to me as she gardened.

She cast a sharp look at me over her shoulder. "Of course not. She—"

A gate on our left creaked open and a man strode into the yard. In a suit and tie, he looked out of place. "I got here as soon as I could," he said. "Is this her?" He frowned at me.

Stacy sighed. "Thad, I told you there was no need to come home. I'm okay talking about Leda. You know that. And, yes, this is Grace Terhune."

I held out my hand but he ignored it. He had a heavy brow bone that overhung his eyes and sunken cheeks like a marathoner. "How do you know she's not a reporter?"

"She's not a reporter," Stacy said. "Go back to work, honey."

"Not with her here." He frowned at me. "Do you have some sick fascination with death? Do you get off on people's grief? What are you really doing here?" His hands balled into fists at his sides, he advanced toward me.

I stepped back as Stacy Wissing slipped between us. "Thad!"

"I'm not leaving until she's gone." He glared at me over his wife's shoulder.

"You'd better go," Stacy said to me. "I'm sorry."

"That's okay," I said. "I'm sorry for disturbing you."

"You'll be sorry," Wissing muttered.

I slid back through the French doors as Stacy hugged her husband. His shoulders shook like he was crying. I retraced my steps to the front door, taking one wrong turn that landed me in a living room. I was about to back out of the room when I noticed a family portrait over the fireplace. A smiling Thad and Stacy stood behind four children—three girls and a boy—who ranged in age from maybe twelve to eighteen. A golden retriever with a gray muzzle flopped at their feet. I pegged the oldest girl, a blond goddess who looked a lot like Stacy must have in her youth, as Leda. The photo must have been taken a year or two before her death. She looked happy in the picture, the sun making a nimbus of her blond hair, no trace of anguish or illness in her shining blue eyes or smooth complexion. What a waste. I was halfway back to the door when something struck me. I returned to the photo, studying the other children. Something about the middle girl . . . It took me a moment, but I finally figured out where I knew her from.

I DROVE AIMLESSLY FOR A FEW MINUTES, NOT SURE where I was going. I was almost certain Daphne, the protestor, was Leda Wissing's sister. Was it possible that she was out for revenge against the pageant or did she really just want to warn other young women about the pitfalls of being obsessed with your looks, as pageant contestants had to be? I felt sorry for her. It must have been dreadful losing her older sister in such a way, and clearly her dad wasn't helping the family get over their grief. Now, Thad Wissing struck me as a more likely candidate for revenge. His anger bubbled at the surface like geothermal pools I'd seen once at Yellowstone. Weird algae thrived in the high temps and turned the pools orange and acid green and blue. Maybe something similar was happening to Wissing; the heat of his grief was allowing revenge fantasies to bloom.

I found myself in front of the Oglethorpe before I knew it, scanning the sidewalks for the protestors. No one. The place looked utterly deserted and I figured it would remain that way until the girls started arriving for the evening's competition. Jodi and Marv had probably finished the tech check and were stealing a few minutes for a nap, a meal, or a workout before returning to the theater. No one else had a reason to be there since the contestants had taken their gowns home.

Chewing at my lower lip, I pulled the car to the curb and dialed information. They had no listing for a Daphne Wissing. Of course, it couldn't be that easy. She might share an apartment with a friend and the phone could be in the friend's name. She might not have a landline. Or, heck, she might still live at home. I lived with Mom until I married Hank, except for my two years at UGA. I could call Stacy Wissing and ask for Daphne's number, but after the way Thad behaved, I didn't want to risk getting him on the phone.

I drove to Mom's. She and Althea were unloading groceries in the kitchen when I arrived. They seemed overdressed for grocery shopping: Mom wore a blue flowered dress with a square neckline and Althea had on a long mustard-colored tunic embroidered at the cuffs over baggy pants. I hugged Mom and greeted Althea self-consciously, uncomfortable with the information Marty had given me about Kwasi. Should I tell her? Not now. Grabbing three bags out of the trunk, I lugged them into the kitchen.

"I just got back from the Piggly Wiggly," Mom said, depositing a bag on the counter. Celery peeked over the top.

"And I showed up just in time to play pack mule," Althea grumbled. She carried a box of detergent to the laundry room. "I think that's the lot. We need to get going, Vi, or we're going to be late. Which wouldn't be all bad. I hope they don't play any of those stupid games, like guessing the poor girl's waist measurement. I can't abide those games."

"We're going to Euphemia Toller's granddaughter's baby shower," Mom said. "What are you up to?"

I quickly filled them in on my morning while Mom stacked cans in the cupboards and Althea stowed produce in the fridge. I folded the reusable bags and put them back in the pantry.

"I can't believe that sweet little Daphne had anything to do with the goings-on at the pageant," Althea said.

"Maybe she didn't," I said, "but I'd sure like to talk to her. I could tell Agent Dillon, I guess, and let him track her down, but it seems unfair to sic the police on her when she might not even be involved."

"Call Kwasi," Althea said.

I looked at her, puzzled.

"The gal's in his class, right? Call him and get her phone number." She looked at her watch. "Oh, wait. He's in class now. But he should be done in twenty minutes. You can call him then."

"Maybe I'll just drive out to GCC," I said, thinking I'd take advantage of the opportunity to query Kwasi about the argument with Audrey that Rachel had overheard.

Mom gave me a long look but Althea merely said, "He's in the Chandler Building, office number 214." She stiff-armed the screen door open and held it for Mom. "Let's get this over with," Althea said. "We don't want that baby to pop out before his mama's got wipes warmers and a baby backpack and forty-two precious little outfits that he'll only wear once. Back in my day . . ."

Chapter Twenty-seven

✄

THE GEORGIA COASTAL COLLEGE CAMPUS LIES JUST south of SR 42 before it meets the interstate. Three or four years ago, it consisted of one classroom building and an administrative building/student union. Now, it boasted multiple classroom buildings, a gym complex, and two dormitories. A pond ringed by cattails reflected the brick and glass façade of Danner Hall, where the administrative offices, bookstore, and student union were housed. Parking in one of the few slots that didn't require a student, faculty, or staff parking sticker, I asked a passing student where I could find the Chandler Building.

"Cut through the coffee bar in Danner and Chandler's right behind it." He pointed.

Following his directions, and stopping for a cup of tea on the way, I found Chandler, a three-story collage of stone, glass, and asymmetric angles. In mid-afternoon on a summer Friday, not too many students clogged the walkways, but one or two lazed on the lawns, textbooks open, eyes shut. It made me nostalgic for my own college days at UGA. Part of me wished I hadn't quit after two years to go to beauty school. Something about college campuses felt separate from the real world, safer, like living in a protective bubble.

A wide staircase led to the upper floors of Chandler and I climbed to the second level, figuring that's where I'd find office 214. Bingo. I studied the half-open door for a moment, where Kwasi had his office hours posted, along with a Calvin and Hobbes comic strip and the Winston Churchill quotation about not quitting. I knocked.

"Come."

Kwasi sat behind a battered wooden desk, grading a paper with quick slashes of a red pen. He looked up as I entered, studying me over the rims of his rectangular glasses. He wore a coarsely woven indigo blue shirt with sleeves that belled slightly at the wrist. His window looked out onto the parking lot and the interstate beyond. Tall bookshelves crowded with books and carvings of wood or stone took up most of the space. A couple of textile pieces and a ferocious-looking wooden mask at least two feet tall decorated the walls. "Hello, Grace."

He didn't sound surprised to see me.

"Althea called to tell me you'd be stopping in."

Ah. Mystery explained.

"Did she say what I wanted?"

He shook his head. "No, just that it was something about a student?" He raised his brows questioningly, creasing his freckled forehead. "Please." He gestured toward a straight-backed rattan chair positioned in front of his desk.

I sat and a lone photo on his desk caught my eye. It

showed Kwasi and Althea standing on the deck of a small boat, strings of fish hanging from their uplifted hands and huge grins on their faces. Althea looked radiant with happiness and the flush of sun.

"You and Althea went fishing?" I asked, thinking that it was sweet he kept the photo on his desk. He must really be serious about Althea.

"Yes, we had a most successful day, as you can see."

"I didn't know Althea fished."

"That woman is up for anything," he said with a real smile. "It is one of the things I particularly appreciate about her."

It just goes to show that no matter how long you know someone, you never really know them. I didn't have time to process this new idea of Althea—or of an appreciative Kwasi—so I put it away for the moment. "What I came by for," I said, "is Daphne Wissing's phone number."

The creases deepened on Kwasi's brow. "I don't have a Daphne Wissing in any of my classes. There's only Daphne Oliver."

It had to be the same girl. How many college-age Daphnes were running around St. Elizabeth? Maybe the Wissings were a blended family. "She's one of the demonstrators, right? About twenty, with sandy hair?"

He nodded reluctantly. "What is your interest in Ms. Oliver?"

"I just need her phone number," I said, not wanting to color his opinion of his student by mentioning she might be sabotaging the pageant.

"I can't give it to you, Grace," Kwasi said in a reproving tone. "The students have an expectation of privacy." He pursed his lips.

Reluctantly, I explained why I needed the number. "It's

important. What if she's planning something for tonight's competition? Someone could get hurt. If you don't give me her number, I'll have to give her name to the police."

He shook his head. "I have trouble believing that Ms. Oliver is a threat to anyone, but if you believe she is, then you should take your concerns to the authorities. I will not betray her trust by giving you access to her personal data."

It's a phone number, I wanted to say, not her social security number or her diary. I switched tacks. "You knew Audrey Faye better than you let on, didn't you? Someone overheard you arguing, heard Audrey say something about 'what happened at Berkeley.' Why haven't you told the police about your prior relationship with her?"

He stiffened and his eyes narrowed. "You take a lot for granted, Grace. My relationship, or lack thereof, with Audrey Faye or anyone else is none of your business. Ditto for what I may or may not have told the police. If you must know, I was surrounded by students from late afternoon until well past the time of Audrey's death. I believe several of them have already corroborated this for the police."

The coldness in his voice intimidated me, but I kept on. "Does Althea know why you left Berkeley?"

He removed his glasses and polished them with a cloth he took from a desk drawer. "Are you implying you do?" he asked, pushing the glasses back up his nose.

I didn't answer.

A sardonic smile twisted his lips. "Whatever you may have heard, I repeat: it's none of your business."

"Althea's my friend," I said heatedly. "I don't want her to get hurt."

"If you were really a friend, you would respect her enough to trust her judgment."

This was not going the way I had planned. Trying to

come to grips with Kwasi was like wrestling the greased pig at the county fair. Every time I thought I had a grasp on him, he slid off in another direction. Time was zipping past and I still didn't have a way to reach Daphne.

"Can you please just give me Daphne's phone number?" I asked, tacitly giving up on discovering what lay between him and Audrey. If she knew about his plagiarism and was threatening to reveal it, that would give him a darn good motive to kill her since it might well cost him his job. Still, it sounded like he had a rock-solid alibi. "Althea's the one who suggested you would have it."

"Are you implying that you'll tell Althea whatever you think you know about my sojourn at Berkeley if I don't give you the number?" His thumb tapped rapidly against his desk.

"Of course not!" I stood up angrily, accidentally knocking a stack of papers off the corner of his desk. They cascaded to the floor and I felt like a clumsy idiot. Damn. "I'm sorry!" I didn't like having to apologize when I was furious with him.

"It wouldn't matter if you were," he said, shooing me away from the papers when I bent to pick them up. "You won't get Daphne's—or any other student's—phone number from me." He managed to make his stubbornness sound as noble as a freedom fighter's refusal to give up his comrades under torture.

I spun around and left, not even bothering with a goodbye. The man was infuriating, even though I couldn't help admiring—a teensy-weensy bit—the way he stuck to his principles. The concept of an ethical plagiarist made my head hurt. The way he refused to give me any information . . . wait a minute! He *had* given me an important piece of info: Daphne's real last name. I fumbled for my cell phone and called information, netting a phone number and address for Daphne Oliver. Hah!

I CALLED DAPHNE'S NUMBER BUT GOT NO ANSWER. Darn the girl. If I hadn't simultaneously felt so sorry for what she'd been through and worried about what she might do, I'd have dropped it. Instead, I drove to the Davenport Apartments, just blocks from the college, and knocked on the door. Cream paint was peeling from it, revealing a puce layer beneath. Tiny balconies fronted the second-floor apartments, and Daphne's first-floor abode had a cement patio with a George Foreman grill and an aluminum folding chair. I was about to knock again when I heard footsteps. Hallelujah.

But my celebration was premature. The girl who opened the door was not Daphne. She was about Daphne's age but was shorter and African American, wearing shorts and a tube top that emphasized a thick waist and generous bosom. A weighty biology textbook rested in the crook of her arm. "Yes?"

"I'm looking for Daphne. Is she here?"

"No."

Miss Monosyllable started to close the door, but I asked, "Do you know where she is? I really need to talk to her."

She shifted the book and sighed heavily. "What's today? Friday? She doesn't have class. And I don't think she'd be at the library on a Friday afternoon."

Great. She was going to list all the places Daphne was *not,* one at a time.

"She might be over to the theater with those protestors." She put a verbal sneer into the last word.

"You don't agree with her about beauty contests?"

"Do I look like beauty pageant material?" Thankfully,

she didn't wait for an answer. "Damn straight I don't. So if I were to protest beauty pageants, it would look like I was just envious of girls who were ahead of me in line when they were handing out Barbie bodies and long eyelashes. I'm a straight-A student and I've been accepted to Wharton for my MBA. I don't have time for pageants *or* protesting. Try the theater."

I stared at a bouncing curlicue of peeling paint on the closed door. Fine. I'd tried to help Daphne, but I had limited resources for my detecting. It was time to let the professionals in on it. I dialed Agent Dillon's number as I returned to the car.

"We've talked to the Wissings, of course," he said when I explained my fears. "In fact, Thad Wissing was on our short list before we nabbed Michaelson; he blames the pageant and everyone associated with it for his daughter's death and he has no alibi for either murder."

I was relieved but a bit deflated to realize the police were ahead of me. "So what about Daphne?"

"I didn't realize there was another daughter in the area," he admitted. "The son lives in Arizona and has a rock-solid alibi for the time of Faye's death. His last name's Oliver, too. All the kids except Leda kept their dad's name when their mom remarried. The youngest daughter's doing a semester abroad in New Zealand." He hissed air through his teeth. "I don't like it that the Wissings didn't mention this Daphne."

I didn't like it, either. "Do you think the same person is responsible for everything—ruining the gowns, the skunk, the murders?"

"The jury's still out on that," he said. "Michaelson looks good for the murders but I can't see him hacking up ball gowns. Unless, of course, he's trying to muddy the waters."

I told him about Morgan Smith being hounded out of the pageant the year Leda died. I felt a bit like a snitch, but couldn't reconcile it with myself not to mention her when she had motive, means, and opportunity.

"Sounds like a long shot," he said dismissively, "but I've heard stranger motives. I'll put her name on the to-do list for when one of my guys has time. Maybe I'll see you at the pageant tonight."

And with that he hung up, leaving me uneasy. Dillon's planning to be at the theater told me he was worried that something might happen. He could add two and two just as well as Marty and I and could figure out that the sabotage incidents were getting more extreme. On impulse, I drove to the theater again, pulling around to the lot in the back. No cats lingered near the Dumpster today and there were no cars in the lot. I drove slowly past the back of the building, looking for reassurance that the theater was secure and no surprises awaited us that night. Something shiny winked from the newly weed-whacked grass near the door I'd found open the day before. Marv must have mown it when he put on the padlock. With a little trepidation, I put the car in park but left it running, getting out to see what had caught my eye.

A lock. I nudged it with my foot. A brand-new padlock with the shackle twisted in two, probably by the bolt cutters lying almost concealed against the building. I crept to the door which hung open a bare inch. The raw scent of gasoline stung my nostrils and I cringed back. I was turning away, headed for my car and my cell phone, when a faint voice inside the theater yelled, "Help!"

I froze, one foot literally an inch off the ground as the panicked voice cried, "I'm trapped! Please help! Someone!"

Taking a deep breath, I plunged into the building.

Chapter Twenty-eight

"WHERE ARE YOU?" I CALLED, STUMBLING ACROSS the crowded basement to the stairs. I banged my shin on the spinning wheel. "Ouch!" I hopped the remaining distance to the stairs and started to climb. The gasoline smell grew stronger as I went, but thankfully I smelled no smoke.

Cautiously, I opened the door to find a single light burning in the hallway. Thank goodness. I'd been afraid it would be pitch-black like yesterday. The meager light showed great splotches of liquid staining the walls and carpet, like someone had sloshed a gasoline can around indiscriminately. I followed the trail of gasoline blotches and was unsurprised when it led to the Green Room.

"Hello? Are you okay?" I called. I hesitated in the hall, made uneasy by the lack of response. I finally forced myself to push at the door, thinking Daphne—I was sure it was her—had been overcome by the gas fumes.

She stood with her back to me, calmly emptying the last of a five-gallon red container of gasoline over an over-stuffed chair by the window that faced the parking lot. Cutoff denim shorts dripped strings down the back of her thighs and her sandy hair was caught in a ponytail at her neck. A green tee shirt with a "Save the Rainforest" message on it showed sweat stains in the small of her back and under her arms. She dropped the empty can, sniffed at her fingers, and then caught sight of me.

"That's okay, then," she said, with no expression in her voice or on her face.

Absolutely nothing in this scenario was okay. Least of all me and her standing in a room primed to burst into flames. My head ached from the fumes. "What's okay?" I asked, starting toward her, intent on dragging her out of the theater.

"You. Here. I just needed to make sure you wouldn't sound the alarm until the fire had truly taken hold. Nothing else worked. I've got to burn this place to the ground. Then it will be over." She pulled a blue disposable lighter from her jeans pocket. "Dad's. He took up smoking after Leda . . . well, you know."

"Lighting that in here would be suicidal," I said, freezing. The fumes would ignite instantaneously. Could I jump her and overpower her before she could flick the lighter? The gap between us was too wide.

"Oh, I know that," she said. She giggled. The sound was eerie coming from a face with almost no affect—no smile, no hint of mirth. "I'm not going to light it in here. I'm going to light it out there"—she pointed to the hall—"and toss it in here. You can come with me."

Come with her? I was closer to the door. I darted through it and was halfway down the hall, thinking maybe I could find a phone in Marv's office when Daphne came into the hall. She clicked the wheel on the lighter. Nothing happened. She shook it, then clicked it again.

"Don't do it—" Instinct took over and I ran toward her. I dove at her knees as a small, steady flame erupted from the lighter. My arms encircled her ankles and she kicked at me as I thudded full length against the floor. My knees and elbow scraped along the industrial carpet and my head whacked against her shin. Stumbling, she still managed to pitch the lighter into the Green Room. I hid my face in my arms. A *whumpf* blasted hot air back at us and the room was engulfed in flames when I risked a peek. Sheets of flickering red and orange ate greedily at the curtains and floor, running up the walls and seeking access to the rest of the theater. Daphne, closer to the Green Room than I and still standing when she tossed the lighter, was flung backward against the wall and slumped there, dazed.

I struggled to my feet, coughing, and grabbed for her hand. "Come on." Using all my strength, I hauled her up and got an arm around her waist. Half dragging her, I started toward the front of the theater. Flames had already spread into the hall and oily dark smoke clogged the air. I was wheezing after just a few steps and remembered the fire safety advice to keep low. Unfortunately, I couldn't drop to my hands and knees and still drag Daphne out of danger.

The crackle of flames behind us kept me moving and I resisted the urge to see how close they were getting. It seemed that the air was just a bit clearer as we turned the corner and I picked up the pace, urging Daphne onward in a hoarse voice. "Come on. Come on."

"Can't see," she croaked.

I flicked a glance at her and caught a glimpse of her face,

reddened as if she'd spent a day in the sun, her eyebrows and the hair around her face singed. Was it possible she'd been blinded? The thought horrified me. She was moving better now, so I dropped my arm from around her waist and grabbed her hand, pulling her after me as I plowed ahead. Sweat dripped down my sides and into my eyes.

A shaft of light pierced the gloomy tunnel of smoke. An open doorway beckoned with natural light promising a window. I ducked into the room, Daphne stumbling behind me and slammed the door shut. A desk. A phone. I rushed to the phone and punched in 911.

"Fire," I gasped to the operator. "Oglethorpe Theater." I eyed the fingers of smoke curling under the door, the fire trying to pry its way in. I ignored whatever the operator was telling me and dropped the receiver on the desk.

Daphne was at the window, straining to open it. She must be able to see *something*. "We're trapped," she said in the same sort of voice someone would say "we're having broccoli for dinner" or "I think I'll take Algebra next semester."

"Move," I said. I picked up the desk chair, an old wood and fabric contraption with casters at the end of the five spokes that spread out from its pedestal base, and ran full tilt at the window. The wheels smashed the glass and my momentum thrust the whole chair out. Its weight ripped it from my hands and it fell, clunking against the side of the building. I leaned out, gulping in great breaths of fresh air. The drop was no more than ten or twelve feet—less than the high board at the swimming pool, I told myself. A thin strip of grass close to the building was bordered by the sidewalk that led around back to the parking lot. Ripping my tee shirt off, I broke the stalagmites of glass out of the window frame so we could hold on and drop down.

Something in the door popped and a tongue of flame licked through the dry wood. "Take your shirt off," I commanded Daphne. "Wrap your hands." I yanked upward on the hem of her tee shirt and helped her pull it over her head. She swaddled her hands as I demonstrated, moving with more urgency now as the door disappeared in a wall of flame.

Sirens sounded in the distance but I knew the firefighters with their ladders would be too late to save us. The fire was eating across the floor.

"Go, go, go!" I shouted to Daphne as the roar of the fire drowned out my voice. She grabbed hold of the sill, swung her legs over, hung for a long moment and then let go. I barely watched her hit the ground before I was slinging my leg over the sill, trying not to slice it open on the jagged glass, and gingerly gripping the window frame with my shirt-covered hands. I hardly felt the glass jabbing into my palms as I cast a fleeting glance over my shoulder at the ground. Heat singed my fingers and I let go.

I landed awkwardly. A searing pain crumpled my leg and I fell back, banging my head on the cement sidewalk. I don't think I was out for long—maybe thirty seconds or so—but when I came to, firefighters were pounding toward me, hauling a hose, and the air shimmered with heat. I pushed up on one elbow, wincing at the ax chops of pain gouging my head, and looked around. Daphne was gone.

THE FIREFIGHTERS HAULED ME BACK OUT OF HARM'S way and attacked the fire. Flames gouted from some of the windows and the streams of water playing over the building seemed to have little effect, other than to create great clouds of steam and add the odor of wet, burned wood to the air. It smelled familiar. It took me only a second to relate it to the smell of my mom's veranda after firefighters soaked it to put out the small fire caused by a Molotov cocktail tossed by Constance DuBois's murderer. I shivered.

The EMT looking at my hands barked an order to his partner, who wrapped a silvery blanket around my shoulders. I tried to tell him I wasn't really cold, but all that came out were hacking coughs that brought tears to my eyes. "Daphne?" I managed to croak.

"Is someone else in there?" the EMT asked, dread pulling at his features.

"No, no. She jumped before me."

"There was no one else here, miss," the man said, forcing me to lie back on the stretcher. A small silver hoop glinted on his ear as he fitted an oxygen mask over my face. I lay quietly for a few minutes, enjoying the play of the cool, clean air against my ragged throat. The EMT gave me an injection "for the pain," he said and I hovered on the brink of unconsciousness as they racked the stretcher up and wheeled me to the ambulance.

Chapter Twenty-nine

A CURTAIN. FOOTSTEPS AND CLATTERINGS. DISINFEC-tant. I awoke disoriented and had just about figured out that I was lying on a gurney in the ER, a white sheet pulled to my chest, my hands feeling clunky and my head pounding, when someone yanked back the curtain shielding my bed with a rattle of metal rings against the rod. Agent Dillon stood there, an expression on his face somewhere between worry and anger.

"What the hell were you doing in that theater?" he asked in a voice that was almost a groan.

Mom nudged him aside and stopped at the end of the gurney, her hand holding my foot through the sheet. "I'm her mom," she told Dillon. "I get to talk to her first. What the hell were you doing in that theater?"

I smiled at them both. "Hi."

Tears slipped down Mom's face and Agent Dillon handed her a handkerchief. "Oh, honey."

"I'm okay."

"Your poor hands."

I freed my arms from under the sheets and looked at my hands. Swathed in gauze bandages with the fingers peeking out, they looked like weird mitts. Now that I thought about it, they did sort of throb. I guessed the tee shirt hadn't done the trick.

"The doc says you'll heal fine," Dillon put in quickly. "No nerve damage. Just a lot of stitches. You won't be holding shears for a while. And your ankle's only sprained."

Right then I didn't care. Mom leaned over and kissed my cheek. "As soon as John's done with you, I'm taking you home. Five minutes." She gave Dillon a minatory look over the top of her glasses, kissed me again, and walked away, pulling the curtain shut behind her.

Dillon scraped a chair up to the bedside. Gurney-side. "What happened?"

His navy blue eyes never left mine as I told him about seeing the cut lock, the cry for help, Daphne setting the blaze and our escape.

"Sounds to me like that girl owes you her life," he said when I finished.

I wiggled uncomfortably under the sheet. "I don't know about that. Have you found her?"

He shook his head.

"She said she couldn't see."

He cocked one brow. "Maybe it was a temporary blindness from the glare. She sure took off fast enough, from what you said."

"Did they save the theater?"

"It didn't collapse, if that's what you mean. But no

one's going to be putting on plays in it any time soon. Or pageants."

I wondered if Marv would be happy or sad. A thought struck me. "My car?"

"What about it?"

I explained about leaving it behind the theater when I went in.

"Not there," he said with a shake of his head. "Maybe Daphne took it." He wrote down the license plate number. "I'll put out an APB. With any luck, she won't have gone far."

"With any luck, my car will still be in one piece. I hope she has the courtesy to fill the tank." Another thought struck me. "My purse was in there! She's probably at the Lenox Square Mall in Atlanta, buying Prada and Gucci with my Visa." Not that my limit would stretch to more than a designer scarf. Still, it was going to be a massive pain in the fanny cancelling my cards, replacing my driver's license . . .

Dillon shook his head slightly and leaned in to lay his hand on my cheek. I could see a patch of stubble on his jaw where he hadn't shaved evenly that morning. His eyes searched mine. "Grace—"

"Time's up," Mom said, popping her head back around the curtain. "There's an aide with a wheelchair right here."

Dillon rose slowly to his feet. He tried to pat my hand but got only gauze. A smile crooked his lips. "I'll stop by later to let you know how things are going," he promised.

"Come for dinner," Mom offered.

"I've got a date," I said.

Dead silence.

"You're not going anywhere this evening," Mom finally said. "Marty can come for dinner, too. And Althea, if she's not tied up with Kwasi—or he can come, too—and Stella. And I'm sure Vonda will stop by to see how you're doing."

"I'll bring beer," Dillon volunteered with a smile so broad it made me want to sock him.

IN THE END, IT WAS ONLY MARTY AND MOM AND ME FOR dinner. Agent Dillon called to say he was tied up at the office and Althea and Kwasi already had plans. I wondered briefly if he'd heard about Daphne setting the theater on fire and regretted not giving me her number. Vonda stopped by earlier, hugged me convulsively, and read me the riot act. I lay passively in my bed upstairs at Mom's, surrounded by the detritus of Alice Rose's and my childhood. I plucked at the tufts on the chenille bedspread as Vonda vented.

"No more investigating," she said, wagging a finger in my face. "You found the real murderer so now you can leave it alone. Let the police and the courts do their thing. I heard Simone is pressing the DA to drop all charges against Stella's hubby in light of the evidence against Daphne."

"I'm not so sure Daphne murdered Audrey and Barnes," I said.

"Of course she did," Vonda said incredulously, widening her eyes under the fringe of platinum bangs. "And she almost killed you, too."

"I'm pretty sure that was an accident," I said, conscious of pain in my palms and head.

"Accident, shmaccident. She lured you into the theater so she could kill you."

"If she wanted to kill me, she had her chance after I jumped from the building."

"She probably thought you were dead," Vonda said. "Or

she didn't have time with the firemen almost there. You need to lay low until the police apprehend her."

"She's a kid, not a criminal mastermind . . . How long can it take for the police to catch up with her?"

DAPHNE WAS STILL MISSING AT DINNERTIME. MARTY filled us in on the chase after Mom dished him a huge serving of meatloaf, mashed potatoes, and collard greens. I got substantially less because I didn't have much appetite. Mom gave me a sharp look but didn't say anything.

"She withdrew the maximum from her account at a bank ATM outside Brunswick half an hour after you called 911 and there's been no trace of her, or your car, since," Marty said.

"Great." If I had to buy a new car, it would be that much longer before I could save up a down payment for a house. I struggled to spear a bit of collard greens with my bandaged hand but gave it up in frustration, dropping my fork on the table. Ignoring Mom who was preparing to feed me a bite off a fork she got from the utensil drawer, I unwrapped the bandages around my right hand and peeked under the dressing taped to my palm. It didn't look as bad as I'd expected: a little red around the stitches—six in one spot and four in another—but not inflamed. I flexed my hand gently. It stung, but I could manage. I removed the bandage from the other hand, letting it spool to the floor.

"Grace Ann—" Mom began warningly.

I gave her the "I'm thirty years old and can be stupid if I want to" look and forked up a bite of meatloaf. I was hungrier than I realized. I inhaled half the meal while Marty talked.

"Michaelson's lawyer is lobbying to have all charges against him dropped. The DA is waffling. The case against Daphne is purely circumstantial, but then so's the one against Michaelson."

"Except for the cape," I reminded him.

He waved his fork dismissively. "Anyone could have dumped it in Michaelson's pickup. The DA knows that's not enough to convict. And Daphne Oliver's motive is stronger: she wanted revenge on the pageant she saw as killing her sister. No one's quite sure why Michaelson would want to kill his girlfriend."

I guessed word of the pregnancy hadn't leaked.

"What about the pageant?" Mom asked. "I hope that's finally been cancelled."

Marty shook his head and swallowed quickly so he could answer. "Nope. Jodi cancelled tonight's evening gown competition, but she's going to combine it with the finale tomorrow night. They'll do the evening gown bit, take a short intermission to tabulate the scores, announce the finalists, and crown Miss Magnolia Blossom."

"Does the woman have no sense?" Mom asked.

"I guess the contestants will have to manage their own hair," I said, holding up my hands.

Marty took one gently in his and kissed my fingertips. "They'll get by," he said. "You just rest."

"I second that," Mom said, rising to stack the dishes in the sink.

"I'm feeling a lot better," I said. "My headache's almost gone. A good night's sleep and I'll be good as new."

Mom peered at me skeptically.

"Don't worry—I'm not going to try to do the girls' hair. I'm going to have a quiet morning looking at houses with Kevin Faye."

"I'd go with you," Mom said, "but I've got a full schedule of appointments tomorrow. Althea's coming in to help. And Stella said she could be here most of the day." She started loading the dishwasher.

"You're really serious about buying a house? Here?" Marty asked, his brows drawing together slightly.

I looked at him, puzzled. "I'm tired of renting, of needing someone's permission before I paint a wall or plant a camellia bush. Why?"

He shrugged. "Houses tie you down. It's harder to be spontaneous, take advantage of situations that present themselves, when you're tied to bricks and mortar. That's why I rent my condo."

"What kind of situations?" I asked, all too conscious of Mom at the sink. Something about the line of her back and the way she held her head still told me she was listening hard.

"Stories. Promotions. Opportunities." He flung his hands out expansively.

"Those aren't the sorts of things that crop up in my life," I observed wryly.

"Walk me to my car," Marty said. He thanked Mom for dinner and helped me stand. My head swam and he put his arm around my waist. He smelled good.

We walked around the side of the house, listening to the *chirr* of crickets and admiring the great golden ball of the moon as it hung low on the horizon. When we reached Marty's MINI, I leaned back against the still warm metal, my feet on the curb, and Marty faced me. The moonlight showed his face plainly, but I couldn't read his expression. He took a couple steps to his right, then wheeled and returned to where I stood.

"I've been offered a job. In Washington," he said. His gaze fixed on my face.

I licked my suddenly dry lips. "DC?"

He nodded.

"And?"

"And what?"

"Are you going to take it?"

"I don't know," he said.

"DC's a long way away. Farther than Atlanta." Ye gods, could I make a more obvious comment? I blamed it on the concussion.

"They have beauty salons in DC, I'm pretty sure," he said, looking at me from the corners of his eyes.

I caught my breath. We'd only been dating a few months—surely he wasn't asking me to move to DC with him?

"Just an observation," he added hastily.

He kicked at a pinecone on the sidewalk and it skittered into the street. A car shushed by on the next street over and someone hollered out his back door for "Omar," stringing the word out for three seconds. I didn't know if Omar was a pet or a kid. I took a deep breath and let myself think how I would feel if Marty left Georgia. Sad. Not brokenhearted, but definitely sad.

"On the one hand, DC is the center of gravity for national politics. On the other, I'd have to give up the Lansky story; readers outside Georgia just won't care that much. The *Journal-Constitution* has matched the salary offer, so that's a wash." He paced to and fro, changing direction with each point he made.

"I'd miss you," I said.

He stopped pacing. "Would you?"

I nodded. He leaned in and kissed me, his lips firm against mine. His hands held my upper arms and drew me tightly against him. I started to tangle my fingers in his hair, but it hurt my palms, so I linked my arms around his neck and pulled his head closer. The kiss grew hotter, more demanding. The veranda light came on, its yellow glow not quite reaching us. Mom. You'd think I was still in high school. Marty pulled away, smiling ruefully. "You'd better go in. Unless you'd like me to drive you back to your place?" His voice was hopeful.

I was tempted, but I didn't want a concussion and stitched-up hands taking the edge off our first time. "Mom would have a conniption fit," I said. "Rain check?"

"Absolutely." He kissed me, quickly and hard, then stood by the car as I ascended the veranda stairs. I turned to wave before going inside and snapping off the light. Mom was nowhere in sight. Marty tooted his horn as he drove off and I floated upstairs, still tingling from his kiss, barely even aware of my aches and pains.

Chapter Thirty

ALTHOUGH MY HEADACHE WAS BETTER SATURDAY morning, it seemed like every other spot on my body ached or stung or just plain hurt. My drop from the burning Oglethorpe had landed me with bruises or scrapes on my elbows, fanny, hip, knees, and cheek. I flexed my hands. The stitches pulled, but the pain wasn't as sharp as yesterday. I swallowed two of the pills the doctor had given me.

Mom was already in the salon with an early client when I came downstairs dressed in lightweight navy slacks and a red and white striped blouse with wide cuffs. We'd stopped by my apartment to pick up a few things on our way home from the hospital yesterday. I might look like I'd gone three rounds with a gorilla, but at least I was well dressed for my house viewings with Kevin Faye. Given the conversation with Marty the night before, I considered cancelling with

Kevin. Maybe Marty was right and owning a house would tie me down, imprison me in St. Elizabeth.

Except this was my home and I felt more comfortable here than I ever had in Atlanta. I was a small-town girl at heart. Which didn't mean I'd refuse to move for the right opportunity . . . or the right man. But I needed to make some smart decisions for myself, and buying a house was definitely a smarter move than pouring rent money down the drain each month. I would look for a house because it's what I needed to do for me right now—that didn't mean I couldn't sell it someday if circumstances changed.

With my decision made and despite feeling under the weather, I was excited by the prospect of looking at houses. Maybe I'd fall in love with something today. And make an offer. And fill out mountains of credit forms. And saddle myself with a lifetime of debt. My stomach churned but I put that down to hunger and ate a bowl of Cap'n Crunch. I was about to leave for Faye's office when a sound like a sob drifted in from the salon.

Barefoot, I hurried down the hall to where I could see my mom's station. Darryl Michaelson sat there, his face in his hands. Standing behind him, shears in her hand, Mom patted his shoulder.

"She trusts you, Violetta," Darryl said, straightening up and talking to Mom's reflection in the mirror. His dark red hair was shorter on one side than the other and strain made him look older. "You're like a second mom to Stel. Can you talk to her for me? Get her to give us another try?"

"Stella's a grown woman, Darryl. I don't have the right to try and influence her when it comes to her marriage. And it wouldn't do any good for *me* to convince her. You have to do it. Have you told her you're sorry about the affair?" Mom asked.

"God, yes!" Darryl pounded the arm of the chair with his fist. "But she—"

I tiptoed back to the kitchen, not wanting to eavesdrop. Okay, I wanted to listen, but it wouldn't be right.

I slipped on my red sandals and pushed through the screen door. Only then did I remember I didn't have my car. Darn that Daphne. I wondered if the police had caught up with her yet. Maybe they had my car safely tucked away somewhere.

"No," Agent Dillon said when I dialed his number from my mom's kitchen phone. Daphne had my cell phone, too; it was in my purse. "No sign of her or your car. We figure she's abandoned your car by now—in an airport lot or a shed somewhere—and has different transportation. We can't reach Thad Wissing this morning—his wife says he's on a business trip—and it's possible he's helping her."

"Is it possible they were in it together all along?" I asked.

"It's not *im*possible," he said.

"What about the baby?" I asked.

"What about it?" His tone said don't even bother asking.

I asked anyway. "Was it Darryl's?" I thought of the anguished man in Mom's salon and found myself praying that the answer would be no.

"Is there anything else the GBI can help you with this morning, Miss Terhune?" Dillon asked with faux politeness.

"Anything *else*? That would imply you've already helped me with something, wouldn't it? But the woman who almost got me killed is still missing, as is my car, and I'm going to be late getting to the Realtor's."

"Then I won't keep you any longer," he said with something that sounded like a chuckle. He hung up.

I stared at the phone in my hand for a moment, tempted

to fling it at the wall, but reason prevailed. I hoofed it the three blocks to my apartment and dug my bicycle out of the garden shed where I kept it. A spider dangled from the handlebars, but the tires looked good, so I brushed off the arachnid and wheeled it into the yard, holding it with my fingertips so I didn't disturb the stitches. Pale blue with a metal basket between the handlebars, the bicycle was old fashioned with no gears. Thankfully, St. Elizabeth is flatter than a bookmark. Realizing I still had some time before I needed to meet Kevin Faye, I let myself into my apartment with the spare key I kept at Mom's.

I smiled at the watercolor landscapes by local artists that hung on my living room wall; it felt good to be home, surrounded by my stuff. Somehow, when I stay at Mom's, I always feel like an adolescent, with all the pluses and minuses that implies. Maybe it's because all my old Nancy Drew mysteries clutter the bookshelves and Alice Rose's old twirling costumes are in the closet. Or maybe there's something in the air at Mom's that zaps me back to my teen years, but I feel more *me*, more adult, in my own place. Even when that place isn't really mine but belongs to my landlady. I couldn't imagine how adult I'd feel in a house I actually *owned*. Well, co-owned with the bank. I grinned at the thought.

I started toward the kitchen, but a dripping sound halted me. I listened. *Plip.* Pause. *Plip.* It sounded like it was coming from my bathroom. I detoured through my bedroom and turned off the tap at the sink. Darn. If I'd left it dripping yesterday, there was no telling how many gallons of water I'd wasted. Probably dozens because the bathroom felt humid, almost like I'd taken a shower. I'm usually more careful. I gave the tap another hard twist and headed for the kitchen. The Cap'n Crunch was already wearing off and

I needed a sandwich before tromping through a bunch of prospective homes.

Pulling the ham and cheddar from the deli drawer, I grabbed the mustard and pickles, too, wincing at the feel of the cold jars on my hurt palms. Depositing my sandwich fixings on the cutting board, I opened the door to my walk-in pantry and yanked on the string that turned on the light. A single slice of wheat bread and a heel was all I could find in the bread box. Had I eaten the whole loaf already? I made a mental note to add bread to my shopping list. It seemed like every time I turned around, I needed more groceries. Slapping the sandwich together, I ate it standing over the sink, drinking a glass of milk.

I glanced at my watch and saw I was going to be late for Kevin Faye if I didn't hustle. I returned to my bathroom to brush my teeth and run a comb through my hair. A slick of rose lipstick and I was ready. As I was crossing the room, I felt a little *pfft* from my shirt and then heard a *clickety-click* as the button bounced on the floor. I looked down at my blouse to see it gaping open, displaying pink bra and cleavage. I did not need this.

I scanned the floor for the button but didn't see it. Probably under the dresser or the bed. Dropping to my knees, I peered under the bed. Whew. I really needed to vacuum under here. Dust bunny central. I stuck my arm under the bed and swept my palm lightly across the floor, snagging the button on the second pass. Placing it on my dresser to sew on later, I stripped off my blouse and walked to the closet. It's really more of a large cupboard with a hanging rod; it wouldn't have surprised me to hear that Mrs. Jones's son got it at Home Depot in the garage organizer section. Luckily, I'm not much of a clotheshorse.

I pulled the door open and stared into a pair of startled blue eyes. "Aaagh!" I jumped back.

"No!" the intruder said, sounding as scared as I was. She half fell, half stepped out of the closet.

I was at the bedroom door, headed for outside and safety when a soft voice said, "Wait. Please."

On the threshold, I turned, still poised to flee. Daphne Oliver stood there, hair straggling damply to her shoulders, wearing a white tee shirt and a pair of khaki shorts with the tag still hanging off them. "I'm sorry I scared you," she said. "I didn't think you'd be here."

She was clearly unarmed and her expression was so pleading—not the blank face of yesterday's firebug—that I stayed.

First things first: "Where's my car?"

She hung her head. "At the airport. In Atlanta. I left it there and took the shuttle back to St. Elizabeth. I couldn't think where else to go."

"Did you buy that outfit with my money?"

She nodded.

Well, at least it looked more like Target couture than Saks Fifth Avenue. "Give me back my purse."

She ducked into the closet, rooted around on the floor, and dragged my purse out by the strap. I snatched it from her and looked inside. Everything seemed to be there, including my keys. It had never crossed my mind that she had my keys, along with my purse and wallet. Like the police, I figured she was long gone from St. Elizabeth, maybe long gone from Georgia.

"I'm really sorry," she said again. She rubbed at her reddened eyes. "After . . . after everything yesterday, when the ambulance took you, I thought you'd be in the hospital for a couple of nights and I could hide out here and think what to do. I really screwed up, huh?"

I bit back the "You think?" that came to mind. "You have to go to the police, Daphne," I said.

"They'll put me in jail. My mom and dad will be so upset. I only wanted to stop the pageant. To stop girls from entering beauty contests and ruining their lives." Water from her wet hair wicked down the cotton shirt, leaving trails like tear streams.

"Like Leda," I said gently.

She sniffed. "She wasn't just my sister—she was my best friend. I used to hear her throwing up in our bathroom, making herself throw up after every meal practically. It was awful. I thought she was getting better—we all did—but then she entered that stupid pageant." Her hands balled into fists. "I didn't set out to hurt anyone. No one was supposed to be at the theater. You weren't supposed to be there." She frowned at me.

Right. It was my fault I got hurt saving her life. And what about poisoning the judges, I wanted to ask. Daphne didn't have the tightest grip on reality and I didn't want to send her to whatever unhappy place she'd been in yesterday. "Why don't we call your folks?" I said, moving toward the phone.

"Dr. Yarrow told us we have to act on our convictions," she said. "He said it's our responsibility as citizens to be bold and make changes. 'Be the change you want to see in the world,' he says."

"I think Gandhi said it first," I said dryly, having seen an inspirational poster with that quotation on it somewhere. It seemed like Kwasi had brought his plagiarism habit to Georgia. I picked up the phone and dialed the GBI number by heart. "Mrs. Wissing?" I said when Dillon answered. "Daphne's here with me at my apartment."

"Are you okay?" Dillon asked, his voice tense.

"Yes, she's fine, but I think she'd like to see you."

"On my way."

I hung up, my hand shaking slightly.

"The things I tried first didn't work, so I knew I needed to be bolder." She punctuated the last word by pounding her fist on her thigh.

"Why don't we sit down," I suggested, backing toward the living room. Daphne was working herself up again and I didn't want to turn my back on her. "Would you like something to drink? Lemonade?"

"Audrey Faye's death should have ended it," she said, sending a chill up my spine. "Shouldn't it?"

Her blue eyes studied my face, searching for an answer. She looked so young, her skin unwrinkled, a smattering of freckles saddling her nose. But the fixed intensity of her gaze was making me nervous. "Absolutely," I said, backing away.

"And then that evil man with the camera. The gun was so loud! There was so much blood! I almost stepped in it." She put her hands over her ears and scrunched her eyes closed as if to shut out the explosion.

I stared at her, horrified. She'd killed Audrey and Barnes. My pulse thrummed. "I'm going to wait for your parents outside," I said.

A knock sounded on the door and I hurried toward it. A glance over my shoulder showed Daphne still standing in my bedroom, her hands clutching her ears like she would pull them off. Agent Dillon burst through the door, gun drawn, followed by two SEPD officers. Sizing up the situation, Dillon holstered his gun and drew me aside as the uniformed officers advanced into the bedroom. Daphne didn't even look up until one of them put his hand on her shoulder. She docilely let them cuff her and lead her out, only asking as they reached the door, "Where's my mom?"

I shivered and Dillon drew me close, hugging me against the solid warmth of his body. "She killed them," I said into his shoulder. Despite my distress, a little tingle fluttered through me at the solid feel of his chest under my cheek. I arched back so I could see his face as I told him everything Daphne had said.

"Nice bra," he said when I finished, stroking his hand down my bare back. His eyes glinted wickedly.

Zing! Electricity shot through me, warming my whole body. I jerked away. I'd completely forgotten I was shirtless. "You stay here," I said, marching into the bedroom and closing the door. I leaned against it for a moment, breathing deeply. At least it was my nicest bra, pearly pink lace that wasn't all stretched out and dingy like some of my others.

"Are you sure?" he called.

No. "Yes." I fumbled in a drawer for a tee shirt and pulled it on, catching my breath when one of my stitches snagged on the fabric. I returned to the living room, hair disheveled, my eyes daring him to comment.

"They'll have processed Daphne by the time I get back," he said, all business now, although I caught the hint of a smile. "I'll see what she has to say about what she told you. Her parents will be there, and I'm sure they'll have a lawyer; it'll be a mess."

"This will get Darryl off the hook, right? Her confession?"

"*If* she confesses and *if* she has the details to back it up," he cautioned. "Keep all this"—he gestured around my apartment, taking in everything that had happened—"under your hat. I'll get back to you when I can, okay?"

Nodding, I walked him to the door. "Thanks for coming so quickly," I said.

"Always." He surprised me with a light kiss on top of my head and strode toward his car, parked askew with the front wheels on the sidewalk.

The sight of his car reminded me that my Fiesta was in Atlanta and I was late for my appointment with Kevin Faye.

Chapter Thirty-one

✂

MY FOREHEAD DRIPPED SWEAT AND MY CRISP SHIRT
was as soggy as the Cap'n Crunch in the bottom of my
cereal bowl by the time I biked the two miles to Faye's
office. He took one look at me and offered me a bottle of
water. "Thanks," I said, gulping thirstily, my hands cupped
awkwardly around the bottle since the bike ride had inflamed my stitches. I sat in the same chair as before while
he seated himself behind the desk.

He looked past me to the bike I had parked on the sidewalk. "What happened to your car?" he asked. "Or are you
on some kind of exercise kick?"

I told him about the fire and about Daphne stealing my
car. Mindful of Dillon's warning, I left it at that.

He sat back in his chair when I finished, looking astonished. "Good heavens! I had no idea. I heard about the

Oglethorpe burning, of course, but I didn't know it was arson or that you were involved."

"Please don't say I was involved with arson." I laughed. "I just happened to be there when the fire broke out."

"That's a little strange, isn't it? That you just happened to be there?"

He gave me a funny look and I wondered if he thought I was behind the sabotage meant to derail his wife's pageant. It didn't matter; soon, everyone would know about Daphne.

I held up my hands in a surrender gesture. "Hey, I'm just trying to prove that—" I broke off, realizing that mentioning Darryl Michaelson, his wife's lover, would not win me any sensitivity prizes. So instead of saying I was trying to prove Darryl innocent by finding the real killer—and had succeeded—I asked, "How many houses are we going to look at?"

"Four." He passed a slim stack of printouts across the desk to me.

I scanned them eagerly, drawn in by the photos on each one. Three were ranch style while one looked like a small, two-story Victorian with carnation gingerbread along the eaves and gabled windows.

"I'll tell you about them while we're driving," he said. "Ready?" He stood and jangled keys in his pocket.

We went around to the back of the strip mall where his black Mercedes was parked. A spatter of bird poop decorated the windshield. "Damn pigeons." Faye stomped to the rear of the car. He got paper towels and a spray bottle of window cleaner from the trunk and scrubbed off the poop. I watched in silence, trying to remember the last time I'd even run my Fiesta through the car wash. March, maybe?

The interior of the car was equally pristine. I buckled my seat belt gingerly, afraid of leaving finger smudges on the metal tab. Keeping up a steady flow of conversation about current mortgage rates, the different kinds of loans, short sales, and foreclosures, Kevin Faye put the car in gear and drove to the first house, located on the south side of town, just a couple of blocks from the beach. The location sounded great and I wondered why the house would be in my price range. One sniff answered the question. The house reeked of cats and never-emptied litter boxes. I was sure the smell had soaked into the walls and flooring. We didn't make it past the front hall.

The second house was more promising. Painted white, it had flower beds full of zinnias, sunflowers, and petunias fronting the house. "The owners are U.S. Navy—they got short-notice orders to Japan," Kevin said, unlocking the front door, "and I think they'd take an offer ten thou under the asking price."

I took notes as we walked through the small rooms, liking the light that flooded through windows on all sides of the house, but wary of what looked like an old water stain on the kitchen ceiling. When we left, Kevin had trouble with the lockbox and I wandered back to the Mercedes while he fought with it. The car was unlocked and I sat in the passenger seat with the door open, studying the printouts. Raucous *caw-caw*s and the beating of wings signaled the arrival of a flock of crows. Soaring low over the car, they settled by the sunflowers. I noticed that one of them had deposited a great white splat on the hood of the car. Since Kevin was still wrestling with the lockbox, I leaned over and punched the trunk button, thinking I'd clean it up before he saw it. I wasn't sure the man's blood pressure could withstand two such besmirchings in one day.

I had just reached the trunk when Kevin trotted down the porch steps. "Got it," he said, then stopped dead. "What are you doing in my trunk?"

The cold snap of his voice startled me. "Nothing. I was going to get the Windex. A bird—"

"I knew you knew." His voice was flat and his eyes glittered.

"Knew what?" I backed up a step as he marched toward me, his steps crisping in the sun-parched yard.

"You saw me in the theater that night. I knew it when I talked to you about Audrey's death and you were so evasive. She was alive when you found her, wasn't she? She told you."

"She was dead. She didn't say anything. I don't know what you're talking about." But I did. He'd killed Audrey. I'd felt all along that Daphne wasn't a murderer, but her jumbled words had sounded like a confession. The lethality radiating off Kevin Faye convinced me he'd done it.

He went on like I hadn't said a word. "And then you tracked me down with this story about wanting to buy a house. Why me out of all the Realtors in town? Huh? I don't know what your game is, why you haven't told the police, but if you think you can blackmail me, you're sadly mistaken. Like that Barnes character with his veiled threats on TV. I knew it was just a matter of time before he approached me, tried to bleed me."

He slammed the trunk shut with an emphatic clang. "You didn't find anything in there, did you? Did you think I'd be so stupid I wouldn't clean it? I even replaced the carpet in case there might be some trace of blood from the clothes I wore that night. Get in." A gun had appeared in his hand. I'd bet my down payment it was the gun that killed Sam Barnes. Kevin Faye kept it pulled in close to his body, hidden from any neighbors who might glance out their windows.

I evaluated my options. I could run—but not faster than a bullet. I could scream and hope someone called 911. I could comply and let him drive me to some out-of-the-way scrap of woods and put a bullet in me. I opened my mouth to scream and he said, "Don't even think about it. If you make a scene, I'll drive straight from here to your mother's place and put a bullet through her while she's blow-drying someone's hair. I've got nothing to lose, so don't try me. Get. In. The car."

I believed him. I got in.

Chapter Thirty-two

✂

FAYE SHOOK HIS HEAD. "UH-UH. YOU DRIVE." HE KEPT the gun trained on me as I walked around to the driver's side and got in. I made a show of examining the dashboard and trying the windshield wipers, playing for every minute I could get.

"Just drive," he ordered.

I turned the key and the door locks *thunk*ed loudly. Great. Locked in a car with a man waving a gun around. "Where to?"

He scrubbed the hand with the gun along the side of his face and then leveled it at me. "I don't know. Just drive. Let me think." One strand of his gelled hair came loose and flopped over his ear.

I backed out of the driveway and drove slowly, hoping to see a jogger or a postal carrier . . . anyone I could signal for help. The street was deserted. When I reached the cross street, Faye said, "West. Head west and take I-95 north."

I drove slowly, trying to use just my fingertips on the steering wheel since my palms hurt like the dickens. We passed Doralynn's restaurant and I noted plenty of tourists on the patio, chatting and eating under the striped umbrellas. I stopped at a crosswalk as a group of preschoolers in tie-dyed shirts crossed two by two under the supervision of a young black man and a woman with long gray hair. No way could I put the kids at risk by trying to alert the adults to my situation. The last kid in line, a Chinese boy with black bangs cut straight across his forehead, waved at me and I forced a smile.

Several blocks later we came abreast of the Oglethorpe. I smelled it before I saw it. Even with the windows up and the air-conditioning humming, the scent of charred wood and chemicals freed from plastics and fabrics by the flames seeped in. The blackened ruin of the building, still square and solid looking, loomed on the left. Both Faye and I turned our heads to study it as the car glided past.

"I shoulda thought of that," Faye said. "After I shot Barnes, I shoulda torched the place."

"Why did you kill Audrey?" I asked as the car approached the on-ramp for I-95.

Faye waited until I had merged successfully before answering. "Do you know what she told me that night?"

I shook my head when he paused for my response. "No."

"That she was pregnant." He ground the words out.

I depressed the accelerator, thinking that if I got stopped for speeding I'd have a chance to alert the trooper. Faye spoiled my plan almost immediately.

"Slow down." The cold muzzle of the gun pressed against my temple and I eased my foot off the pedal. "If we get pulled over, I'll shoot the cop first and then you." He kept the gun at my head for a few moments and then pulled it back. "She told me she was pregnant."

"And you knew it wasn't yours."

I caught his startled response out of the corner of my eye. "That's right," he agreed after a moment. "It couldn't have been mine. We had all the tests done when she didn't conceive. It seems my sperm aren't lively enough." He barked out a bitter laugh. "Well, she's not so lively now.

"I'd already been thinking about killing her, you know," he said.

I arched my brows in surprise and he nodded. "Oh, yes. I knew she was screwing around on me, seeing that Michaelson guy, and I needed the insurance money. My properties in Florida are being foreclosed on . . . the Delta Bayou project isn't getting off the ground . . ." He paused and worried at the mole on his temple with his left hand. "But I wanted to plan it all out, have an airtight alibi, do it right. But then she told me about the pregnancy, said she was divorcing me, and I just snapped. You can understand that, can't you?" He slewed his body in the seat so he was almost facing me.

"Sure," I said.

"I grabbed up that file thing and stabbed at her. God, what a mess! Blood everywhere. All over my shirt, my hands . . . I wasn't expecting that. I had to think fast, grab the cape off the rack to cover my clothes. And then you saw me when I was leaving."

I didn't bother telling him that I couldn't have picked him out of a lineup featuring Brad Pitt and Ronald McDonald.

"I got rid of the cape in the parking lot—tossed it into Michaelson's truck. I'd followed Audrey to one of her hook ups with him so I damn well knew his truck. The bastard! I put the police onto him by telling them about him screwing my wife."

I glanced over to see a smile of grim satisfaction twisting his face.

"And I know she said something to you. What did she say?" His skin pulsed under his jaw and his eyes bored into me.

I was tired of him not believing that Audrey was dead before I entered the room. "She said she loved you, that she forgave you," I said.

"Liar!" He screamed into my ear from inches away.

Spittle landed on my cheek and I flinched away from him.

"Audrey never forgave anyone anything. She could hold a grudge like nobody's business." He sank back against the seat and the gun settled onto his thigh. "She didn't really say anything, did she?"

"No."

We drove in silence for another ten minutes. Just when I was hoping that Faye had drifted off, he gestured with the gun. "Get off at the next exit. There's a cabin that's been on the market for months—I showed it once a couple months back. Nobody lives in it. It's out in the middle of goddamned nowhere without a neighbor for miles. If anyone hears the shot, they'll just assume it's a hunter a little bit ahead of the season. There's bound to be a shovel in the garage," he muttered to himself.

My fingers tightened on the steering wheel. I tried to clear my head so I could come up with an escape plan, but random images and thoughts whirled in my brain. I pictured my mother's grief if I never turned up again and it nearly brought tears. I felt sad that my young nephews, Alice Rose's boys, wouldn't remember me in a few years. I hoped Vonda and Ricky would tie the knot again. Enough!

The practical side of my brain tried to stifle my morbid imagination. What we need here is a plan, it said, not maudlin thoughts.

All I knew was I couldn't afford to let Faye drag me into a deserted house. If we got to the cabin, I was dead. I was actually considering hitting the brakes and trying to leap out of the moving car when a flash of lights in the rearview mirror caught my attention. A swirl of blue and red strobed from the light bar atop a state patrol vehicle. My heartbeat sped up and I kept my eyes glued to the mirror, certain the trooper was going to pass us on his way to an accident up the road. But the blue car with red lettering stayed behind us and gave a single whoop of the siren. The silhouette of a lone cop, familiar Smoky the Bear hat on his head, sat behind the steering wheel.

Faye shifted to look over his shoulder. "Shit! What did you do? Are you speeding?"

"No." I tried to sound calm but my voice shook. "Maybe the taillight's out or something."

His eyes narrowed and he brought the gun up again. "Get off here." He pointed at the upcoming exit. "Then pull over."

He didn't spell out his plan, but I saw the implacability in his eyes before he dropped them to the gun, ejected the cartridge, and slammed it home again. If I did what he told me to, an innocent state trooper would die. And me, too.

I signaled for the turn and slowed. A sloping off-ramp led to a four-way stop at an intersection surrounded by nothing but piney woods. Not a McDonald's or 7-Eleven in sight. The state trooper followed us off the highway and suddenly I knew what I had to do. Saying a quick prayer, I gunned the engine and drove straight for the stop sign. The car's sudden acceleration flung both Faye and me back against the seat. Thirty miles an hour . . . forty.

"Don't—" Faye shouted, then raised the gun and fired at me.

The noise deafened me and my hands jerked on the wheel. The window beside me blew out, showering safety glass chunks over my head and chest and into my lap. Hot air streamed in. Before Faye could fire again, I stomped the brake pedal as hard as I could and the car slid the last few feet into the stop sign, impacting near the passenger-side headlight. *Crunch.*

I whipped forward into the exploding air bag. "Unh!" It punched my breath out and smothered my face. A powdery substance drifted through the car, making me cough. Faye coughed beside me and I couldn't tell if he was seriously hurt or not. Panicking now, I fought the deflating fabric and scrabbled at the seat belt, desperate to get out of the car before Faye got loose. I pulled up on the door handle and rammed the door with my elbow, sending a zing of pain shooting up my arm. I hardly noticed it as I leaned my whole weight against the door. It popped open.

I tumbled to the ground, instinctively trying to break my fall with my hands. Loose gravel and roadside debris dug into the already wounded palms and I cried out.

"Police! Lie face down on the ground!" It was a woman's voice, harsh and authoritative.

I complied, lifting my head a fraction of an inch to see where the trooper was. I couldn't see her so I glanced under the car. Faye lay on the ground, his hands behind his head, while a pair of black boots and blue-trousered legs were planted wide six feet in front of him.

"Miss Terhune," the trooper called. "Are you okay?"

How did she know my name? "He's got a gun," I warned the trooper, sitting up and brushing ineffectually at my hair and clothes. Blood from my palms streaked the blouse where I touched it and I stopped. Steam hissed from the car's radiator as I struggled to my feet.

"Not anymore," she said with satisfaction. Metal clinked on metal and she hauled Faye to his feet, his hands cuffed behind his back.

"She's a crazy woman," Faye babbled, jerking his head at me. His hair fell in disordered spikes around his face. "She tried to steal my car. I was trying to stop her—"

A car flew down the exit ramp and screeched to a halt, interrupting Faye. Agent Dillon and another GBI agent got out. Dillon's sharp eyes took in the scene with a glance and he strode toward me. I smiled involuntarily at the sight of his trim figure with the gun holster showing as his sport coat flapped back in the rising wind. "Why the hell didn't you just pull over?" he greeted me.

I glared at him, the sudden pang of happiness I'd felt on seeing him fading quickly. "Faye said he'd kill the cop first, then shoot me if we got pulled over," I told him. My lower lip trembled and I bit it. "How did you know what was going on?" The breeze teased my hair into my eyes and I pushed it back impatiently.

"Daphne. During the interrogation it became clear she hadn't killed Audrey or Barnes, but that she'd seen Barnes get shot. She was in the theater that night, leaving the skunk carcass, when she heard Barnes arguing with someone. She caught a glimpse of them on the stage and hid when she heard the shot. She picked Faye out of a photo lineup."

"How did you know I was with him? Where we were?"

"We drove to his office to arrest him and saw your bicycle there. I thought my heart was going to stop," he admitted. "I put out an APB on Faye and his car and it was less than half an hour before Trooper Garrity radioed in that she'd spotted you." He gently touched an abraded spot on my cheek. "Hurt?"

"Everything hurts," I admitted. I held out my palms.

"Good God," he said. "The doc's not going to be happy with the way you've torn up his handiwork. Does the ER give volume discounts?"

I managed a weak laugh as the other GBI agent stuffed Faye into the back of the state patrol car. A red-tailed hawk soared overhead and I followed it with my eyes until it landed atop a loblolly pine.

"I don't want to go to the hospital," I said. "I just want to go home."

Chapter Thirty-three

✂

HOME WASN'T IN THE CARDS, OF COURSE. AGENT DIL-
lon insisted on carting me off to the ER in his car and
stayed with me while the doc cleaned my hands and re-
bandaged them. At least Dillon honored my request not to
call my mom. I wasn't at death's door and she didn't need
to know I'd ended up in the hospital for the second time
this week. Dillon made a good mom substitute, insisting
I swallow my pain meds on the spot and reading over the
discharge instructions before tucking them into his jacket's
inside pocket. When we were done at the hospital, he took
me to GBI headquarters where I answered questions about
the kidnapping for the better part of two hours. I'd get to
repeat the experience on the stand when Kevin Faye came
to trial. Oh, goody.

Just as I felt myself fading, Agent Dillon, who'd been
watching me closely, called a halt, dismissing the other

agents who were sitting in on the interview. "We can finish this tomorrow," he said. "I'm taking you home." He bullied me into taking more pills with a swallow of warm root beer before escorting me to his car.

I was tired and achy enough not to argue. Sinking back into the seat of his Crown Victoria, I suddenly remembered something. "It was Darryl's baby, wasn't it?"

Dillon shot me a look as he pulled into traffic. "No."

I jerked upright. "No? Then it was Kevin's after all? How ironic."

He shook his head. "We're guessing it was Barnes's. We found some correspondence in his e-mail that suggests the two of them were involved. We're running the tests now. If it's not his . . ." He shrugged. "It's not like we can DNA test the entire male population of Camden County."

Thank God. I leaned back again, immensely grateful that Stella would be spared that particular sorrow. Audrey Faye had led a complicated life, juggling her husband, her ex-husband, and a boyfriend. Something still puzzled me. "But how did Faye leave the death threat and rip up the bikini when he was with you after Audrey's murder?"

"Daphne left the note. She wasn't referring to Audrey's death—she didn't even know Audrey was dead. She was talking about *Leda's* death."

Another thought floated randomly into my narcotic-dimmed brain. "What about Barnes's film? Did that ever turn up?"

Dillon turned onto Mom's street. "He'd uploaded it to an online storage site. There was absolutely nothing remotely related to the murder on it. He got himself killed for nothing." Disgust and regret sounded in his voice. He hadn't liked the man, but he was saddened by a pointless death; I liked that about him.

We pulled up at the curb and Dillon came around to help me out. I stumbled when I stepped out, more woozy than I'd realized, and he caught me with an arm around my waist. The salon door burst open and Mom and Althea tumbled out, followed by Marty. Glancing around, I spotted his yellow MINI across the street. Marty reached us first, his long legs carrying him past the women.

"Agent Dillon," he said neutrally. He and Dillon had met during the DuBois case and their different goals—the age-old tension between reporters and cops—had resulted in some antagonism.

"Shears."

The men nodded at each other.

Mom broke the silence by bustling up and hugging me and Agent Dillon together. "Oh, thank goodness! Marty was telling us what happened—"

"Police scanner plus a couple phone calls," Marty said, looking pleased as Dillon's jaw tightened.

"—and we've been frantic for the last hour."

"I'm sorry," I mumbled.

Althea turned a sharp eye on me. "Don't be keeping Grace standing around out here when anyone can see she's about to fall flat on her face," she scolded the others. She slipped an arm around my waist and Mom got on my other side, nudging Dillon aside gently.

Dillon fell back a step and gave me a half smile. "Looks like you're in good hands," he said.

"You boys run along and find something useful to do," Althea told Dillon and Marty over her shoulder. "We're putting Grace Ann to bed."

Chapter Thirty-four

I DOZED MOST OF THE REMAINDER OF THE AFTER-noon. With only an hour to go before the pageant finale started, I rested in the hammock just below the veranda, half drowsing as the sun warmed my face. My newly gauze-mittened hands rested on my stomach and I let the scents of magnolia and pine drift over me. I didn't even look up when a car door slammed and someone climbed the steps to the veranda. A hair client, I assumed, although I'd thought Mom was done for the day.

Apparently, she was because her voice filtered to me a few minutes later, along with the clink of ice cubes in tea glasses. "Why don't you sit a spell?" Mom asked someone.

I considered opening my eyes to see who it was, but that would be too much effort.

"I don't want to be a bother . . . It's just that . . . Oh, Vi, I don't know what to do."

It was Stella. A bee hummed past my face and I snorted air at it. The painkillers the doc had given me were numbing more than my hands; I felt like my brain was working at half its normal speed.

"Should I try to work things out with Darryl or make our split permanent?" Stella asked. A chair scraped against the veranda.

"Do you love him?" Mom asked.

"I do," Stella said, sounding sad about it. "I always have. Do you think I'm terminally stupid?"

"To love your husband?" Mom sounded surprised. "Of course not."

"But he cheated on me. He slept with another woman!"

"That will take some forgiving," Mom admitted, "if you decide you want to stay with him."

"I don't know if I've got that kind of forgiveness in me," Stella said.

"I wouldn't worry about that. No one's got that kind of forgiveness all on their own—it comes from God. But I think we have to at least want to want to forgive before He blesses us with it."

"Jess would be devastated if we got divorced."

Mom didn't respond to that and I breathed in deeply. Someone was barbecuing not too far away.

Stella spoke again. "You know, Vi, Darryl betrayed me. He did. But there's all kinds of betrayals that happen every day in a long-term relationship of any kind. I betrayed him, too."

At least, I thought that's what she said, but her voice had dropped to a whisper and I wasn't sure.

"How?" Mom asked calmly.

Clearly, she wasn't expecting a confession of orgies or domestic violence or anything too heinous.

"After Audrey was murdered, I thought . . . I wondered . . . just for a moment, if maybe Darryl . . ."

"If he'd done it?"

"Mm-hm."

Mom was quiet again and it struck me how much she said when she didn't say anything. How had I known her for thirty years and not noticed that before? I yawned and wondered vaguely if I should let them know I was here. Too late, I decided. I was drifting off again when Mom finally spoke.

"Every marriage goes through its rough patches, Stella, whether it's an affair, or neglect, or just getting bored with each other. And like you said, there's the everyday betrayals like telling a story on your spouse that would embarrass him, or refusing intimacy as a way of getting back at him, or sharing things with a friend—even a girlfriend—that you ought to be sharing with your mate. When Gene and I had been married a little over six years, I let myself get interested in another man."

That jolted me awake. My eyelids popped open and I stared up at a cornflower sky shredded with clouds that looked like lint from a giant's dryer filter.

"It doesn't matter who it was—he's long gone from St. Elizabeth's—and nothing ever happened between us beyond a conversation or two that was more intimate than it should have been. But I thought about him. I'd iron or mop or weed the garden and let myself think about what it would be like to be with him. It turned me away from Gene for a few months."

Sorrow colored my mother's voice and I couldn't decide if I wanted to comfort her or shout at her. How come she'd never told me this?

"And then one day I woke up and looked at the wrongness of what I was doing. And I worked hard at putting that other man out of my mind and focused on loving my Gene the way I'd promised at the altar, forsaking all others. You know," Mom said, her voice brisker, "you don't have to make up your mind right this minute. Give it time. See how it feels."

"Darryl wants me to go to counseling with him," Stella said, some quality in her voice acknowledging Mom's story without actually commenting on it. An airplane droned past overhead and obscured part of her next sentence. ". . . I will."

"I think that's a good idea," Mom said. "Sometimes— almost all the time—it takes more guts and grit to work on a marriage than to walk away. Will we see you at the pageant tonight?"

"Wouldn't miss it," Stella said. "Rachel's wearing an old dress of mine and I can't wait to see her in it. I think she's got a real shot at winning the crown. Can't you just see it? Our Rachel as Miss Magnolia Blossom?"

I lay in the hammock long after Stella left and Mom cleared away the tea glasses, thinking about relationships and the pure, deep color of the sky as it expanded into space.

Chapter Thirty-five

THE PROTESTORS, MINUS DAPHNE, LINED THE SIDE-walk outside the high school when Mom and I showed up for the beauty pageant. The sun, low on the horizon, warmed the red brick of the old building and softened the graffiti sprayed on the sidewalk and bike racks. If I squinted my eyes so I couldn't read the words, the fat letters and bright colors almost looked like modern art. In honor of the occasion, I wore a red sundress with a deep flounce and high-heeled sandals. I'd removed my gauze wrappings again, but left the bandages on my palms. Mom had French braided my hair and tucked the ends under, leaving my neck bare. She had on a floral patio dress with cap sleeves. It fit loosely and fluttered playfully around my ankles. Scanning the ranks of the protestors, I spotted Althea standing beside Kwasi. I nudged Mom, who looked over at her old friend and sighed.

Althea caught sight of us and her jaw tipped up. She looked like she was going to come over, but Kwasi took her hand and leaned in to say something. I decided on the spot that I wasn't going to tell Althea what Marty had learned about Kwasi "Chuck" Yarrow and his plagiarism. Even if it was true—and I reminded myself that I didn't have proof—it wasn't like he was a Bluebeard or a Madoff or a Ted Bundy. He clearly cared about Althea and if she wanted to know his secrets, she'd ask. Or hire a PI.

Just past the cozy twosome, I spotted a large poster of Leda Wissing. Candles glowed in front of it and a stuffed rabbit leaned against it. I hoped Daphne knew about the makeshift memorial and that it brought her some comfort. The rest of the protestors seemed subdued, hefting their placards halfheartedly and spouting slogans with all the energy of the last-place finisher in a marathon collapsing across the line.

Mom and I had no trouble snaring good seats; even with all the publicity about the murders and the arrests, the auditorium was less than half full. I guessed the townspeople figured all the drama was over. Marty sat between Renata Schott and the other judge at a narrow table shoehorned in front of the first row of seats, just below the stage. The judges were going to have to tip their heads back uncomfortably to even see the contestants. I'd had to watch the premiere of the second Spider-Man movie that way—from the front row—and left the theater with a hideous headache. Marty looked around, saw me, and waved. Renata stole his attention with her hand on his arm and snuggled up a lot closer than necessary to whisper something in his ear. I glared at her back.

Stella, accompanied by Darryl and Jessica, a reed-thin girl with her parents' red hair and braces, slipped into the

seats beside us just as Jodi Keen came onstage and asked
for a moment of silence for Audrey Faye and Sam Barnes.
People obediently bowed their heads and stopped chatting
and texting for the requested minute. The show kicked
off with the contestants performing the dance number I'd
watched them practice. It seemed a little lopsided with only
five girls instead of the twelve or so it was designed for.
Still, they kicked and shimmied enthusiastically and the
applause was generous.

While the contestants scurried offstage to change
into their evening gowns, Jodi introduced the judges and
showed a ten-minute video montage of the contestants at
the nursing home (no footage of vomiting judges made it
into the video) and snuggling kittens at the humane society,
gamboling on the beach, inspecting displays at the marine
museum, and enjoying ice cream on the boardwalk. Then,
the first contestant appeared in her evening gown, and
crossed the stage with a smile glued to her lips. Morgan
came next, in a gold lamé number that was a far cry from
her battle dress uniforms. She got raucous applause and
whistles from a group of young men in the back whose
short hair suggested they might be her army buddies.

As Brooke started across the stage in a sophisticated
maroon dress that crisscrossed over her chest, someone
stepped over people's feet and scrunched past knees to
claim the seat next to Mom. It was Althea. I grinned at her,
surprising myself by how relieved I was to see her.

"Rachel's my friend," she said gruffly. She faced forward, smoothed her brown caftan over her lap, and focused
on the stage. Mom winked at me.

Jodi announced Tabitha and the young woman glided
onto the stage. She looked like Helen of Troy in a Grecian-
style white dress that draped across one shoulder and dipped

low—really low—across her bosom. The skirt looked relatively modest until she moved and a slit revealed her leg up to her hip. Her golden hair shimmered under the lights, a shampoo-ad swathe of blond falling to mid-back. The audience drew in its collective breath and then clapped wildly. With a seductive smile, she waltzed offstage as the judges made notes.

"And our final contestant for tonight's evening gown competition—Rachel Whitley," Jodi announced.

Rachel appeared. Stunned silence.

Beside me, Stella gasped.

"Oh, my," breathed Mom.

Marty turned his head to find me, both brows raised comically, a look of unholy amusement on his face.

"That is too cool," Jessica said, leaning forward. "Can I have an outfit like that?"

"No," her father and mother said together.

With a huge grin on her face, Rachel swayed to midstage. A sleeveless black leotard with a scoop neck hugged her torso while a skirt—a tutu, really—of black netting drifted over a pair of black tights that disappeared into Converse high tops. Black, of course. Her nails gleamed black and kohl rimmed her beautiful eyes. Fingerless black lace gloves covered her arms to the elbow. For a moment, the grape-colored tips of her heavily gelled hair made me wince for the perfection of the cut I'd given her, but then I grinned. This was vintage Rachel.

Sporadic applause sounded around the auditorium until Althea stood and began clapping strongly, giving Rachel a standing ovation. Rachel looked over and smiled gratefully as the rest of us surged to our feet and smacked our hands together. It hurt like hell, but I clapped louder than I ever have.

Rachel waved as she trotted offstage and Jodi said they would tabulate the judges' scores and crown Miss Magnolia Blossom in ten minutes. Feedback squealed from the microphone and people covered their ears.

"She didn't wear my pink dress," Stella said mournfully.

"Oh, get over it, Stel," Althea said. "She's not a pink kind of girl. She's just trying to be true to who she is."

And I knew from the look in her eyes that she was wondering how much of her true self she had sacrificed to be who Kwasi thought she should be. I thought that we might see her clad in J.C. Penney separates the next time she came into the salon.

"I'll bet Jessica can wear that dress one day," Mom consoled Stella, leaning across me to smile at the girl. "Maybe to a prom. It would look gorgeous with your coloring."

Jess smiled back, bouncing in her seat as Jodi came back, an envelope raised high in one hand. For once, she didn't have the clipboard. "If the contestants will please join me on stage," she said and waited while the five girls filed out and stood, holding hands, in the center of the stage. Their expressions ranged from nervous to complacent.

"These five young women are our finalists and I and the whole Miss American Blossom staff congratulate them on their accomplishments." She beamed and led another polite round of applause, setting the mic to screeching again.

"Now, without further ado . . ."

Thank goodness. I was tired of ado.

She named the fourth- and third-runners-up, the girl whose name I couldn't remember and Morgan. Rachel was the second runner-up. As she accepted a bouquet of yellow roses and left the stage, only Brooke and Tabitha were left in the spotlight's glare. I noticed they weren't holding hands anymore.

"Drumroll, please," Jodi tittered, and a recorded drum-roll reverberated through the room.

I inched forward on my chair, finding myself chanting mentally, Let it be Brooke, let it be Brooke.

Jodi went through the rigmarole about the first runner-up taking over if the winner couldn't fulfill her responsibilities, yada-yada, and then said, "The first runner-up is Brooke Baker."

Brooke kept her head high as she left the stage with an armload of flowers, but I glimpsed the searing disappointment on her face. I knew she'd find the money for vet school another way, though. She was the kind of woman who made her own luck, who found a way of turning an apparent loss into a win.

I was still looking at where Brooke had disappeared behind the curtain when Jodi crowed, "And our new Miss Magnolia Blossom is . . . Tabitha Dunn!" Tabitha did her best to look stunned as Jodi secured the rhinestone tiara on her head. She slapped her hands to her face and even squeezed out a tear or two, but the smugness shone through.

Oh, well. Sometimes losers win big. It wouldn't surprise me if Tabitha ended up with the Miss America Blossom crown. I hoped it worked out better for her than it had for Audrey Faye. I kissed Mom's cheek; hugged Althea, Stella, and Jess; nodded at Darryl, and went to congratulate Rachel. I bumped into Marv on the way, carrying microphone cables draped over his tattooed arms.

"Marv! What are you doing here?"

"Running the lights and sound. I've gotta keep my hand in until the theater's rebuilt."

"You're rebuilding?" Given his negative attitude toward the theater, the news surprised me. "I thought you wanted out from under it."

Rubbing his fleshy nose, he said, "Me, too. Until it burned. I couldn't believe how sad it made me to see the bricks all blackened like that. So, I'm rebuilding. If I'm lucky, maybe the fire got rid of the mice. I should reopen by next summer. I've already got a production of *Waiting for Godot* booked in. It's one of my favorites."

I congratulated him and caught up with Rachel in the hall. She was talking to a good-looking blond kid she introduced as Braden after giving me a hug. If the look in his eyes was any indication, he appreciated the real Rachel; he didn't even glance at Tabitha when she swept by in a fog of roses and triumph.

"Stella's not, like, totally upset about the dress, is she?"

"No," I said with a smile. "She understood."

"Great!" Rachel beamed. "Let me change and we can go," she said to Braden.

He shoved his hands in his jeans pockets. "Why don't you just wear that? You look great."

Nice kid, I thought, as another high school–aged girl with waist-length brown hair elbowed her way past a clump of people and stood in front of Rachel and Braden, arms akimbo. She quirked one dark eyebrow. "I didn't think you'd do it, Whitley, but you kicked butt." She lobbed something metallic toward Rachel, who snatched it out of the air. A key ring. "One week, okay?"

"Thanks, Shannon." Rachel jangled the keys victoriously as she and Braden headed off for whatever after-pageant celebration they had planned.

"Ready?" Marty's voice sounded behind me.

I turned with a smile that got broader as I studied his elegant figure in the well-cut tux. His closeness made my tummy do loop-de-loops.

"Well?" he prompted.

"I think I just might be," I said.

My mischievous tone kindled an answering smile that curved his lips and lit his brown eyes. "We are talking about dinner, right?" The look in his eyes said he hoped we weren't.

I tucked my arm in his. "Among other things."

Organic Skin-Care Recipes

Mocha Body Scrub

2 cups coffee grounds
¾ cup kosher salt or brown sugar
1 tbsp. cocoa oil (other oils work fine, too, including olive
     oil) or cocoa butter

Pour oil or place cocoa butter in a medium bowl. Add coffee grounds and salt or sugar. Mix well. Use to exfoliate arms, back, chest, etc. by massaging gently into skin during or just after shower. (If using during shower, ensure you have a wide enough drain to wash the coffee grounds down.)

Eucalyptus Bath Salts

3 tbsp. Epsom salts
10 tsp. baking soda

6–8 drops eucalyptus essential oil (or sandalwood or
  vanilla)
5–6 drops food coloring (your choice of color)

Measure Epsom salts into small bowl. Add baking soda
and crumble together, mixing well with your hands. Add
6–8 drops of your essential oil. Don't overdo it or your bath
salts will dissolve. Mix well. Using gloves, mix the food
coloring into the bath salts, making sure the color perme-
ates the mixture evenly. Transfer to a glass jar with tightly
fitting lid. Use within two weeks (or they lose a lot of their
scent). To use, add a handful of salts to the tub while the
water's running.